REIGN OF FLESH

Naomi H Brown

Puddin' Pants Press

ISBN: 978-0-6482768-8-3 (Print)

ISBN: 978-0-6482768-7-6 (eBook)

Cover design by roosterrepublicpress.com

One

S urvivors refer to life after the drones as Before and After. The day before the modern, mundane existence was scorched beyond recognition is referred to as Before. After consists of a life where the overwhelming prospect of survival in a hostile new world fills every waking moment. A place where nerves are so raw and frayed that one's greatest hope is for a few uninterrupted hours of sleep free from terror-filled dreams.

When I think back to that day, I remember every moment with perfect, painful clarity, despite the insanity that unfolded. It was a glorious Sunday morning, the type of picture-perfect weather printed on dusty postcards found on rotating wire racks in a forgotten corner of mom and pop gas stations across the country. The sky was a bright, cloudless blue. The sun warm and welcoming when I pulled back the block-out curtains to let light into my twelve-year-old sister's bedroom.

She had recently ditched her habit of waking up with the sun and had taken to sleeping in-a foreboding precursor to adolescence, which I stubbornly refused to acknowledge. I'd barely survived *my* teenage years, limping out the other side with a broken heart and a collection of questionable tattoos. How was

I supposed to navigate Sasha's tumultuous hormones while still figuring out how to manage my own fluctuating emotions?

With the morning light streaming in through the window, casting a beautiful glow across my sleeping half-sister, her eyelids began to twitch as she drew closer to consciousness. "Wake up, sleepyhead," I commanded in a nauseatingly cheerful voice. I knew she heard me, but I went along with the ploy anyway. I busied myself tidying her room, gathering up yesterday's discarded clothes, noisily rearranging a jumble of books on her postage-stamp-sized desk, and just generally making as much noise as I could short of pulling out the vacuum cleaner. "Come on. It's time to get up. I've made pancakes for breakfast, and we have church this morning," I reminded her.

I heard an exaggerated moan from the direction of the bed before Sasha tossed the covers aside. My little sister grudgingly pushed herself up onto her elbows. She rubbed her puffy eyes and glared across the room at me. "Why do we have to go to church?" she asked. Sasha asked the same question every Sunday morning. And every Sunday morning, I provided her with much the same answer. "Because that's what Mom would have wanted. Besides, the cakes they serve after the service are out of this world."

I could have explained that I thought it was essential to make meaningful connections with the people in our community since we had no family left of our own. I wanted her to see other families interact in a caring and thoughtful manner, not just have me and my slightly dysfunctional way of going about life as a reference point. Plus, on more than one occasion, I had been able to call on one of the parishioners to keep an eye on Sasha for me when a job had taken longer than anticipated.

For me, it had nothing to do with religious beliefs. I didn't believe in God Before and had even less faith After, although I was careful not to share that particular nugget with my sister. If Sasha wanted to believe in God, then that was okay with me. Each to their own and all that. I'd ceased believing in a higher power years ago. Watching my mom die a slow and agonizing death from cancer while my stepfather drank away the family income night after night down at his favorite bar quickly stripped me of any belief in God.

Despite my complete lack of faith, connecting with the same group of folks each week helped ground me. Raising Sasha on my own could be challenging, and it was reassuring to know there were people out there who would happily give us a hand with no expectation of receiving anything in return.

While Sasha might have questioned the need to sit in the pews listening to the Reverend's weekly sermon, I knew she enjoyed spending time with the other kids that attended church. It didn't take her long to make friends with a couple of girls, and they had recently started meeting in the park alongside the church each Sunday before the service even though we'd only been attending regularly for a couple of months. I figured with careful cultivation, she might create some lasting friendships that would help steer her through her teens.

Sasha climbed out of bed and lumbered across the room. She was almost at the door when I cleared my throat of an imaginary tickle. Rolling her eyes in that infuriating way young girls seem to have instinctively perfected, she turned on her heel and returned to the bed, flinging the covers up without bothering to smooth out the wrinkles or plump the pillow.

I stood watching her performance with my arms crossed, her dirty clothes dangling from my hand, and I wondered how I would survive the next six or seven years. I was beginning to understand why all those moms I saw at school drop-off all seemed to share a similar pinched expression. No wonder so many women were running to their cosmetic surgeons for Botox injections. My free hand crept up to my face self-consciously, and I quickly forced it back down. *Damn it,* I thought in alarm. I needed to call Brent and arrange a night out. Too much time playing mommy was starting to do my head in. I was overdue for a night of heavy drinking with my boyfriend, all thoughts about my newfound responsibilities shelved while I got reacquainted with my old pal JD.

I made a quick detour to the bathroom to toss the dirty laundry into the hamper, which was already overflowing before I joined Sasha in the cramped kitchen of our apartment. I sat down opposite her and grabbed a couple of pancakes from the plate on the table. They were the sort that came in a plastic bottle, and all you had to do was add water and shake the mixture vigorously to form a batter before pouring it into the pan to cook. While they weren't anything special, we liked to drizzle them with maple syrup, which then became our weekend 'treat.' We ate breakfast in silence. It wasn't because of any underlying tension or a bad mood on either part. We were simply too busy enjoying the syrupy pancakes to bother talking.

When we had reduced the stack to a single overcooked pancake that bordered on being pure charcoal, Sasha offered to help with the post-breakfast clean-up. Which I had to give the kid credit for. Not many twelve-year-olds' volunteered for chores. I shook my head and shooed her away. Although I appreciated the offer, church started in half an hour, and we needed to hustle if we didn't want to be the last ones to arrive. I quickly cleared the table and washed the dishes while Sasha got dressed and brushed her teeth. It didn't take long. I don't mess around when it comes to doing the housework. Some women may find household chores therapeutic, but not me. I prefer to smash through it as quickly and painlessly as possible. And if that involves cutting corners here and there, I'm all for it.

Sasha has a similar approach to fashion and personal grooming, and when I use the term fashion, I'm using it loosely. Very loosely. When it comes to getting dressed in the morning, my sister only has one rule-don't wear anything that smells like week-old cheese. Other than avoiding anything that is overtly odorous, anything goes. She doesn't care about her appearance, which isn't necessarily a bad thing. I'm glad she is more concerned about her schoolwork and getting good grades. It's refreshing that she is utterly oblivious to the superficial fluff that fills most young kids' heads. Correction- used to fill their heads.

Even so, I was her age not so long ago, and I remember how nasty girls can be to each other. Especially to kids that they don't understand or perceive to be different somehow. With that in mind, I made a point of grouping her clothes together in acceptable combinations when I did the laundry. Although she never came right out and said so, I think she was grateful for the help. Not that I'm a fashionista. Most days, I got around in faded black jeans and a t-shirt. But I scrubbed up alright when the occasion called for it. I guess I don't need to worry about fancy dresses and strappy sandals anymore.

After I sent Sasha back to her bedroom to run a brush through the bird's nest that was her hair, we made our way downstairs and walked through the breezeway to the pothole-riddled car park at the rear of the apartment complex. I unlocked the passenger door to the truck and held it open while my sister climbed into the cab. Once she was safely inside the vehicle, I closed the door and gave the F-150 the once over as I did a quick lap around the truck. The truck was my pride and joy, and I found myself checking it for dents and scrapes whenever I was about to get behind the wheel. I swear if I discovered a scratch in the paintwork, I would be banging on my neighbor's doors until I found the culprit.

Most people probably wouldn't look twice at my ride, but until eight months ago, I'd been running my landscaping business from the back of an unreliable hatchback that was so riddled with rust that I feared my feet would bust through the bottom of the footwell. The truck might have been almost as old as me, but she had less than thirty thousand miles on the odometer, and her previous owner had treated her like a frigging princess. I suspect she looked almost as good now as she did when she first drove off the dealership lot nearly twenty years ago. Even better, I'd only paid a fraction of what she was worth.

One of my regular clients, Mrs. McCleary, offered me the truck after her husband died from a massive stroke that dropped him where he stood. One minute he was standing in the refrigerated goods aisle of the supermarket pondering which brand of soft cheese Mrs. McCleary wanted; the next minute, he'd collapsed dead, a wheel of Brie rolling across the floor to bump against a shopping cart.

The couple was in their mid-seventies when they enlisted my help to keep on top of the yard. I had been maintaining the garden for them for over two years when Mr. McCleary died. They always came out to chat with me whenever I arrived to tend the lawn and surrounding garden beds, which I appreciated. Not all my clients were so friendly and respectful.

Mr. McCleary's sudden death shook me, and I rearranged my work schedule to attend the funeral, leaving a small posy of flowers with my condolences for his widow. With Mr. McCleary gone, I expected his wife to sell their home and move into one of those dreadful retirement communities where folks have oversized panic buttons in every room of their tiny condos. Mrs. McCleary had other ideas. She called me the day after her husband's funeral and asked if I could increase my fortnightly visits to once a week.

Her voice was thick with grief, and I briefly wondered how she could be thinking about something as trivial as gardening so soon after her husband had died. It wasn't my place to judge, so I agreed to take on the additional work, and after a brief negotiation on the price, she hung up.

The following week when I arrived at the McCleary residence, the old woman came out to the curb to greet me, leading me past the house to the garage, her gnarled old hand gripping my forearm for support. She must have lost ten pounds in the week or so since I had last seen her. It was little wonder that she required assistance navigating the uneven flagstones that ran parallel to the clapboard house.

She asked me to open the garage doors, which I was happy enough to do. Built long before automatic doors were a thing, the doors were solid hardwood. It would have been difficult for Mrs. McCleary to swing them open at the best of times, damn near impossible in her weakened state. I assumed she wanted help sorting through the contents of the garage. It would have been one hell of a job, a lifetime of tools and memories too precious to throw away, stored on the hand-built shelves that lined the garage walls. But I was willing to do the work if she was willing to pay.

Mrs. McCleary produced a set of keys from the pocket of her skirt and handed them to me. "Be a dear and reverse the truck out of the garage. You can drive stick, can't you?" she asked.

"Sure. I had a boyfriend who taught me how. He was a real purist when it came to cars. When he found out that I could only drive an automatic, he flipped. As far as he was concerned, if it was an auto, it wasn't a real car."

Mrs. McCleary nodded. "I can still drive, but I'm afraid the truck is a bit more than I can confidently handle. I'd probably end up backing the thing into the side of the house."

"No problem." I entered the garage and unlocked the driver's door. Although the truck was an older model, it was beautifully maintained, and the interior was as spotless as the outside. I climbed up into the cabin and started the engine. It rumbled to life enthusiastically, and I couldn't help smiling. My battered Toyota sounded like a terminal vacuum cleaner compared to the truck. I shifted the gearstick into reverse and backed out of the garage, rolling to a stop beside Mrs. McCleary.

She tapped the window with an arthritic knuckle. The truck didn't have power windows, so it took me a moment to wind the window down manually. "So, what do you think of it?" she asked with more enthusiasm than was strictly necessary. I chalked it up to the emotional roller coaster she must be riding since losing her partner of the last fifty-odd years. "It's a sweet ride. Mr. McCleary took great care of her."

For a second, the older woman's face crumpled in grief, and I could have kicked myself for being such an insensitive asshole. Why did I have to go and mention her husband? What the hell was wrong with me? To her credit, she was quick to recover her composure and even managed a watered-down smile. "It's true. He loved that darn truck. Fred had already retired when he decided to buy it. It was one of the few times we ever fought. I thought he was a foolish old goat spending our retirement funds on a second vehicle, and I told him so. But he had his heart set on it, so I gave in, and he got his truck."

I didn't know what to say, so I just nodded.

"My son-in-law checked on the internet how much they are selling for, and he thinks I could get around eight thousand for it since it's in such great condition." I thought that sounded about right for a truck with low miles and the one owner who had kept it garaged. Mrs. McCleary ran her hand along the door, and her eyes grew distant. She must have been lost in a bittersweet memory of her husband and the truck that almost came between them years ago.

"Jess, I'd like to sell you the truck. There's no point leaving it in the garage when it could go to someone who would enjoy it the way Fred did."

I was stunned by her thoughtfulness during such a difficult time, but there was no way I could ever come up with the eight grand to buy it. Before I could say as much, she continued.

"I'd like to gift it to you, but my well-meaning family would toss me in an old folk home before the week is through if I tried doing something so outrageous. So, I thought we might be able to come to some sort of mutually beneficial arrangement that won't make my family think I've gone soft in the head."

"An arrangement?" I asked, perplexed. The conversation had taken me by surprise, and I was struggling to keep up.

"Yes, an arrangement. I have already spoken to my lawyer and had the papers drawn up. I will sign the truck over to you in exchange for your gardening services until you work off the market value. Or I die. Whichever comes first," she added with a wink. "How does that sound to you?"

I'm sure I sat there staring out the window at her like a slack-jawed half-wit.

"Well? What do you think?" She prompted me when I didn't reply. I forced my mouth shut and nodded dumbly.

"It meant so much to Fred. He spent every Saturday washing and polishing the truck before taking it out for a drive. I cannot stand the thought of it going to a stranger. And, frankly, it's painful watching you wrestle your garden tools in and out of the boot of that old wreck." She waved dismissively at my car parked out on the street. "Plus, it doesn't look very professional." She was right about that. It was a constant struggle to fit a lawnmower and all my other equipment in the Toyota's trunk.

"Mrs. McCleary, you are far too generous. I couldn't possibly accept the offer."

"Nonsense. It's not a freebie; I expect you to work for it. The papers are in the glove compartment, ready to be signed. All you have to do is say yes." She smiled encouragingly as I eyed the interior of the truck covetously. It had air-conditioning, central locking, and a working stereo. I just had to say one little word.

"Yes!" I squealed, and Mrs. McCleary laughed happily. I was giddy with excitement and hopped down from the cab and hugged my newly designated fairy godmother. She wrapped her bony arms around me and squeezed back. When we finally pulled away from each other, we both had tears in our eyes.

***

I hoisted myself into the cab beside Sasha and reminded her to buckle her seatbelt. She's a smart kid, but for some inexplicable reason, she almost always forgets to buckle up. During my more cynical moments, I wonder if she does it deliberately, just to give me something to nag her about.

It took longer than I expected to drive across town. You would think the roads would be empty on a Sunday morning, with folks opting to relax and have a sleep-in instead. But no, apparently, people had swapped a leisurely morning spent in bed with a coffee and the paper for a mad determination to head over to the massive homemaker center in search of weekend markdowns before the place had even opened its doors for trade.

My fingers drummed an impatient tattoo on the steering wheel while we sat through a second light change at the intersection opposite the home improvement depot.

"Quit it." Sasha finally erupted, unable to endure the annoying tapping any longer. "It won't be the end of the world if we show up late. I mean, it's not like you even believe in God anyway. So, what's the big deal?" I glanced across at her out of the corner of my eye. Despite the sassy edge, I couldn't argue with the kid's logic.

"I don't want people thinking we're tardy," I countered lamely. She made a point of turning toward me and rolling her eyes for a second time that morning. "Tardy? I see someone has downloaded a word of the day app. Cute."

Ignoring her jibe, I managed to cross the intersection with the next green light, and the traffic thinned once we were past the homemaker center. I made a mental note to take an alternate route the following Sunday to avoid the weekend renovation warriors. I turned into the church parking lot a few minutes later and barely managed to squeeze into a narrow space between two people movers in the far corner of the lot. I frigging hate people movers. There is something about them that shits me to tears. I can't help thinking the people that drive them should get a goddamn hobby and stop pushing out so many stinking brats.

Having such uncharitable thoughts right before attending church wasn't lost on me. I climbed out of the truck and forced myself to smile. I had no idea how many of the faithful followers of Jesus Christ believed my act, but since they were yet to call me out, I figured it was safe to continue the charade. It was also possible that they knew I was a non-believer and were willing to let it slide for the sake of Sasha's eternal soul.

We hurried across the parking lot and made our way along the sidewalk that ran parallel to the church. When we reached the steps outside the entrance, I was relieved to discover we wouldn't be the last ones to arrive. A family of five scurried toward us from the street. The father struggled to control his young sons, who were eager to escape into the park next door.

I ushered Sasha up the steps and quickly slipped inside the open double doors, ignoring the faces that craned around to ogle the latecomers. There weren't any empty pews left, so we had to squeeze in beside a grey-haired couple that smelt faintly of mothballs near the rear of the church. Once everyone was sitting quietly, the Reverend began his sermon. I tried to listen for the first few minutes, but it wasn't long before my mind began to wander.

It was warm inside the church, the bright morning light filtering through the numerous windows. The sun touched the golden lacquer on the pine seating and created a feeling of being cocooned in a warm and soothing embrace. The cynic in me wondered if the effect was intentional. A ploy by the church's builder to help convince people God was right there with them in the building. It didn't make me feel closer to a higher power.

The heat from the light streaming in just made me drowsy. I wondered if it would be a terrible sin to close my eyes for a little bit. I'd been squeezing in a lot of extra jobs lately to try and make ends meet, and the additional work was beginning to wear me out.

At some point, the combination of the warmth inside the building and the Reverend's monotonous drawl must have lulled me to sleep. I woke to a sharp jab to the ribs by the old guy sitting next to me. I looked around in confusion and wiped the drool from the corner of my mouth. How attractive. I hoped nobody other than the old codger with the pointy elbow noticed my faux pas. I turned to Sasha and whispered, "I'm sorry." She frowned and replied, "You were snoring," before returning her attention to the pulpit and the middle-aged woman reading a passage from the Bible. I simultaneously felt ashamed of being such a shitty role model and proud of managing to sleep through most of the hour-long service.

After the Reverend thanked the congregation for listening, he invited everyone to stick around and join him for cake and coffee. You don't have to ask me twice. Sasha and I remained seated on the pine bench until she spotted her friends walking down the aisle with their parents. She stood up and joined the girls, the smiling trio headed straight for the refreshment table. I sat watching for a moment as the group deliberated over which of the tasty-looking baked treats to load onto their paper plates, and I envied their innocence. I rarely have time to catch up with my friends anymore. If I'm not working, I'm usually hunched over our table in the apartment deciding which bills to pay.

Once the crowd thinned, I made my way over to the urn and took a chipped cup from the stack. I filled it with coffee and remembering that it was the cheapest and nastiest coffee the volunteers responsible for the weekly morning tea could provide; I added plenty of sugar to mask the brew's burnt dirt taste. It was remarkably unsuccessful. I must have grimaced as I took a sip because the Reverend appeared beside me and smiled sympathetically. "It's not a fine Arabica blend, but it's better than nothing, right?"

I swallowed the mouthful of coffee the wrong way, and I began to cough. I could feel the heat rushing to my cheeks and knew I must be turning an unflattering shade of red as I gasped for air. The Reverend patted me on the back, his smile replaced with a genuine look of concern. Eventually, I began to breathe normally, and I apologized for my coughing fit. "No need to apologize. I've been trying rather unsuccessfully to convince Mrs. Halstrom to upgrade to a slightly more palatable brand of coffee since I first came here. Sadly, my pleas appear to fall on deaf ears. Might I recommend the Hummingbird cake? It's devilishly good," he suggested before reminding me to talk to the President of the Church Committee regarding the grounds keeping contract that was about to open for bids. The previous contractor had his tenure terminated due to repeated drink driving offenses.

The Reverend must have spotted the magnetic sign on the side of my truck because I didn't recall ever mentioning I owned a landscaping business. And I hadn't realized the church would even consider hiring a non-believer. I made a mental note to look into it and snatched up a piece of the Hummingbird cake before it was all gone. I took my burnt dirt coffee and cake outside and wandered across the adjoining park to a vacant bench beneath one of the leafy oak trees shading the area. I knew I should make an effort to mingle with the other members of the congregation. However, I was happier sitting on my own sipping the dreadful coffee and nibbling the cake, which was every bit as delicious as the Reverend had promised. If I could cook for shit, I would have found out who baked it and begged them for the recipe.

For the second time that morning, I admired the perfection of the day. The sky was bright, the sun was warm, and beneath the shade of an oak tree, there was the barest hint of a breeze to cool my skin. I kept a watchful eye on Sasha, sitting on the ground under a nearby tree with her friends. The three girls looked happy chatting to each other as they sipped juice from disposable cups. I could almost believe she was as innocent and carefree as the two girls beside her. Unfortunately, I knew better. Watching our mother suffer as cancer ate away at her body profoundly impacted Sasha. Some days were more difficult than others, and judging by my sister's smile and the relaxed slope of her shoulders, she was happy and enjoying the moment. It was good to see.

Two

While I was pondering my sister's resilience, I noticed a shadow darken a patch of grass between the park and the concrete sidewalk flanking the church. My eyes were drawn upward to the sudden smudge on an otherwise cloudless day. Hovering fifteen yards above the ground was what appeared to be a metal wasp. It wasn't an exact likeness, more like a streamlined, mechanized interpretation of the insect. Its body was curved and sleek; the metal surface a matte maroon color that appeared to absorb light rather than reflect it.

I was trying to figure out what the hell it was when a flash of light shot from its underbelly, streaking across the clearing before ending in a God-awful explosion that left my ears ringing and my eyes stinging. I stared in disbelief at the charred spot on the sidewalk outside the church where only moments ago, one of my fellow parishioners had stood. Now all that remained of them was a greasy red smear and one lone shoe.

Before I realized what I was doing, I dashed over to Sasha and snatched her away from her friends. I'd already dragged her halfway across the park, careful to conceal our retreat under the canopy of leafy branches when people finally understood they were in danger and started screaming. There were more explosions behind us, and I risked a glance over my shoulder. I saw an entire family standing on the church steps vaporized. An ugly red mist the only clue they had even existed. People were running in every direction, screaming and staring up at the metal monsters hovering in the sky above them.

I continued toward the street, yanking on Sasha's hand, urging her to move faster. We reached the edge of the park, and I paused beneath a tree while I scanned the street. We needed to get as far away from the church as possible, but I had no idea where we could go. Returning to my truck was out of the question. It was behind us, right in the middle of the carnage unfolding on the grounds surrounding the church. Without the pick-up, our only other option was to break cover and seek refuge at one of the houses across the street. I held Sasha close against me, too afraid to step out into the street in case one of those wasp/drones was hovering out of sight, waiting to blast us to bits.

While I stood at the edge of the park, crippled by indecision, Sasha looked back over her shoulder for the first time. The trees blocked any view of the metal insects hovering above, but there was no shielding her from the gory mess we were fleeing. She cried out in horror as chunks of charred flesh flew through the air when an elderly woman was caught trying to escape toward the car park and exploded in a blinding flash. I could feel her trembling beside me, and I squeezed her tight, hoping to reassure her. She looked up at me, and I could see my fear reflected in her eyes. For an agonizing moment, the responsibility to keep my little sister safe overwhelmed me.

"Quickly," I urged, pulling her after me as I cautiously approached the street. We needed to leave the park and find shelter. Immediately. I scanned the sky above the road. It was clear. At least for the moment. I turned to Sasha, "See that house on the corner? The one with the porch?" I pointed across the street to a brown brick home with an attached carport. She nodded doubtfully; her eyes locked on the property with the porch stretching across its length.

"We're going to run across the road to that house as fast as we can. Do you understand?" She mumbled something that was lost as another blast rocked the park. I felt the heat of it on my back but didn't dare check how close it was. "Come on," I half screamed. I rechecked the sky for any sign of the metal wasps. I couldn't see any, but I knew they could be hovering just out of sight, waiting for some poor schmuck to step out from beneath the trees and make a run for it.

Shit. We'd never escape if I kept thinking like that. "We run on three," I told my sister. "One, two, three." We sprinted in unison, our feet barely touching the ground as we bolted across the empty street. Sasha started to lag behind as I reached the curb on the other side. It wasn't her fault. I was wearing my trusty motorcycle boots while she had opted for more church-friendly ballet flats. I yanked her along the narrow footpath, not caring if she lost one of the impractical shoes slowing her down.

When we finally reached the house, I melted against the wall beside the front door. The wide porch, coupled with the overgrown shrubbery crowding the front yard, provided us with a reasonable amount of cover. Nevertheless, I whispered for

Sasha to remain still. She nodded and remained focused on the street while I gently tapped on the front door. When there was no response, I knocked again, this time a bit louder—still nothing. "Shit," I cursed under my breath. We needed to get inside the house. There wasn't time to fuck around. The longer we remained outside, the greater the chance one of those killer drones would notice us and try blasting us out of existence.

Sasha looked up at me nervously. "It's alright," I said in a half-hearted attempt to reassure her. I didn't know if there was anyone inside. Nobody came to the door when I knocked. Considering what was happening in the park across the street, I couldn't blame someone for ignoring my desperate knocking. I hadn't seen a car parked in the driveway, so perhaps nobody was home. If nobody were there to let us inside, I'd have to break in. I'm not a criminal, and up to that moment when the sky filled with killer metal insects, I'd never done anything more serious than deface public property when I was on a drunken rampage with a bunch of friends as a teenager.

I motioned for Sasha to follow me, and I led the way along the porch to the carport at the side of the property, hoping there would be another entry point to the house. There was a side door beneath the carport, as I'd expected. All I had to do now was figure out how to open the damn thing. I pointed to the pair of trash cans lined up neatly against the brick wall a few feet back from the door. "I don't think anyone is home, so I'm going to have to find a way inside. I need you to crouch down beside those trash cans and wait for me." She looks at me like I've suddenly sprouted a second head. "You're going to break into the house?"

There wasn't time for a lesson on morality. "Get down, stay still, and don't make a sound."

Once she ducked behind the rubbish and recycling, I began searching for a spare key. I've always thought people were plain stupid, leaving a key to their home lying around for any old asshole to find. It was practically an invitation to have anything of value stolen. Or worse, waking in the middle of the night to discover a stranger holding a knife to your throat. On this occasion, I was hoping the owners were too stupid or trusting to worry about such things.

I checked under the doormat, and the pot plants positioned either side of the door, but there wasn't a key hidden beneath them. I guess the folks that lived there were sensible like me and didn't want to make it too easy for some desperate meth head to steal their flat-screen when they weren't at home. I was out of options. I would have to force my way inside. Having never committed a break-in before, I took a moment to ponder the best approach to gain entry to the house. Picking the lock was out since I had zero skills in that department, and I'd probably break my leg if I tried kicking the door in as it was solid cedar. That only left one option-I'd have to smash a window.

I didn't like the idea. It would be noisy and could draw unwanted attention, but it was the only way to gain access, and I had to make sure Sasha was safe. There was an explosion close by, followed by screaming that sent me scuttling behind the metal trash cans with Sasha. I don't know how long I remained crouching beside my sister, but it must have been a good stretch of time because my legs were numb when I finally stood up. I didn't want to take my eyes off Sasha. However, she would be safer hidden where she was than if she followed me. "I'll be back soon," I promised with more conviction than I felt and left her to go find a way inside.

I crept back along the front of the house, clinging to the bricks, hoping that I would go unseen. I tried to avoid looking across the street at the park we had barely managed to escape, but I found myself searching for the source of the pitiful screaming that was slowly beginning to wane. My eyes locked on a scorched figure, slowly crawling across the grass toward a picnic table. Their progress was painfully slow, and it took me a few seconds to realize they were missing an arm from just above the elbow. I felt compelled to run across the road and help them. But I didn't. There wasn't anything I could do for them. I had no medical training beyond basic first aid and there was no way I could get them to a hospital without risking my own life. Once I was safely behind a climbing rose wrapped thickly around a trellis, I tried calling 911. An automated voice informed me the lines were busy and advised trying again shortly. No surprise there.

Unable to help the wailing stranger across the street, I slipped around the far side of the house and discovered a narrow window set high in the wall that was open a couple of inches. I reached up and tried to slide it all the way open, but the window didn't budge—it must have been locked in place. Stretching up onto tiptoes, I pressed my face to the opening and peered inside. It was the laundry room. The homeowners probably kept the window slightly open to avoid condensation build-up. It was too bad they weren't less security conscious-it would have been much easier if I could have climbed in through an open window.

I scrounged around in the narrow garden along the side of the house until my hand settled on a concrete garden ornament that had long ago been overshadowed by a prehistoric-looking fern. Picking it up, I adjusted my grip on the moss-covered angel. Shielding my face with my free arm, I lobbed the ornament at the window. I cringed as the window shattered, shards of glass flying into the laundry along with the angel. The thud of the angel landing on the floor, combined with the almost musical tinkle of broken glass hitting the tiles, had me glancing around nervously. Surely everyone and everything in a half-mile radius had heard my desperate act of vandalism.

I waited for an irate neighbor to pop their head over the fence with a shotgun pointed at me, or worse still, one of those murderous machines hovering in the sky across the road to appear. A minute later, when I remained alone and alive, I figured my destructive efforts had gone unnoticed. I carefully knocked the remaining slivers of glass out of the window frame before hoisting myself through the opening.

Landing heavily on the other side, a twitch of pain shot up my ankle, and I prayed that I hadn't done any serious damage. When I took a tentative step forward, although it hurt to do so, I could tell it was nothing serious. I hobbled out of the laundry, pulling the door shut behind me. At some point, I'd have to figure out a way to block off the window, but first, I needed to get Sasha inside.

It was easy enough to find my way around the ranch-style house's simple layout, and I didn't have to worry about disturbing anyone. If I weren't alone in the house, I figured someone would have appeared by now with guns blazing. I hurried down the tiled hallway and passed through a doorway that opened into the living room. I crossed the dated brown shag pile carpet and flipped the deadbolt on the door. Sasha's head popped up from behind the garbage cans, and I ushered her inside.

I eased the door shut behind her and secured the lock before turning to my sister. I wrapped her in a fierce hug, and she groaned, whacking me on the back. I reluctantly loosened my grip on her. "Let's find somewhere safe for you to hide while I close the curtains and block off the window in the laundry," I said. Sasha looked up at me, perplexed. "Why do I have to hide? Aren't we safe now that we're inside?" I shook my head. I could understand how she might think we were safe now that we were indoors, but I wasn't taking any chances. "Stay here while I close the curtains. It's better if no one knows we are here." I led her over to one of the overstuffed armchairs positioned opposite the outdated television and pushed her down onto the floral upholstery.

While Sasha sat in the armchair, I went from room to room, draping the house in shadow as I closed the curtains. "What now?" Sasha asked when I returned to the living room a few minutes later. "I need you to help me secure the laundry." She followed me down the hallway, waiting off to the side of the laundry door while I slowly turned the handle. It was probably overkill, but I half expected some murderous drone to blow the door off its hinges the second I cracked it open. Feeling foolish, I pushed the door back against the wall and gestured toward the linen cupboard. "I need you to help me drag the cupboard across the window to stop anyone from getting in. You push, I'll pull."

Spare bedding and a boggling collection of mismatched towels filled the cupboard, making it much heavier than I'd anticipated. "Damn it," I complained as we pushed and pulled to no avail. We managed to shift it a couple of inches before I unloaded some of the bulkier stacks of sheets and blankets, tossing them in a pile in the corner. Once I'd cleared some of the shelves, we tried moving the cupboard once more, and with the weight reduced, we managed to shift the linen cupboard across the broken window. Wanting to prevent anyone from being able to push the closet aside, I jammed as much of the linen back on the shelves as would fit before hustling Sasha out of the laundry room.

I ushered my sister into the guest room at the rear of the house and pulled the door shut behind us. Sasha plonked herself down on the bed while I eased back the heavy block-out curtains and checked the backyard for signs of trouble. When I peered out at the neatly paved yard, it was difficult to believe the terror unfolding in the park across the street. Sighing loudly, I let the curtain fall back into place and sat down on the bed beside my sister, draping an arm around her slender shoulder. She looked up at me expectantly, and I shrugged. I had no fucking clue what was happening outside, and I admitted as much. "I don't know what those things are. Or why they are blowing people up."

Smoothing my hair back from my face, I tried not to see the charred parishioner crawling across the ground when I closed my eyes for a moment. Shaking away the gruesome image, I turned to Sasha and asked, "Did you see them?" She shook her head. "No, not really. One second I was with Ellie and Nora, then you were dragging me across the park. I saw a flash of light and people exploding. That's it. What do you think is happening?"

"Honestly, I have no idea. Until we can figure out what's going on, I think the best thing we can do is lay low and stay out of sight."

"If they can't see us, they can't kill us," Sasha stated calmly. I eyed my sister warily. Perhaps I had underestimated her. I'd been treating her like a regular twelve-year-old, but maybe Mom's death had wizened her beyond her years.

"Yeah, hopefully," I agreed, squeezing her hand. " Since we might be stuck here for a few days, I'm going to have a look around the kitchen and check out the food situation."

"Is it that bad?" Sasha asked. Not wanting to alarm her any more than necessary, I replied, "It's just a precaution. It's better to be safe than sorry, right?" She nodded slowly, and I felt her eyes on me as I stood up and left the room. Somehow, we had to survive this madness, and if that meant being super vigilant and taking crazy precautions-I was okay with that.

Hours later, after we had been cooped up in the guest room, thumbing through old copies of craft magazines Sasha found in the built-in wardrobe, I ventured out to investigate what was happening outside. I made my way down to the formal living room that overlooked the park and put my eye to a crack between the curtains. It was late afternoon, and the sun was beginning its descent toward the horizon. I stood transfixed by the complete lack of activity out in the street.

A dog trotted down the middle of the road, pausing opposite the park to sniff the air. I watched with grim fascination as it hopped up onto the grass and enthusiastically approached what I suspected was a chunk of barbecued human meat. The dog took its time investigating the charred remains, circling the exotic flesh with its nose to the ground before eventually taking a tentative bite. The flavor must have been to its liking because the dog began gnawing at the remains with gleeful abandon. My stomach roiled, and I quickly turned away.

Although the park was quiet, I could still hear the chilling sound of explosions going off in all directions. None sounded extremely close, but that was little comfort. I'd heard gunshots and wailing sirens in the distance while we'd been sitting on the bed flipping through magazines. So, whatever was happening, it wasn't over yet. The action had just moved on to a different part of town.

Three

The following day, I awoke shortly after sunrise. Despite barricading the guest room door with a set of drawers the night before, I'd barely gotten any sleep. I'd doze off briefly, then jolt awake a short time later when a blast ripped through the night somewhere nearby. Sasha slept better than I'd expected. She mumbled fretfully a couple of times during the night, but she quickly settled when I reached out and wrapped her hand in mine.

My limbs were heavy with fatigue as I pushed the drawers aside and let myself out of the bedroom. With any luck, the homeowners were coffee drinkers because I desperately needed a caffeine fix. Before making my way into the kitchen, I quickly checked all the doors were still secured. Early morning light filtered through the frilly lace curtains covering the kitchen windows, and I wondered if life would return to normal with the beginning of a new day. As I rummaged through the pantry shelves in search of coffee, my heart sank. Whatever hopes I'd held for the madness of yesterday to be over were shattered when I heard muffled screams accompanied by what sounded an awful lot like a shotgun blast.

My hand fell on a canister of coffee, and relief washed over me. If I'd had to deal with caffeine withdrawals while coping with the end of the world, I think I would have lost my shit completely. It was cheap, nasty instant coffee, the sort that required a bucket load of cups to feel any type of buzz, but I wasn't in a position to be picky, so cheap nasty instant it was. Thankfully, the power supply was yet to be affected, and I filled the kettle and flicked the switch to bring it to the boil. If people continued to die, I guessed it wouldn't be long before there was no one left to run the power plants, plunging us back into the dark ages.

While the kettle came to the boil, I found a box of cereal. It was the stuff that tasted like cardboard that oldies eat to help keep them regular. Sasha wouldn't be impressed, but it was better than nothing. I placed the box along with a couple of bowls on the kitchen counter, ready for when she eventually woke up and wanted some breakfast.

I was sipping on my second dreadfully unpleasant cup of coffee when my pocket vibrated. I'd forgotten all about my cell phone and was digging in my pocket to retrieve it when an engine revved out in the street, followed by a blast and the piercing shriek of twisting metal. Scalding coffee sloshed over my hand as I flinched at the terrible noise. Ignoring the pain, I dumped the mug on the counter and ran through the house to the window in the living room. Pulling back the curtain, I peered out into the street.

An SUV had jumped the curb and slammed into a power pole almost directly in front of the house. The sizable bonnet had crumpled around the pole while the rear of the vehicle was a mess of twisted metal and melted plastic where one of the drones must have hit it. I glanced around fearfully, wondering if the wasp-like machine was hovering nearby.

"What happened?" Sasha mumbled from behind me, her voice thick with sleep. It took all my self-control to refrain from whirling around and punching her out. My nerves were already frayed, and my sister creeping up behind me didn't help the situation. "Jesus, Sasha," I hissed. "Try not to sneak up on me like that, alright?" She looked at me silently before returning her attention to the mangled vehicle out the front. "We have to help them."

"No. We can't do that," I told her.

"Jess, we can't just leave them to die. Please," she implored. I understood her concern. She was a kind and thoughtful girl, and her compassionate nature compelled her to go and help the people trapped in the SUV. But I wasn't so kind or decent. There was no way I was about to risk our safety for random people, who, more than likely, were beyond saving. One of the occupants had smashed through the windscreen headfirst and now lay motionless across the crumpled bonnet. The driver wasn't granted such a swift demise. She sat slumped over the steering wheel, blood leaking from a gash on her forehead. Even from inside the house, I could easily hear her agonized groans.

"We have to go and help them," Sasha urged.

"If we go out there right now, one of those things could be lurking just out of sight, waiting to kill us too."

"I'd rather be dead than live the rest of my life, knowing that I let someone burn to death because I was too scared to help them." Shit. I didn't think twelve-year-olds were capable of such profound and selfless thoughts. Despite her naivete, I couldn't argue with her logic. Frigging hell, the kid had me well and truly backed into a corner. If I stood back and did nothing to help the injured woman, I'd look like the world's biggest asshole, and Sasha would never forgive me. If I did venture out and try to help, there was a damn good chance I'd end up medium-well done like yesterday's parishioners.

"Alright," I snarled, turning away from the window. "You wait here while I go see if I can help," I instructed my sister. I was furious and terrified at the same time. Although it wasn't Sasha's fault, I couldn't help but feel she had forced my hand. I ran into the kitchen and looted the drawers for a pair of kitchen shears. Seat belts lock in place in the event of an accident to keep the occupant secure, so I would need to free the driver from the restraint as quickly as possible. With the shears in hand, I slipped outside and was overwhelmed by the stench of burnt flesh. Covering my nose with my free hand, I fought the urge to puke and quickly made my way to the end of the carport and stepped up onto the front veranda. It was hard to imagine how many bodies it had taken to create such a dreadful smell. After another twelve hours of roasting in the summer sun, the decay would be unfathomable.

Before stepping out from under the veranda onto the path, I looked back over my shoulder, and sure enough, Sasha's pinched face was peering out at me from between the curtains. The weight of her expectation pressed so heavily on my chest that it was hard to breathe. With immense reluctance, I turned away from her and returned my attention to the SUV. It couldn't be more than ten steps to the wreckage, but it may as well have been a mile. Admonishing myself for being such a gutless wretch, I scanned the sky for signs of the metal wasps before stepping out onto the path.

It took all of three seconds to reach the driver's door of the SUV. Hopped up on adrenalin, I yanked on the door handle harder than was strictly necessary, and the door swung open with such force that I stumbled backward. Recovering my balance, I reached into the car and gently prodded the injured driver. The woman moaned, blood bubbling between her lips. She was in even worse shape than I'd expected. Airbags and a seatbelt could only do so much when you slam into a power pole at high speed.

A lick of yellow flame flickered in the back of the car, a nasty chemical smell filling the air as the upholstery caught alight. Although I doubted it would explode like they inevitably do in every action movie I'd ever watched, I figured it wouldn't be long until fire engulfed the entire SUV.

Mindful of not inflicting further pain on the injured driver, I gently pushed her back from the steering wheel and rested her head against the seat. Her eyes fluttered open, and for a moment, she seemed to see me. She reached out, but then her chin slumped forward, and her hand dropped into her bloody lap, and she was unconscious again. As I'd suspected, the seatbelt was locked in place and wouldn't budge, so I attacked the belt with the kitchen shears. They were blunter than I'd hoped, and it took considerable effort to hack through the tightly woven material. When the shears made their final snip through the belt,

I quickly removed the sash from across her lap and grabbed hold under her arms as best I could.

I'm lean and wiry, and doing yard work every day has helped keep me fit and strong, but I'm only five foot two, and this woman had a good three inches and thirty-something pounds on me. Extricating her from the SUV was no easy task and as I half dragged, half lifted her out of the seat, she cried out in pain. Her breath came in ragged gasps, and she started to cough. A crimson spray of blood erupted from her mouth, and I recoiled from the shower of droplets that splattered my face and chest. I almost dropped her in revulsion, my grip loosening as I shrank away from the bloody exhalations.

Unable to carry the much larger woman, I dragged her away from the vehicle, pulling her along as I shuffled back along the path. One of her tennis shoes got caught on a paver protruding like a chipped and worn snaggletooth, and her foot slipped free. It seemed to take forever to drag the unconscious woman along the path. By the time I reached the veranda, I was sweaty and out of breath.

After lowering the woman to the ground, I squatted beside her and carefully brushed aside the bloody strings of hair plastered to her face. "Damn it," I muttered when I noticed her unblinking eyes. I put my hand close to her face to check for any signs of life, but she was gone. Anger swelled in my chest as I thought about the risk I had taken trying to rescue her. It had all been for nothing since she went and died on me, although it was probably for the best. Without medical assistance, she would have died eventually anyway. It just would have taken longer, and she would have suffered the entire time.

With the woman lying dead on the veranda, I shifted my focus to the flames that flickered and danced inside the SUV. I had to extinguish the fire before it spread to the power pole and caused even more problems. Sasha tapped the glass behind me, and I turned to see what she wanted. She gestured to a spot near the mailbox, and I followed her gaze. There was a hose coiled beside a faucet, partially concealed by a thriving lavender bush. I snatched up the nozzle and turned on the tap before running over to the burning car.

The flames crackled and hissed as the spray from the hose dampened the burning interior of the vehicle. It took a few minutes to douse the fire, and I alternated between checking the sky for drones and watching for any smoldering areas inside the car. Afraid that the fire would reignite after I turned away, I made sure the car was thoroughly soaked before I turned off the water and ran back up to the house.

It was a relief to step under the veranda once more. I wanted to retreat into the safety of the house, but I still had to do something about the dead woman lying at my feet. I couldn't leave her there to rot right outside the window. I stood over her body, wondering who she had been. There was a wedding band on her neatly manicured hand, and I guessed the dead guy hanging across the bonnet was her husband. I hadn't noticed any child restraints in the back seat of the SUV. Hopefully, that meant there wouldn't be children somewhere waiting for their parents to come home.

I pressed the palms of my hands to my eyes and took a steadying breath. I couldn't afford to dwell on the dead, and the lives being so brutally snuffed out. It was too demoralizing. Aware that Sasha was watching, I pulled myself together and motioned for her to unlock the window. She slid open the window, and I stepped over to the gap. I asked her to grab the quilt from the master bedroom, and she nodded in understanding.

While Sasha was gone, I crouched down and got a sturdy grip under the woman's arms so I could drag her away from the middle of the veranda. Now that I knew she was dead, it wasn't necessary to be so careful with her body. If her bare heel rubbed across the rough concrete, it wasn't like she would wake up and complain about the skin missing from her foot. Still, I tried to be respectful.

Once I'd wrangled her body off the veranda, I grappled with her heavy limbs, dragging her beneath the shady undergrowth in the garden. As far as final resting places go, it wasn't ideal, but it was the best I could manage. I gently lowered her head and shoulders to the ground before placing her arms at her sides. Sasha walked around the side of the house, dragging a bedspread behind her. "She's dead, isn't she?" I nodded, and Sasha looked past me at the woman lying amongst the greenery. "At least she didn't burn to death. That would have been worse."

"I guess so," I agreed. It felt like an awful lot of effort, not to mention the tremendous risk I'd taken for minimal reward, but I kept it to myself. Sasha handed me the bedspread and I carried it over to the dead woman and carefully draped it over her body. It felt woefully inadequate, but what more could I do? At least she was covered, which was more than could be said for the dozens of people lying dead in the park.

Although it couldn't be much past seven-thirty, the day was already heating up. I made a mental note to make sure we moved on before the body got too ripe. Beside me, my sister was mumbling a prayer for the dead woman, and I felt my cheeks flush with shame. Sasha was doing her best to pay her respects to the stranger I'd tried to help, and all I could do was ponder how long we had until the woman's rotting remains became a problem.

As soon as I heard her say the word 'Amen,' I took Sasha's hand and led her back inside the house. I pushed the door closed behind me and slid down onto the floor. I felt utterly wrecked. The sun had been up for less than an hour, and all I wanted was to crawl into bed and forget that I'd ever woken up that morning.

Sasha knelt beside me and placed her hand on my shoulder. "You look like the lone survivor in a horror movie. It's kind of scary to look at. Why don't you go take a shower, and I'll find you a clean top." I nodded slowly and stood up. She was right. Hopefully, a shower would help clear my head and wash away the stink of fear that clung to my pores. I walked down the hallway to the bathroom and pushed the door most of the way shut for some privacy. A stack of clean towels sat on a shelf above the toilet, and I pulled one down before checking out my reflection in the mirror over the vanity.

My sister hadn't been kidding when she told me I looked like something from a horror movie. The dead woman's blood stained my cheeks, and my eyes were huge and haunted with circles so dark they looked like bruises. It's incredible what a real-life doomsday scenario will do for a girl's self-esteem. I've never been particularly vain, but the image staring back at me wasn't very flattering.

Repulsed by my appearance, I quickly peeled off my clothes and turned on the shower. It took a moment for the hot water to come through. Once the shower cubicle was steaming up, I adjusted the temperature and stepped under the showerhead. A powerful jet of hot water massaged my scalp, and I delighted in the sensation. With my eyes squeezed tightly shut, I allowed the water to wash over my face, dissolving much of the blood, dirt, and sweat. I scrubbed myself clean with a zesty citrus body wash I found in the shower caddy and took the opportunity to shampoo my hair as well. If I didn't make it through the next few days, at least I'd die with clean, shiny hair.

While it was tempting to remain in the shower until the hot water ran out, I figured Sasha would probably appreciate the chance to dive under the shower and freshen up. After reluctantly turning off the water, I toweled myself dry and put yesterday's underwear back on. Dirty underwear on a squeaky-clean backside was a bit of a letdown, but I wasn't quite ready to subject myself to a pair of big granny panties. I shimmied into my jeans and was wrestling with the zipper when I remembered my cell phone. I dug it out of my pocket and checked the screen.

There was a missed call from Brent, my on-again, off-again boyfriend. My stomach did a little flip. It always happened whenever I thought about Brent. Even after three years, he still had that kind of effect on me. The intense physical reaction I experienced around him was part of why I insisted on breaking it off on a semi-regular basis. Having such strong feelings for another human being made me uncomfortable, and sometimes it became too much for me to handle.

Brent understood my neuroses and deep-rooted commitment issues. He'd learned not to take it personally when I retreated for a while. And truthfully, I was beginning to suspect he secretly enjoyed the solitude when I needed a breather and pushed him away. It gave him an excuse to pack up his truck and go fishing for a few days. Sometimes he'd take off with his buddies, but usually, he'd go out alone and enjoy the time away by himself.

I considered sending him a text, afraid that if I called, I'd lose my composure when I heard his voice. I kept trying to construct an adequate message, but I couldn't possibly convey what was happening in a few hundred characters. Frustrated, I tried calling instead. I'd just have to keep it together and refrain from turning into a blubbering mess. The last time I'd tried using my cell phone, it was to call the emergency services, and I hadn't been able to get through. So, I didn't hold out much hope of being able to make contact with my boyfriend.

I waited impatiently as the phone rang. On the fourth ring, he picked up.

"Hello? Jess?"

"Yeah, it's me."

"What the hell is going on down there? Are you alright?" I shook my head. How could I explain the unexplainable?

"It's crazy. People are being blown to bits in the streets. Sasha and I barely made it to safety."

"Jesus. I saw it on the news last night when we got back to the cabin. CNN is claiming it must be a foreign invasion by Russia, or maybe China. They're using high-tech drones to do their dirty work, decimate the population before sending in troops to secure the country. But there have also been reports of attacks in other countries as well, and I can't imagine any superpower having the capabilities to launch such large-scale attacks around the globe."

As far as theories go, it was plausible enough. But I wasn't completely sold on the idea. Why would they go to all the effort to kill regular folks that posed no real threat to them? Surely, it made more sense to target the army bases scattered around the country, minimizing the chance of an armed response? But what did I know? After all, I cut lawns for a living, so I probably wasn't an expert strategist, privy to the intricacies of a hostile takeover.

"Yeah," I agreed, "I'm not sure any nation could manage an attack like this. The technology is pretty scary."

Changing the subject, Brent asked, "Are you guys at the apartment?"

"Nope. We were at church when this all started. I managed to grab Sasha and get the hell out of there just in time. Right now, we're holed up in a house across the street from the park."

"Is it safe? Are there any drones around?"

"It's safe enough for now, but we'll have to move on soon. I need to figure out where to go first."

"Fuck," Brent cursed, his voice thick with emotion. "I need to come and get you."

"No frigging way!" I squawked.

"I have to fucking help you!" he bellowed into the phone. I flinched and pulled the phone away from my ear. As big and scary-looking as Brent is, with his arms heavily tattooed and a thick ginger beard to make even the roughest biker jealous, he is extremely slow to anger. It was a new and unnerving side to him. However, emotional extremes were probably the new normal in these strange and distressing times.

"Brent, please calm down. You're scaring me." I heard him taking a steadying breath. I did the same.

"I'm sorry for yelling. I'm worried about you and Sasha, and I feel like I can't do anything to help you while I'm up here in the mountains."

"It helps just hearing your voice," I assured him. There was a long silence, and when I was about to ask if he was still there, he said, "Look, I don't know how much longer we'll have phone service. I'm going to hang up and try to figure out a plan, and I'll call you back soon. In the meantime, I want you to stay put."

"Okay. When do you think you'll call back?" After hearing his voice, I couldn't stand the thought of never hearing from him again. In the hours after the drones appeared, I'd been so focused on getting Sasha out of harm's way that I hadn't had a chance to think of anything or anyone else. Speaking to my bear of a boyfriend made me long for him to wrap me in his comforting embrace.

"Give me an hour. That should be enough time to sort something out. I want you to do something for me while you're waiting."

"Alright. What is it that you want me to do?"

"The newsreaders are starting to report cases of looting. You'd think a foreign invasion, or whatever the hell it is, would be bad enough, but apparently, the lowlifes are taking advantage of people getting killed. I want you to find a weapon, preferably a firearm. If you can't get your hands on a gun, find something else. A baseball bat would be good, or in a pinch, an ax will do."

"Jesus, Brent."

"Don't argue with me, Jess. Just do it. You need to prepare yourself. I'll call back soon. I love you."

"I love you too." Too bad it took a national disaster to prise the words out of me.

There was a gentle knock on the bathroom door before Sasha poked her head into the room.

"It's okay. You can come in. You should take a quick shower while I get us some breakfast." She entered the bathroom and handed me a gray t-shirt. It was a few sizes too big, but it would do the job. I pulled it over my head and checked my reflection in the mirror. "What do you think?"

Sasha eyed my outfit dubiously. "You look like a poorly dressed dude, but everything else was bright and ugly. Also, I think the lady that lives here has an unhealthy obsession with cat t-shirts. I examined the oversized t-shirt. The color was okay; I often wore gray clothes anyway. The only problem was the size. I reached around and took hold of the hem of the t-shirt, twisting it into a knot at my waist. That took care of the excess fabric. "Better?" I asked.

"Better," she agreed. "I heard you talking to someone. Was it Brent? Is he okay?"

"It was Brent, and he is fine. He's thinking of a way to get us out of here and somewhere safe. He'll call back in a while. Hop in the shower, and I'll go pour us each a bowl of yummy bran flakes for breakfast."

"Bran flakes? Gross. I'd rather starve." I smiled at the small exchange, a moment of normalcy in an otherwise crazy situation. I scooped up my bloody top and left Sasha to shower in private.

We each munched on a bowl of tasteless cereal with a distinct lack of enthusiasm. While the bran flakes lacked flavor, the cereal certainly lived up to its fiber-packed promise. By the time we'd scooped out the last mouthfuls, we felt like we'd eaten three times as much as we had. I was rinsing the bowls when my cell phone started to ring.

"Brent. That was quick."

"Hey babe. Is everything still alright where you are?"

"Yeah. We just had some breakfast." I refrained from mentioning the ear-splitting blasts going off with increasing frequency in the nearby streets. Hopefully, he wouldn't hear them in the background. There was no point freaking him out more than he already was.

"Good. According to the news reports, the attacks are concentrated in the more densely populated areas. I know you aren't gonna like this, but I think you need to haul ass up here to the cabin. It's deep in the heart of nowhere, and I haven't spotted a single drone yet. Plus, the guys have all left to try and reach their families, so there are loads of supplies."

I considered his proposal. It made sense. Brent was off on a boy's weekend at a remote cabin that was more than an hour's drive from the nearest town. There was only one major flaw in the plan. The place was over five hundred miles away, a remote getaway that had been in Brent's family for decades. Brent had bought the cabin from his father and uncle when they decided to sell the property a few years back. I think Brent dreamed of retiring there one day when his working years were behind him, and he could fill his time hunting and fishing and staring into a crackling fire on cold winter nights. It was idealistic, but people need their dreams. Without them, life can be unbearably grim.

"Jessica? Are you still there?" He only ever called me Jessica when shit was getting serious.

"Sorry. I was thinking about what you said. The cabin would probably be the safest place for us, but you're so far away. I'm not sure we can get there. You have no idea how bad it is here."

"Listen, I'm the only one left up here. The other guy's bailed as soon as they heard what was happening. With just the three of us to feed, we could easily survive for months if I do the occasional supply run. Plus, the isolation means less chance of being attacked by drones or assholes."

"It's over five hundred miles," I repeated.

"I know that. It's gonna be hard, but I don't think you have any choice. It's not just drones that pose a threat. The major cities are already experiencing power outages and, with it, looting and murders. You have to get your sister out of town. It's too densely populated. Soon getting blasted to all hell won't be the only danger you have to worry about. Did you end up finding a weapon?"

"Jesus, Brent. I think you're letting your redneck inclinations get the better of you," I protested, but even as I said the words, I knew he was right. Being hit by a drone wasn't the only risk we needed to watch out for. That's why I'd been so careful to secure the house after breaking in.

"I'm not trying to scare you, Jess. I'm trying to prepare you. Now go find a pen and paper- I need you to write some stuff down."

By the time we said goodbye (possibly for the last time until Sasha and I found our way to the cabin) and hung up, I'd written over three pages of notes. I had a reasonably concise strategy for reaching Brent and the secluded getaway. Of course, having a plan and being able to follow through with it were two completely different things.

"What was that all about?" Sasha inquired when I rejoined her in the dining room where she was seated at the table, piecing together a puzzle she'd found collecting dust on a shelf in the family room.

"Brent wants us to meet him at the cabin in Wyoming." Sasha's eyebrows climbed her forehead, and she scoffed at the suggestion. "Does Brent the lumberjack realize how far away that is?"

Brent isn't a lumberjack. He's a bartender, but with the beard, tattoos, and penchant for flannel shirts, Sasha teases him for looking like a woodcutter.

"He knows how far away it is," I replied with more patience than I felt. "His cabin is in Wyoming, and that's where he is right now."

"So why doesn't he come to us?"

"Because it's not safe to stay here. It would be better if we went someplace quieter where there are fewer people."

"So, it's going to be safer to travel nearly four hundred miles into another state when those machines are blowing up anything that moves than to stay here?"

"The cabin's five hundred miles away," I corrected, and she rolled her eyes. "And I think the drones are specifically targeting people."

"Just so we're clear, you're not exactly selling me on the idea. If the drones are targeting people-people like us, how is it a good idea to leave the house and expose ourselves like that? We would have to cross a lot of open country."

"How do you know that?" I asked.

Sasha gave me a withering look, "We studied it in Geography last semester. I got an A+, remember?"

I nodded. "Of course, you did."

"Well? You haven't answered my question." She wasn't about to let it go.

I sifted through the puzzle pieces until I found one that fit. "I know that it seems like this is the safest place for us right now, but that will change. The longer those things are out there killing people, the more dangerous it's going to become. We need to leave town, and we need to leave soon."

"Why? I don't understand why we can't stay here." I explained to my sister what Brent and I had discussed, and to her credit, she listened quietly, only interrupting a couple of times to ask questions. By the time I finished talking, she had agreed that the idea had some merit.

The remainder of the day passed uneventfully. Sasha and I sacked the house for anything that might be useful on our impending journey to the cabin. Brent had provided me with an exhaustive list of items that we would need, and I wondered how they would all fit into a couple of backpacks. Backpacks I was yet to acquire. Sasha managed to find a nifty pocketknife with half a dozen handy attachments, squirreled away in the back of a drawer in the buffet. And I found a torch with replacement batteries that I could cross off the list. Aside from those two things, it appeared that I would need to venture out on a scavenging mission to find the rest of the items on Brent's list. I hated the idea of leaving Sasha alone in the house while I searched the neighborhood for supplies, but I had no intention of taking her with me. It was an unnecessary risk-I'd end up spending my time watching out for her rather than focusing on the task itself.

I was hunched over the kitchen bench studying the list when Sasha came bounding over with far more enthusiasm than our current situation warranted. Looking particularly pleased with herself, she urged me to guess what she had found. For a second, I wondered if she had discovered a handgun. I'd been through the entire house and found nothing more dangerous than a dull-edged Chef's knife in the utensil drawer.

"What have you got?" I asked, more out of a sense of obligation than interest. She drew her hands from behind her back and revealed her great discovery. In one hand she held a small sewing kit, in the other a basic first aid kit.

"Wow." I was hoping for a handgun. A sewing kit was a bit of a disappointment, but Sasha didn't share my opinion. 'Don't you think this will come in handy?" she enthused.

"We could use the first aid kit," I agreed.

"And the sewing kit."

I shrugged noncommittally. "I'm not so sure about the sewing kit." Her face fell, and I felt like a royal bitch. "But we can take it anyway. Just in case." Her smile returned, and she said she would place them with the other things we would be taking with us. I returned my attention to the list. Brent and I had agreed it would be best to set out at first light. Hopefully, it would be quieter then, and I'd be less likely to encounter trouble. I was anxious for the day to end so that we could go to bed. I was tired and worried about the supply run I'd be doing the next morning. Although it was unlikely that I'd get much sleep, I longed to lay my head on the pillow and close my eyes. At least for a little while.

Four

I slid the pocketknife into the front pocket of my jeans, doubtful it would be of much use if I had to defend myself, but it made Sasha feel better, so I agreed to take it with me. Sasha grudgingly followed me into the bedroom we had shared for the last couple of nights, her complaints falling on deaf ears. She wasn't strong enough to push the drawers against the bedroom door on her own, so I'd decided she would hide in the closet until I returned.

The closet was a repository for old dresses, only a decade or two out of fashion, and some winter coats stashed away for the season. I pushed the clothes to one side of the rail and nodded with satisfaction at the amount of space inside. My sister could easily fit into the closet without feeling too cramped. She would undoubtedly be bored senseless, but at least there was room to move about and change positions. "Do I really have to hide in the closet?" she asked yet again.

"We've already discussed this," I replied, my patience wearing thin.

"I know you said it would be safer if I hid in the closet while you were gone, but don't you think it's a bit excessive?"

"Yeah, it might be, but you're doing it anyway."

"But it's dark and boring in there," she protested.

"Dark, boring and safe," I agreed sweetly. Too sweetly. Sasha eyed me dubiously, aware of the dangerous territory she was entering. "Grab a pillow and your bottle of water and climb in."

Accepting her fate, she snatched a pillow off the bed and crawled into the space I'd cleared for her. She scooted back against the wall and hugged the pillow to her chest; the sassy attitude replaced with anxiety. I crouched down in front of her and took her hand in both of mine, "I know you're scared, but you'll be fine." Tears glimmered in her eyes, and she blinked them away. "I'm not scared for me. I'm scared for you," she clarified.

"I'm gonna be super careful, I promise."

She nodded glumly. "I can't lose you, Jess. Now Mom's gone, you're all I have left," she said, choking back a sob. Why did she have to go and get all emotional on me? I swallowed the lump in my throat and leaned over to hug her. "You're not going to lose me," I admonished in the sternest voice I could muster. I hope she bought it. I had no way of knowing if I would make it back to her, but I'd do whatever was necessary to return.

"Just stay put, and remember-I might be gone for a few hours or even longer if one of those drones is hanging around. But I promise I'll be back by sunset."

"Have you got the list?"

"You know what? I think it's still sitting on the kitchen bench," I admitted sheepishly. "I'll grab it on my way out. I'll see you in a few hours." I stood up and eased the closet doors shut, shrouding my little sister in darkness.

I stopped in the kitchen, folded Brent's list into a small rectangle, and stuffed it in my bra for safekeeping. I flung an old gym bag I'd found under one of the beds over my shoulder and headed for the door. Before slipping outside, I checked my pockets to make sure I had everything I needed-pocketknife, cell phone, list, and gym bag to carry everything. It was time to go—no more fucking around. I let myself out of the house and stood under the carport for a minute, listening.

A dog barked a couple of houses over. It sounded lonely and anxious rather than alarmed. Even though it was still very early, I heard a blast in the distance, somewhere off to the south, maybe four or five blocks down. There was nothing close by, and that reassured me. When I'd spoken to Brent, he had suggested trying to locate the items we would need for the journey in the nearby houses rather than risk heading over to one of the malls. I toyed with the idea of making my way back to the Home Depot I'd grumbled about on our way to Church a lifetime ago, but first, I'd raid the surrounding streets. The closer I stayed to the house, the better.

I walked around the back of the house to the paved, undercover courtyard. It was a sweet setup, low maintenance with some potted greenery and a spacious table and chairs for enjoying a meal outside on a balmy evening. I ducked beneath some trousers hanging from a retractable clothesline and wondered if the couple that lived there would ever return to take them down. Pushing aside such maudlin thoughts, I crossed the courtyard. Ferns grew across the narrow path that led to the street running perpendicular to the road opposite the park.

Poking my head over the top of the gate, I cautiously checked for drones or any other potential danger. While there weren't any wasp-like machines hovering in the air, I did spot a man across the street skulking along the footpath three or four houses down. He looked up, scanning for drones before he approached a parked car and unlocked the driver's door. He quickly climbed inside and wasted no time starting the engine. I waited for him to pull out onto the road and turn left at the t-intersection across from the park before I unlatched the gate and slipped out into the street myself.

I felt very exposed standing out on the median strip with nowhere to hide. Eager to begin my search, I hurried up the walk of the house next door. I was climbing the porch steps when I noticed the curtains twitch over the window to my right. I saw someone's silhouette by the window, no doubt watching as I turned tail and ran back down the walk. Feeling like a criminal (which I was, even it was borne of necessity), I jogged down the street until I was out of sight of that first house with its watchful occupant.

I stopped outside a two-story house painted duck-egg blue with crisp white trim. It had a real Hampton's vibe going on, and I could just imagine the fancy type of people that lived there. With any luck, they wouldn't be home, and I could raid the place. I hopped up the front steps and knocked on the door. When there was no response, I knocked a second time. Either nobody was home, or they weren't answering the door. I tried the door handle, but it was locked. The windows were securely latched too. "Goddamn it," I muttered in frustration.

I ran back down the steps and made my way around the side of the house, preferring to minimize my chances of being seen committing an offense, although the cops undoubtedly had more pressing concerns. The side gate had one of those annoying childproof locks, and I wasted precious time trying to figure out how to open the damn thing. Gravel crunched loudly beneath my boots with every step, the noise magnified by the stillness of the morning. At this rate, the entire neighborhood would know what I was up to.

As I rounded the corner of the house and the backyard opened out before me, I suddenly understood why my knocking at the front door had gone unanswered. The family that lived there couldn't hear me because they were in the backyard. Bile, hot and bitter, crawled up my throat, and I heard a mournful sob and was surprised to discover the sound had come from me. I blinked back tears and covered my mouth as I fought the urge to vomit.

The mother and child must have been outside enjoying the sunny morning last Sunday when the metal wasp-like drones hit. A half-empty basket of washing sat abandoned beneath the clothesline. The clothes hanging on the line fluttered ever so slightly, casting a flickering shadow across the body of the woman lying on the ground beneath them. A mass of maggots writhed in the gaping hole where her chest had been.

Her baby lay scattered a few feet away beside a blanket and toys. There wasn't much to see. All that remained was a small, chubby hand that looked disturbingly like a starfish and a few globs of meat wrapped in the tattered remains of a pink jumpsuit. I felt myself growing woozy as I stared at the tiny dismembered hand. Taking a deep breath, followed by another, I reached out and steadied myself against the house, slowly moving toward the French doors a few yards away.

When I reached the doors, I grabbed the handle and flung open the door with enough force to rattle the glass panes in the frame. My foot caught on the threshold as I entered, and I fell into the house, landing heavily on my hands and knees. My breathing came in huge, ragged gasps as I bawled uncontrollably for the woman and child outside. I don't know how long I cried for, it could have been a minute, or it could have been ten. Eventually, the sobs slowed to the occasional hitch of my chest, and I forced myself to stand up.

My eyes felt hot and puffy, and a combination of snot and tears streaked my face. I crossed the airy open plan living and dining room and stopped in front of the kitchen sink. I flicked on the mixer and splashed my face with cold water until I felt calmer, and the heat disappeared from my cheeks. After slurping some water to moisten my throat, I dried my face on a dishtowel. Feeling marginally better, I walked over to the fridge and examined the photo of the smiling family that had called this house home. It was impossible to reconcile the happy trio with the dead mother and her baby. I wondered where the man in the picture was. Did he discover the ruined remains of his wife and child, or had he been out running an errand at the time and simply never returned? I hoped it was the latter. I doubted anyone could survive the devastation of finding their loved ones like that.

Reminding myself why I was even standing in the dead family's house, I checked the refrigerator's contents. There were plenty of leftovers stacked neatly in colorful Tupperware containers and a carton of milk that had gone sour. I collected a couple of tomatoes from the crisper and some carrots that were still firm and crunchy. I debated taking the carton of eggs. It seemed probable that the half a dozen remaining eggs would break before I could get them back to the house. Fuck it. The prospect of sharing a plate of fluffy scrambled eggs with Sasha made it worth the risk.

While there hadn't been much happening in the fridge, the freezer section was another story. Cuts of meat I could only dream of being able to afford were carefully wrapped in plastic film, and I sorted through them, settling on a pair of fat steaks, some ground beef, and a portion of bacon to go with the eggs if they survived the trip. There was no point in taking anything else because we wouldn't be sticking around long enough to eat it.

The pantry was stocked like a mini supermarket, and I loaded cans of beans, tuna, and tinned fruit into the gym bag. A box of crackers and an unopened packet of trail-mix were tossed in the bag too. There was a massive tub of some deliciously named protein powder at the bottom of the pantry, and although it wasn't on my list, I figured it would be a useful addition. I just had to find a suitable container to store some in since there was no way I could lug a large five-pound tub around with me.

I found the dead woman's Tupperware stash stacked haphazardly in the cupboards under the kitchen island. It took a minute or two to find a matching lid and container. Then I filled it with the sweet-smelling protein powder. In a pinch, it would keep Sasha and me from going hungry when we were on the road.

There was only so much food we could take with us, especially since I didn't even have a vehicle lined up yet. My first choice would be the truck, of course, but I didn't know if it was damaged in the initial attack. Or if I'd even be able to reach it when the time came to take off. I left the gym bag on the island bench and looked for the other items on the list.

I let myself into the garage and squeezed around a BMW sport utility vehicle that must have cost five times my annual income. Nice ride if you could afford it. An impressive home gym setup filled the far side of the garage. I wondered whether it was the husband or wife who enjoyed working out, and then I reminded myself that it didn't matter. They were dead. And all the shiny stainless-steel dumbbells and fancy elliptical machines were frigging worthless now. I wasted a few minutes poking around in the garage, but there wasn't anything I could use. The family that had lived here hadn't been outdoorsy types.

I returned to the gym bag that I'd left on the counter and examined the contents. Half the food I'd collected would need to be used back at the house. The rest would last us three or four days, tops. Aside from that, I'd found nothing of use. I was deeply disappointed. With nothing of consequence marked off my list, I'd have to continue breaking into houses and risk crossing paths with a drone or being shot by some trigger-happy homeowner.

Sighing, I zipped the bag and made my way over to the front door. I flipped the deadlock and stepped out onto the porch, pulling the door shut behind me. I wished that I could erase the image of the dead mother and her baby from my brain, but I knew I'd never rid myself of the terrible memory.

I jogged across the lawn and skipped the next house as I'd seen a scowling face watching me from an upstairs window when I'd been making my way along the side of the duck-egg blue house. I continued down the street, pausing beneath a tree while I considered whether to continue straight or turn left at the next intersection and work the opposite side of the block. Wanting to remain as close to Sasha's location as possible, I opted to make my way around the block rather than venturing further away.

The house on the corner was concealed by a six-foot-high fence that stretched around the property's perimeter. From my position under the tree, I could see an automatic gate with an intercom. Mentally crossing that house off my break and enter list, I forced myself out from under the tree and jogged past the gated home. A security camera mounted above the automatic gate followed my progress.

I ducked around the corner into the next driveway and nearly ran into a burnt-out car parked across the concrete drive. The front passenger door stood open. The rotting remains of a woman in purple leggings and an equally bright tank top lay half out of the car, her blackened face resting against the concrete. The driver was missing from the waist up. The smell was horrific. I covered my nose as I darted across the lawn, leaving the dead behind. In their haste to escape, the dead duo must have forgotten to lock up, allowing me to slip inside with a minimum of fuss.

A fluffy tortoiseshell cat shot out from behind the couch and rubbed against my ankles, loudly meowing as it gazed up at me with big amber-colored eyes. I lowered the gym bag to the floor and crouched down to pat the friendly ball of fur. Judging by the ripe smell of its owners, I assumed the poor creature hadn't eaten for a couple of days. No wonder it wouldn't leave me alone.

It trotted after me, its meows growing in intensity as I entered the kitchen and found a box of kibble in the pantry. The sound of the kibble rattling inside the box sent the poor, hungry cat crazy. It circled my legs, almost tripping me over as I found its food bowl on the floor beside the breakfast bar. The cat started gobbling down the food before I'd even finished feeding it. Feeling sorry for the poor, abandoned animal, I poured more biscuits in a pile on the floor beside its food bowl and refilled its water. There was enough food to keep it going for the next two or three days. After that, the cat was on its own. I opened the window behind the kitchen sink just wide enough so the cat could comfortably hop in and out as it pleased.

With the cat taken care of, I set about searching the house for anything usable. Despite knowing the couple that lived in the house were both dead and decaying in the driveway, I still felt awkward rifling through their personal belongings. I had to remind myself that no one would be playing the extensive collection of country music CDs displayed in the lounge room. Nor would they get to finish reading the romantic thriller on the coffee table. There would be no more travel snaps added to the framed prints on the wall.

For some reason that I couldn't quite pinpoint, I stood examining the photos of the country music-loving couple. In one shot, they stood in front of a shimmering lake wearing bulky yellow life jackets. In another picture, the woman was grinning at the camera, her sweaty hair plastered to her head as she held a water bottle, a rocky outcrop jutting from a wooded hillside, the picturesque backdrop. Nearly all the photographs were of the couple involved in outdoor activities. Was it a stretch to think a couple that went hiking and kayaking for leisure might also enjoy camping?

A thrill of excitement rippled through me. Where to look? The garage seemed the most likely place. I found the door to the garage and flipped the switch. A long fluorescent bar flickered to life. Like in the previous house, shelves lined the walls. Tools and outdated computer equipment thick with dust were stacked haphazardly on the shelves, along with a heap of junk too precious to toss in the garbage. Feeling disheartened, I sighed. I'd been so sure I'd find a tent and a sleeping bag or two.

As I turned to go, something on one of the shelves caught my eye. Nestled behind a grubby keyboard and a tangle of auxiliary cords was a pair of two-way radios. I picked one up and pressed the button. Nothing happened. I flipped it over and removed the back cover to check the batteries. There were none, which explained why the damn thing hadn't worked. Still, if I could get my hands on some fresh batteries, I figured a pair of two-way radios could come in handy during our journey to the cabin.

After scoping out the rest of the house and coming up empty-handed, I stopped in the laundry and eased the curtain aside to check the backyard. There was a small aluminum shed nestled in the far-right corner of the yard that looked promising. Although I was reluctant to waste any more time searching the property, it would only take a minute or two to peek inside the shed.

It was as hot as hell inside the shed, the lack of ventilation creating an unpleasant sauna effect, and I felt like I'd been slapped in the face by the steamy air. Sweat beaded above my lip, and I wiped it away with the bottom of my t-shirt. The familiar scent of grass clippings and motor oil filled me with longing for the mundane activities undertaken before this nightmare had begun. I wondered glumly if life would ever return to normal or if this *was* the new normal.

I didn't have an opportunity to ponder further what the future might hold because there was a loud boom, and the thin aluminum walls of the shed shuddered violently. For a moment, I thought the entire shed would collapse around me, and I crouched beside the lawnmower, waiting for the end to come. A few seconds later, when the shed was still standing and I hadn't been pinned beneath sheets of aluminum, I slowly stood up and put my eye to a crack in the door.

Although the yard was clear, smoke rose in lazy tendrils from out in the street. It couldn't have been more than a few houses up, and I eased the shed door shut, afraid of being discovered. Venturing out during daylight had been a mistake. I made a mental note to avoid traveling when the sun was up; the risk of being spotted during the day far outweighing the drawbacks of trying to find our way around in the dark.

As my heartbeat slowly returned to normal, I stood in the one spot with sweat dripping down my back, too scared to move in case a drone heard me through the thin metal walls. I counted to three hundred before daring to resume the search.

I found a large backpack in a corner, a pair of tennis rackets concealed within the main compartment. Since I didn't foresee us playing any epic tennis matches on our way to the cabin, I ditched the rackets. Figuring I could either pass out from heatstroke or take a gamble and return to the house, I opted for the latter. I was crazy thirsty and wanted out of the cramped garden shed.

Back in the house, I cracked open a can of Coke that I took from a stash in the bottom of the fridge and guzzled it down in about three seconds flat. The bubbles made my eyes water, and I had to stifle a massive burp that rumbled up from my belly like a volcano. A sugar hit was just what I needed after the draining heat inside the shed. Ready to move on, I transferred everything from the gym bag to the backpack and slung it over my shoulders, securing the strap around my waist for added security. The cat wandered over, and I gave it a quick farewell scratch before heading out into the street once more.

Five

The source of the smoke I'd seen when the shed shook and shimmied was immediately apparent when I walked out onto the front lawn. Across the street, there was a smoldering black crater in a townhouse where an upstairs window had been. Wisps of smoke continued to trail from the burnt-out hole, but surprisingly the rest of the house hadn't caught alight. It was little wonder the shed had felt like an earthquake was rocking it. The damaged townhouse couldn't have been much more than a hundred yards from where I stood.

There was no sign of the drone responsible for the damage, so I ran across the street to the first townhouse in the row of three and rattled the door handle. Unsurprisingly, it was locked. Not wanting to waste more time out in the open the necessary, especially so soon after an attack, I skipped back down the steps and bypassed the next property since it had a For Let sign in the window. There was no point in trying to get inside a vacant property. I needed to find a place filled with the trappings of everyday life, not an empty shell.

I ran up to the door of the final townhouse-the one with the blown-in window, and despite my reservations about entering a house that could catch alight at any moment, turned the handle: desperate times and all that. The door was unlocked, the handle turning in my hand, but when I pushed, I met resistance. I threw my shoulder against it, and the door opened an inch or two. "What the fuck?" I grunted, wondering if some asshole had barricaded themselves inside. I pushed against it again, harder this time, ignoring the pain that shot along the length of my arm. It gave a little but nowhere near enough for me to squeeze through. "Hello, is anybody there?" I asked, convinced there must be someone inside the house pushing back against the door. When there was no response, I shoved as hard as I could, throwing my full weight into it.

As the door gave in, I thought I saw a flash of movement out on the footpath, but the street was empty when I turned to look. More concerned with gaining entry to the townhouse, I shrugged it off and squeezed through the partially open door, pulling the backpack in after me.

A melted, lidless face stared up at me from the floor, and I leaped back in surprise. My feet tangled, and I fell backward, landing on my backside hard. I scrambled to my feet as fast as my aching ass would allow and kept a safe distance from the burnt figure slumped behind the door. As I recovered from the shock, I noticed the dreadful smell of burnt tissue and clasped a hand over my nose.

The poor guy's face and chest were horrifically burnt. I couldn't even begin to imagine the excruciating pain he must have endured as he stumbled downstairs, trying to escape the drone. The fortitude and determination required to navigate a flight of stairs in his condition were stupefying.

His hand shot forward, his fingers stretching toward me, and I screamed. The unexpected movement had caught me off guard, and I felt ashamed of my reaction. He continued to stare at me with his creepy lidless eyes, and he made a croaking sound. I thought he was trying to talk, but it was difficult to tell with his lips seared off. Despite my reluctance to move any closer to the man, I took a step forward and crouched down beside him.

I thought I'd shit my pants if he reached out and tried to touch me. Thankfully, his hand stayed at his side as he mumbled something while his right eye remained locked on mine. Without lips to help shape his words, it was almost impossible to understand what he was trying to tell me. "Ill e." I frowned, not comprehending. "Ill e," he repeated. My mouth dropped open as I realized what he was trying to say. I shook my head. No way.

"Yes," he insisted.

"I can't," I whispered in response to his tortured plea.

"Ill e. Lease," he begged, reaching out to me. This time I didn't shrink away. I took his hand and held it in mine as I considered my options. As things stood, nobody would be coming to help this miserable wreck of a man. The drones were still roaming the streets seeking out people to kill. The emergency services were either incapacitated or completely overwhelmed by the high volume of callouts. I strongly doubted that the situation would be resolved anytime soon and certainly not fast enough to be of any assistance to the man on the floor beside me. I couldn't stand by and allow him to suffer a slow and painful death.

"Okay," I heard myself agree. Even with the man's face all burnt and crispy in places, I observed his relief at my assent. I gently lowered his hand and stood up. I looked around the lounge room, searching for a suitable weapon. It needed to be quick and painless. The miserable bastard had already suffered enough. Tastefully arranged furniture and a carefully curated collection of homewares that put my thrift shop style to shame decorated the room. I picked up an ornate bookend off a shelf and checked its weight. It felt like it was both heavy and solid enough to get the job done. I turned it over in my hands until I found a comfortable grip and forced myself to return to the man by the front door.

"Is this really what you want?" I asked, desperately hoping he had changed his mind so I wouldn't have to go through with it. "Do it. Now," he croaked.

"I'm so sorry this happened to you."

He nodded almost imperceptibly. "Thank you,' he sighed and looked away, waiting for the blow that would end his suffering.

I raised the bookend in the air with an anguished cry before swinging it down against his head. His skull caved in, and blood splattered the wall behind him. I smashed his head, again and again, crying out each time the bookend connected with his ruined skull. When I could no longer raise my arms, I dropped the bookend, turning away from the specks of bone and brain matter clinging to the murder weapon. Sickened by my actions and trembling uncontrollably, I picked up the backpack and fled the townhouse, all thoughts of ransacking the place forgotten.

I bounded down the steps and out into the street, my thoughts preoccupied with the man I'd just killed. Ending his life may have been an act of mercy, but it didn't feel that way to me. I'd just bludgeoned a stranger until his face looked indistinguishable from roadkill flattened by a big rig. I was officially a murderer. I sprinted down the middle of the road, trying desperately to outrun my sense of guilt and absolute horror at what I'd just done.

A shadow appeared on the road ahead of me, accompanied by a low thrumming sound that I could barely hear over the sound of my boots pounding the asphalt as I ran. Fuck. I'd been so caught up in the emotions competing for attention inside me that I'd neglected to keep an eye out for the drone responsible for the gaping hole in the townhouse. With no way of knowing if it had seen me, I veered off the road and dived under a cluster of hydrangeas, the large flowering heads starting to brown from too much sun.

I curled my body into a tight ball, ensuring my limbs were concealed beneath the drooping foliage, and dragged the backpack in front of me. Unsure if the drone was coming for me, I squeezed my eyes shut and waited. The seconds slowly ticked by, and nothing happened. Could my mad run for cover have gone unnoticed? Time and again, I'd had near misses with the flying machines while the people around me were picked off one by one. My luck was due to run out soon.

I forced myself to reach out and part the branches shielding my body and looked out at the street from my limited viewpoint. While it was impossible to get a clear view of the sky from where I was lying, I did manage to spot a collection of feet huddled behind the car parked in the drive of the yard I was hiding in.

"It's gone," a female voice called shakily. "You can come out from under the bush now." I didn't know if I should trust a stranger with my safety, but what alternative did I have? I couldn't very well lie in the dirt under the hydrangea for the rest of the day.

I rolled out from under the bush and brushed myself off as I got to my feet and walked over to the car. I could see the tops of three heads hunkered down in the narrow gap between the vehicle and a neatly trimmed hedge used as a fence between the properties. The woman peered up at me cautiously, an arm wrapped protectively around each of her children. "I won't hurt you," I stammered, shocked that someone would be crazy enough to drag two small children out into the open. They couldn't be more than three and four years old.

She slowly rose from her crouching position behind the car and dragged the children up after her. I could see she was younger than I'd first thought, probably no older than myself. All three sets of eyes watched me warily. Their misgivings about me seemed somewhat extreme, considering I was a lone female who had been cowering under some greenery up until a few seconds ago. Not precisely threatening behavior, but who was I to judge? I tried to reassure them that I was friendly. "You don't need to be afraid. I promise that I won't hurt you."

"Did someone hurt you?" The little boy asked shyly.

"Huh?" I had no idea what he was talking about. He pointed at my face. "You have blood on you. Did someone hurt you?" Puzzled, I wiped at my face, and my hand came away smeared with blood. Maybe I'd been scratched by a branch when I'd dived under the hydrangea, although I couldn't recall feeling the sting.

Nor could I detect any injuries on my face. Then I realized the blood wasn't mine. Back at the townhouse, I'd been liberally splashed with blood and other things I couldn't think about without a stiff drink to ease my conscience. No wonder they were suspicious. I looked like the bloody murderer that I was. I backed away from the car with my hands raised in a consolatory gesture, hoping to appease their misgivings about me.

As I stepped away, I wondered how she had managed to survive with two small children in tow. I was still trying to reconcile the need to lead Sasha out into the streets, and she was much older and capable of following directions. Running around in the open with children too small to keep pace with an adult, let alone not break down into a blubbering mess at the sight of a body, was unfathomable.

None of that mattered, though. I was done for the day and needed to return to Sasha. I'd already been longer than I'd expected and didn't want her worrying. Plus, I felt physically and emotionally exhausted. Too much had happened since I'd sneaked out of the house this morning. If I pushed on, I was likely to slip up and make a mistake that could get me killed.

As I turned to leave, the woman called out. "Wait." I glanced back to see her dragging the little boy and girl around the front of the car toward me. I was impatient to be on my way, not wishing to stand around only a few houses down from the man I'd killed, covered in the evidence of my crime. I watched as the woman brought her children over to where I stood, slightly bemused by their scrunched-up faces peering at me from behind their mother as they hid behind her legs. "Can we come with you?" she asked hopefully.

It occurred to me that she must be awfully desperate if she was willing to team up with someone as suspicious-looking as myself. "Why would you want to do that?" I finally asked. She looked down at each of her children in turn before returning her attention to me. "We haven't eaten in over twenty-four hours. And I don't know how much longer we can last out here with those things flying around. I was trying to reach the church. I thought someone there might help us, but I'm scared we won't make it. We barely avoided being seen by that last drone." Her eyes teared up as she clutched her children protectively.

"You're only a block away from the church, but there isn't anybody there to assist you anyway," I explained.

"Please help us," she begged. All three of them looked hungry and desperate. I unzipped the backpack and removed a box of granola bars I'd found at the house with the cat. "Here, take these." I passed her the box and watched as the children greedily snatched at the bars as she unwrapped them. I gently herded them over to the covered entry of the house we were standing in front of, hoping if anyone were inside, they wouldn't begrudge us sheltering on their front stoop for a few minutes while the trio gobbled down the granola bars.

I watched the street, wondering what the hell to do with the young mother and her two little ones. I was eager to put some distance between myself and the townhouse, aware that the longer I lingered nearby, the greater my chance of being linked to the dead guy inside. But the woman, who wasn't much more than a girl herself, had asked to come with me. Sasha and I would be setting out to meet Brent at the cabin soon, and it would be a long and dangerous journey for the two of us. Impossible if I had a stranger and her toddlers in tow.

The young woman thanked me for the food after she'd swallowed the last mouthful of her granola bar. She brushed aside a stray lock of blond hair from her face and watched as I hoisted the backpack over my shoulder and adjusted the straps. "I have to go," I told her. "You should get those kids off the street. If that drone returns," I didn't finish the sentence. She would know what could happen.

"I don't have anywhere to go. My boyfriend left to buy some groceries on Sunday morning, but he never came back. We waited for as long as we could, but when the food ran out, we had to leave."

"You should have left them at home and gone out to find some food by yourself." She shook her head vehemently. "There's no way I'd leave them alone." Maybe she was right. The children were probably too young to be left alone.

"I tried my neighbor's apartments, but nobody would answer their doors. They know I have two kids. What sort of asshole turns their back on a hungry child?"

What sort of an asshole, indeed? I wondered if she was playing me and decided it didn't matter. She had a valid point. I couldn't leave them there. All three of them watched as I considered my options. I might have stamped my foot in a fit of childish petulance and cussed under my breath loud enough for everyone to hear. The boy stifled a giggle with his hand, and his mother scowled at him.

"I can take you to a house where you should be safe for a couple of days at least," I grudgingly offered. The young woman's face split into a grateful smile, and I felt like a heartless bitch for even considering leaving them to fend for themselves. "How far away is the house? The kids are pretty tired, and I don't think they're up for a massive trek."

I shook my head. "It's right around the corner. If nothing goes wrong, we'll be there in a few minutes."

She crouched down to the children's level and explained they only had to walk a little further, and then they'd have somewhere safe to rest. The girl began to sob, and her mom wiped away the tears glistening on her plump cheeks and told her to shush. Telling her to be quiet had the opposite effect. The girl began crying even louder, exhausted, and overwhelmed, and beyond reason. I glanced around nervously, sure the kid's caterwauling would draw unwanted attention.

Without thinking, I picked up the boy and told his mother to follow me. She grabbed her crying daughter and placed the toddler on her hip, following so close behind me that I could hear her labored breathing over my shoulder. I jogged back the way I'd come, crossing the street opposite the cat house. I could have easily dumped them there, but I didn't want them to see the dead couple in the car. I made sure the children were facing out into the street to spare them the sight.

I jogged past the house with the large fence and security camera and turned the corner, grateful we didn't have too much further to go. The boy didn't look like he weighed much, but my legs were starting to burn under the added burden. I heard an explosion a few blocks over, followed by another, and I picked up the pace, ignoring the lead boots it felt like I was wearing. A minute later, I reached the yard of the first house I'd broken into and ran up to the porch steps. I lowered the kid and dragged him up the steps beside me. His mom joined us, the little girl no longer crying. I pushed the boy toward his mother and opened the front door that I hadn't bothered to lock earlier.

As I was about to usher them inside, I heard the unmistakable click-click of a shotgun behind me. I froze, wondering if the day could get any worse. "Turn around slowly with your hands raised, and don't think about trying anything stupid. I don't want to pull the trigger, but I will if I have to," a gruff male voice informed me. I didn't want to find out if he was only bluffing, so I raised my hands as directed and slowly turned to face him.

I was surprised to see a regular-looking middle-aged man watching me intently. I realized he must be one of the neighbors. My suspicions confirmed when he said, "You're not going back inside the Jacobson's place. I saw you break in earlier. I wasn't ready for you then, but I am now." He kept the shotgun pointed in my direction, and I was under no illusion as to what would happen if he pulled the trigger. I'd have a hole the size of a dinner plate where my abdomen should be, and Sasha would be left to find her own way to the cabin.

Ignoring the cold sweat dripping down my back, I found my voice. My throat was as dry as fuck, my tongue a thick wad of cotton wool inside my mouth. "The Jacobson's are dead. This woman and her children are alive. They need food and water and somewhere safe to rest. I found them around the corner. They were hiding behind a car while one of those drones prowled the street. It's a miracle the damn thing didn't discover them."

He glanced over at the young woman and her children, scrutinizing their sweaty faces before returning his attention to me. "Please. They haven't eaten for days," I pleaded. His shoulders slumped, and he exhaled loudly before lowering the shotgun. "Alright then," he finally agreed. I stood there gaping at him, unsure if I'd heard correctly. Could it be that easy? Tug the old heartstrings and open sesame. "Are you sure?" I asked for clarity. I wasn't about to second guess a man with a loaded gun.

Judging by his bemused expression, I'd gone from being a threat to being someone who might not be operating on all cylinders. "Would you like me to reconsider?" he asked, losing patience.

"No." I shook my head so hard that I practically gave myself whiplash. "I'll get them settled in and make sure they are okay, and then I'll be on my way."

"You're not together?"

"We just met," the kid's mom spoke for the first time during the encounter.

The man shrugged as if it made no difference to him. "Okay then. I'm going to go back home. It's best if you don't let the little ones look in the backyard." She waited for him to explain, but his mouth turned down in a pained expression, and he said nothing.

"There are bodies in the backyard that you don't want to see. Besides, you need to keep clear of all doors and windows. A drone blew out the window of the townhouse near where we met to get at the guy inside." I didn't like sounding so dramatic, but it was something she needed to hear. Plus, nobody needed to see what remained of that poor dead baby and its mother, especially not someone who had children of their own and was already struggling in this crazy new world.

The young mother escorted her children inside the house while I remained out on the porch, waiting for the gun-toting neighbor to depart. He gave me the once over before turning to check for drones and clunking down the steps, and disappearing next door. Once he was out of sight, I followed the others inside and secured the door behind me. I dumped the backpack on the floor and began closing all the drapes across the front of the house. When I reached the French doors that opened onto the back deck, I stood well back and pondered how I could cover the glass panels to make it difficult for a drone to spot the family hiding inside.

The woman walked over and joined me. "Why don't you try using a couple of bedsheets? That's what I did in my apartment. Curtains are so expensive, but you can pick up some old bedsheets at the thrift store for a couple of bucks. It doesn't look fancy, but it keeps the sun out."

"Yeah, that sounds like a good idea. I'll run upstairs and check the linen cupboard."

"You'll need a hammer and some nails too," she added.

"Right. I'll be back in a minute, and we'll cover those doors, and you can fix something for the kids to eat. There's plenty of stuff in the freezer."

I forced my legs to carry me upstairs despite the physical crash I could feel coming. The adrenalin from my experience at the townhouse had worn off, leaving me feeling like I'd pulled an all-nighter and then some. While I was upstairs, I went from room to room, closing the curtains before finding a couple of high thread count sheets in the linen closet beside the bathroom. I rubbed the fabric between my fingers and wondered how much they had cost. They felt cool and impossibly soft and silky to touch. Sticking them with nails would be a terrible waste, but what did it matter, really? Quality bedlinen probably wouldn't be a priority for most people in the foreseeable future.

With a pocket full of nails, I dragged a chair over to the French doors, being mindful to place it off to the side so I wouldn't be visible from outside. I was struggling to hold up the sheet, position the nail, and swing the hammer when the woman came over and held the sheet up for me while I hammered the nail into place. "Thanks, I appreciate the help."

She smiled and introduced herself. "I'm Fiona, and my kids are Harry and Charlotte. In all the excitement, we didn't get a chance to tell you our names."

"Harry and Charlotte, huh? I guess you have a thing for the royals." Fiona blushed, and the color to her cheeks made her look even younger. "You could say that. I've been collecting royal memorabilia and following the Princes since I was a little girl. The British just seem so proper and refined."

"Well, okay then." I climbed down off the chair and carried it to the other side of the doors. Fiona was a few inches taller than me and could hold the sheet above the door without much effort.

"I'm Jess," I told her while I hammered the nail into the wall. "There. That should do the job. I'd still keep Harry and Charlotte away from them to be on the safe side. Why don't you go and get something to eat? There were some frozen meals you could pop in the microwave."

I returned the chair to its place at the dining table and took a moment to observe the kids snuggled against each other on the lounge. Little Charlotte had a thumb firmly planted in her mouth as she watched her mother moving about the kitchen. I hoped they would be okay now they had somewhere secure to hide out, but I knew it was only a temporary solution. If the situation with the drones didn't resolve itself soon, they would find themselves without food once more, and I couldn't imagine Fiona would venture out alone to scavenge while Harry and Charlotte stayed behind. I reminded myself they were no longer my problem. I'd done what I could for the family. The rest was up to Fiona.

"I can't stay any longer," I announced. "My sister is waiting for me, and I've already been away for too long." Fiona's face fell. I could see that she didn't want to be left alone, but that wasn't my concern.

"Can't you go get her and bring her back here? There's plenty of room for you both."

I was already halfway to the front door. "I'm sorry, but that won't work. We're leaving town tomorrow. I understand you're scared and don't want to be alone, but I can't help you."

"Where are you going?" she asked, trailing behind me. "Maybe we can come with you. Once Harry and Charlotte have had something to eat and have had a rest, they'll be fresh and ready to go. I promise. Please don't leave us. I can't survive out there on my own." She tucked some loose hair behind her ear nervously and crossed her arms across her chest. I knew she was right. She'd be lucky to last out the week if she remained on her own.

"We're headed for Wyoming. My boyfriend has a cabin up in the mountains. I just don't think you could keep up with two young kids." I gestured to the siblings who were poking their heads up over the back of the lounge, looking cute and grubby and making me feel guilty with their big blue eyes. I could tell she was calculating the distance to Wyoming. Her brow furrowed as she realized the logistics of such a journey. "We can do it," she blurted in desperation. "I swear we can."

It occurred to me then that she wouldn't let me leave without them. I was her best shot at survival, and she wasn't about to let me slip away without a fight. I couldn't blame her for clinging to me. Although I probably looked like a murderous psycho, I'd been the only person to reach out and help her and her children since the world turned to shit.

"Okay. Feed the kids, then take them upstairs and throw them in the bath while I go and get my sister."

"Really?" Fiona clapped her hands together in excitement and lunged forward, wrapping me in a tight embrace. I remained stiff and unresponsive, waiting for her to release me. After an unbearable length of time, she loosened her grip and stepped back out of my space.

"Thank you so much. I promise we won't be any trouble."

"Yeah, sure. I have to get my kid sister. I'll meet you back here before dark."

"We'll be waiting," she assured me.

"Just remember to keep quiet and stay away from the windows," I reminded her.

Believing I would return for them later in the day, Fiona allowed me to leave without further drama. I stepped out onto the porch and closed the door behind me, relieved to be free of the burden of the young mom and her children.

Six

Sasha must have crept out from her hiding place in the closet and stationed herself on the other side of the door, waiting for my return, despite explicit instructions to stay put until I let her out. Before I even had a chance to slot the spare key in the lock, the door swung open, and Sasha threw herself against me and gave me a brutal bear hug, taught to her by Brent in one of his more mischievous moments. I pushed her back inside the house and carried the backpack through to the kitchen. "I thought I told you to remain in the closet until I came and got you," I said irritably.

I placed the backpack on the counter and began unpacking my bounty. Once everything was spread out, and I could take inventory, I realized I'd risked an awful lot for minimal reward. All I had was a backpack, some walkie-talkies, minus the batteries required to make them work, and a small amount of food. Luckily, I'd only broken one of the eggs during my foray, so that was something. We'd still get to enjoy some scrambled eggs before we set out for the cabin.

"It was dark and boring in the closet, and you were gone for ages," she complained. She was right, but I was undeterred.

"What if it hadn't been me at the door? What would you have done then?" Sasha flinched at the harsh tone of my voice, and I immediately regretted speaking to her that way. Being stuck in the closet with nothing to do would have been miserable. Just because I was having a rough time didn't mean I needed to take it out on my sister. "I'm sorry, I didn't mean to get snappy. It was pretty tough out there, and I've hardly got anything to show for it."

"You're covered in blood. Again." She gave me the once over before removing a clean dishtowel from a drawer and running it under the faucet. When it was thoroughly soaked, she wrung it out and handed it to me. "I can put this stuff away. You go sit down and wipe your face." I smiled gratefully, although it felt more like a grimace, and walked over to the dining table and collapsed into one of the chairs. Sasha went ahead and placed the meat and eggs in the refrigerator before slicing up one of the tomatoes. She opened the box of crackers and arranged the tomato on top. "Salt and pepper?"

I nodded. The level of my hunger took me by surprise. My tummy started rumbling, and my mouth was watering in anticipation. Considering everything I'd seen and done today, I hadn't expected my appetite to return for some time. I finished scrubbing at my face, knowing nothing short of a high-powered gurney would do a thorough job of removing the bits of the dead guy from my body. The dishtowel had turned a muddy reddish-brown color, and I pushed it off to the side so that I could eat the tomato crackers Sasha placed in front of me. Sasha sat to my left and nibbled at her crackers while watching me thoughtfully. It might have made me feel self-conscious if I hadn't been so damn hungry. "What happened out there?" she finally asked.

"Nothing," I answered too quickly and stuffed another cracker into my mouth to cover my lie. I began picking at the filth caked under my nails, determined to avoid further questions regarding my morning's activities. "It's just scary out in the open, and I'm worried about how we'll go tomorrow when we leave this place."

"Bullshit."

My eyes flew up to meet hers, my mouth silently working as I struggled to think of a suitable chastisement. Sasha never swore, at least not within my earshot. "Stop treating me like a baby. Be honest and tell me what's going on. I can handle it." I rubbed my temples, feeling the beginnings of a terrific headache. "Alright," I agreed and launched into an abridged version of everything that had happened since I left the house, omitting the part where I beat some poor guy to death with a bookend. I didn't think she needed to know about that. Not now, nor ever. That was my secret, and I didn't plan on sharing it with anyone, not even Brent.

When I got to the point of the story where I met Fiona and her children, Sasha perked up, sitting straighter in her chair, her eyes wide and engaged. I think because we had faced so much death over the past few days, she was desperate to hear about anybody that still had a pulse.

"So, where are they now?" she interrupted.

"I was getting to that."

"Well? Where are they?"

I bit down on the irritation threatening to bubble up. It had been a brutal day, and I was exhausted. My patience all but spent. "I took them to a house around the corner where they would be safe. They have enough food to last a week or more if they ration it carefully."

Sasha scowled, clearly displeased with my answer. "You just left them to fend for themselves?" she asked.

"Yes," I snapped. My sense of guilt getting my back up as much as my sister's incredulous expression.

"How do you expect her to survive on her own with two little kids?" she pressed, unaffected by my salty reply.

"I guess she'll have to manage like everyone else." Sasha made a sound of disgust and stood up, thrusting her chair back with such force that it toppled over, clattering loudly on the tiled floor.

"I'm going to find them and bring them back here where they'll be safe."

"Like hell you are," I exploded.

"You might not care what happens to them, but I do," she fired back.

"It's not that I don't care, Sasha. You have to try and understand that we can't save everyone, and tomorrow we are leaving to meet up with Brent."

"I know we can't save everyone. I'm not stupid. But we *can* help a young mom and her little kids."

"Do you honestly think we'd have any chance of making the five-hundred-mile journey with a couple of toddlers slowing us down?"

"I don't care! I'm going to find them, and you can't stop me."

I took my time rising out of the chair and stepped closer to her. She must have seen something in my face that unsettled her because she took a cautious step back.

"If you try and leave this house, I will tie you to a chair, and you won't even be able to scratch your butt if it gets itchy. Do you understand me?" I said. Sasha nodded, her lower lip quivering as she fought to hold back tears.

"I'm going to check the news," she mumbled before retreating to the family room. I heard the television's muffled sound and wondered what sort of grim vision was being aired by the television networks. Although it was tempting to see what was happening everywhere else, I respected her need for space. I'd never spoken to her that way before, and it rattled her. I made a mental note to apologize to her later, once we had both had a chance to calm down.

I sank back down onto the chair and buried my face in my hands. There had been enough drama for one day, and I felt dangerously close to breaking point. With everything that had happened, I needed some time alone to decompress. Hopefully, a long hot bath would help calm the emotions battling inside me.

***

That night I woke from a deep sleep and lay in bed, waiting for the brain fog to clear. Soaking in the bath earlier had done the job, and I'd crawled into bed afterward and fallen asleep almost immediately. I didn't know what time it was, but darkness swathed the house, and it had still been daylight when my head hit the pillow. Wondering what had caused me to wake so suddenly, I reached out to shake Sasha and felt the empty bed beside me. What the hell?

I jumped up and switched on the lamp, willing myself to remain calm despite the panic clawing at my chest. She probably woke up and needed to use the bathroom. "Sasha," I whispered as I poked my head out into the hallway. I crept down the hall and gently knocked on the bathroom door. When there was no answer, I opened the door, and although it was dark, enough light filtered through the frosted glass window for me to see that the bathroom was empty.

Okay. My sister wasn't in the bathroom. Maybe she was having a hard time sleeping after our argument. Sasha preferred to avoid conflict if she could, so it wasn't a stretch to think our blazing fight had upset her enough to keep her awake. Since we were sharing a bed, she might have got up and left the room so as not to disturb me. "Sasha? Where are you?" I called out as I checked the other bedrooms. They were empty too.

I went from room to room, and still no Sasha. When I reached the kitchen, and she wasn't there, I began to panic in earnest. I'd checked every room in the house. I clutched the sides of the counter and concentrated on my breathing. Now was not the time to flip out. I needed to figure out what had happened while I was asleep. Could someone have broken in and taken her while I was unconscious? Surely, I would have heard if an intruder was trying to break in or Sasha would have woken me.

Ignoring the sense of urgency that spurred me to rush to conclusions regarding her whereabouts, I methodically checked all the doors and windows in the house. Everything was locked.

The cupboard in the laundry was still flush against the broken window. If nobody had taken Sasha against her will, then she must have run off on her own. Why would she do something so reckless? I knew she was upset with me over the way I'd spoken to her earlier when she'd challenged me about not helping Fiona and her children, but surely, she wouldn't run away over it. A few harsh words didn't warrant such an extreme reaction.

As I stood there freaking out, it hit me. "Fucking hell!" I screamed into the silence. She'd gone out looking for the mom and her two children. Shit. I'd never even considered the possibility that my kid sister would attempt to find the hapless trio on her own. I raced down the hallway and ducked into the bedroom to retrieve my boots. I tugged them on and quickly tied the laces before snatching my cell phone off the nightstand and pressing the power button. I waited impatiently for it to power up. Once the screen lit up, I frantically typed a brief message to Brent explaining what had happened. At least that way, if we didn't make it to the cabin, he'd have some idea about what went wrong.

Pushing aside all thoughts relating to Brent and how badly I wished he was here, I ran back to the kitchen and grabbed a goodish-sized knife from the knife block. I regretted having not yet found myself a handgun capable of scaring off potential attackers. Pausing midway to the door, I backtracked and dug around in the utensil drawer until my fingers wrapped around the metal handle of a meat tenderizer. It had a nice heft, and I imagined the pointed tips across its surface would stop someone in their tracks if I wielded it with enough force.

Wasting no more time, I left the house and crossed the covered outdoor area, shuffling across the pavers to avoid tripping over a potted plant in the dark. I felt my way around the outdoor setting and made my way to the path that led to the side gate. Something brushed against the side of my cheek, and I leaped back, barely stifling a shriek. Realizing it was nothing more than the wispy leaves of an overhanging climber that had touched me, I chuckled nervously at my histrionics.

I opened the gate and stopped dead, stunned by the brilliant light show in the distance as blossoming orange fireballs lit up the sky across the city. Cocooned inside the house each night, I'd been unaware of the true breadth of the invasion. There must have been dozens of explosions flaring at random intervals as I stood transfixed, mentally calculating the number of drones patrolling the streets around me. A crippling sense of doom settled over me while I watched the sunset-hued flashes of burning light, aware countless people were being hunted and killed as I stood helpless and afraid.

I might have given up just then, accepted the hopelessness of the situation, and stood waiting until one of the drones sought me out and ended it all. Still, Sasha was out there someplace, alone and vulnerable and probably scared witless. As frightened and overwhelmed as I felt, I had a duty to look out for my sister.

Pulling myself together, I closed the gate and made my way down the footpath, careful to sidestep the circle of light beneath the streetlamp. All the houses looked dark and menacing without the warm and inviting glow that usually spilled out from behind their curtained windows. Only a few homes further down the street had their lights on, and I wondered how long it would be before a drone honed in on such easy targets.

I crossed the yard of the house where I'd left Fiona and her children and climbed the handful of steps to the front door. I tried turning the door handle, but it was locked as I'd expected. Fiona might be young and gentle-natured, but she'd grown up poor, living in a rough neighborhood with Harry and Charlotte. Keeping all the doors locked would have been second nature. I wasn't judging her; it was merely an observation. Sasha and I weren't much better off. No doubt if I'd gone and got myself knocked up as a teenager, I'd be wandering around helpless and alone in flip flops and cheap denim cutoffs.

I knocked on the door, hoping she would hear and let me in. I waited a minute or two in case she'd been asleep upstairs, but she didn't appear. Whether because she didn't hear me knocking or she was simply too scared to come to the door, I didn't know. If I had to force my way inside, I figured it would be easier going in through the French doors at the back of the house, so that's what I did.

It only took a gentle tap with the meat tenderizer to smash the pane of glass beside the door handle. I knocked the remaining shards of glass out of the frame and reached inside to turn the lock. My boots crunched on the broken glass as I entered the house and swept the sheet aside. Before I'd had a chance to secure the door behind me, I heard a familiar hissing sound followed by a horrible burning sensation as an aerosol was sprayed directly into my face. My eyeballs felt like they'd been set alight, and I cried out in pain.

"Fiona, it's me, Jess. For fuck's sake, stop spraying that shit in my face!" I wailed as Fiona advanced on me. She depressed the trigger again, releasing another cloud of bug spray, and I ducked to the side and swatted the can out of her hand. "Relax, it's Jess," I repeated.

"Oh, shoot. I'm sorry. I thought you were an intruder."

"Don't worry about it. I guess you didn't hear me knocking."

"I guess not," she agreed sheepishly. I found the kitchen sink for the second time that day and splashed my eyes with water until the stinging began to subside. "Damn, that hurt." I patted my face dry before feeling around for the light switch on the rangehood. The low wattage bulb provided enough illumination for us to see each other easily without being bright enough to advertise our presence in the house. "Where's my sister?"

Fiona shrugged. "I have no idea. We waited all afternoon for you to show up, but you never returned," she replied angrily.

"She came looking for you. Where is she?"

"I already told you. She's not here. I've been alone here with Harry and Charlotte until you came smashing your way inside and scared us half to death," she explained. I let out a shaky breath and collapsed on the couch. "I'm sorry for scaring you." I could feel myself teetering on the edge of a full-blown meltdown, and I didn't know if there was anything I could do to stop it. Luckily, Fiona sensed my agitation and sat down beside me. She suggested I take a few deep breaths. I nodded and focused on my breathing for a minute or so. I felt stupid sitting there breathing like I was in a birthing class, but it seemed to do the trick.

"Why do you think your sister came looking for us?" Fiona asked once she could see I was feeling better.

"She was furious that I wasn't going to come back for you," I admitted. Fiona's face tightened, her lips pursing in a mixture of hurt and anger. After a tense pause, she finally asked, "Did you tell her which house we were in?" I thought back to the heated conversation we'd had when I'd returned earlier in the day. I slowly shook my head. "I don't think so. I don't remember mentioning anything specific. Maybe I told her it was a blue two-story house, but I can't be certain."

"So, you didn't tell her the street name or number?" She pressed.

"No. It's not like I needed her to send you a postcard or anything."

Fiona glared at me, "You don't have to be a jerk about it." She had a valid point. I could be a real asshole sometimes, and it seemed now was one of those occasions. "I'm sorry. I didn't mean to be rude; I'm just really freaking out right now."

"I understand. If Harry or Charlotte went missing, I'd go crazy. That's part of the reason I begged you to take us with you. I'd do anything to keep my kids alive, and I knew straight away that you're a survivor. You're tough and willing to do things other people couldn't. Your sister can't be too far away. Maybe she thought you meant we were in a house on the other side of the block."

I appraised Fiona with fresh eyes. Perhaps I'd been too harsh, thinking she was just another ditzy blond popping out kids she couldn't afford to support. "That's possible," I agreed. I wanted to question her about what she meant by my willingness to do things other people couldn't do, but it would have to wait until another time. I had more pressing matters to deal with at present. "I'm going to look for Sasha. I'll try around the block, as you suggested. If she shows up here while I'm gone, make sure she stays put."

"Of course, I will. Be careful out there."

Seven

O ut on the porch, I stood watching the balls of fire lighting up the night at sporadic intervals while deciding which way to go. There was no telling how far Sasha had gotten in her quest to find Fiona and the kids since I didn't know when she'd decided to venture out by herself. She could have slipped away only minutes before I woke up, in which case she should be relatively easy to locate if nothing terrible had happened to her. Or she could be long gone if she'd left earlier and become disorientated in the dark, wandering further than she intended.

I walked down to the sidewalk and checked both directions, wishing my sister had badgered me for a cell phone like other kids her age. I wouldn't be standing around at a complete loss right now if I could send her a quick text and find out exactly where she was. Wishful thinking wasn't going to help find her; neither was procrastinating the night away. I just needed to pick a direction and go with it.

An explosion only a few houses down on the opposite side of the street jolted me into action. I took off toward Park Street, distancing myself from the commotion as a second blast blew in the large bay window of a nearby home. It was lit up like a

Christmas tree, with only the sheerest of lace curtains blocking the light within. *Fucking idiots*, I thought as I ran from the high-pitched shrieking coming from within the burning house.

Afraid the drone responsible for the blast would turn its attention on me, I willed my legs to pump harder, my boots pounding along the sidewalk as I neared the corner of the block. I turned right onto Park Street, grateful for the cover provided by the large crepe myrtle planted near the street corner. I jogged past the SUV that had crashed into the power pole days ago and turned my head away from the sickening stench of decaying flesh wafting from within. The bodies were ripening much faster than I'd anticipated. A combination of warm, humid temperatures and seemingly endless sunshine beating down on the remains was accelerating decomposition.

I thought of all the bodies and body parts littering the park across the street and wondered how long it would be before the smell became unbearable. Plus, all that organic matter was bound to create some sort of nasty biohazard given enough time. It was yet another reason why we had to hit the road and head for the mountains. I just hoped Brent was still alright. He hadn't replied to my earlier text, which worried me.

Confident that I was out of the drones firing line for the moment, at least, I slowed to a walk so that I wouldn't run right past my sister without even realizing it. I took the time to look around the house's front yard next to us, although it was doubtful she'd be hiding so close to home. The faintest hint of light seeped from around the window along the side of the house, confirming my suspicions that the people next door had holed up inside, waiting for the disaster to pass. Good luck to them.

About midway down the block, I heard an approaching car engine. I melted into the shadows and waited while it rumbled past, watching as it turned right onto Church Street. It surprised me that a drone hadn't targeted the car, and then it dawned on me how it was traversing the streets without being accosted. Some smart cookie had knocked out the headlights, reducing the vehicle's visibility. The brake lights still glowed like tiny red embers as it slowed to take the corner, but that was the only source of light illuminating the car. I wasn't sure how the drones identified their victims, but movement and light seemed to draw their attention, as did sound.

I emerged from the shadows and continued down the sidewalk, checking over my shoulder every few strides for any sign of the drone. Knowing it was less than a block away unnerved me, and it was difficult to remain focused on searching for Sasha when I kept expecting to hear the high-pitched whine of a killer metal wasp as it closed in on me.

I spotted a sedan hastily parked with its nose touching the curb and its tail poking out into the street a few yards back from the stop sign on the corner and briefly wondered what had become of its driver. They had probably panicked when everything had started exploding and fled from the car, thinking it would be safer anywhere but inside a metal and glass coffin on wheels.

I spun around and saw the top of a head drop back down below the window. It was too dark to see clearly, but there was something vaguely familiar about their outline that made me believe it could be my sister. "Sasha?" I ran over to the car and tried the door handle, but it was locked. I knocked on the window with my open palm as I tried to get a decent look at the person cowering inside. "It's Jess. Open the door."

Sasha's pale, frightened face peered up at me from her hiding place in the footwell behind the driver's seat. It took her a moment to realize it was me, and I had to point to the lock a couple of times before she got the idea and unlocked the car so that I could open the door and help her out. We hugged each other for what felt like an eternity. I eventually unwrapped her arms from around my waist and took a step back to prevent her from latching onto me again.

"What the hell are you doing out here? There are drones everywhere," I hissed, anger quickly replacing my relief at having found her.

"I had to find Fiona and her children. We can't just leave them to die," she explained, her voice choked with emotion. Her distress managed to dampen the anger inside me, and I bit back the furious reprimand threatening to spill out of my mouth. "You could have gotten yourself killed. How would that have helped Fiona and her kids?" She snuffled and gave a slight shrug of her shoulders. "What were you doing in that car anyway?" I led her over to a sheltered spot under someone's carport, squeezing in between a minivan and a thick hedge of fragrant lavender. When she didn't answer, I took her by the shoulders and forced her to look at me. "Answer me, please."

"I was looking for the house you described when I heard voices." She kept looking back over her shoulder nervously, and

I had to encourage her to continue. "I barely managed to duck behind the car before a group of guys came out of a house nearby. They were armed with baseball bats and machetes. I think they were going through the empty houses and stealing stuff."

I thought about Fiona and the kids hiding in the flashy-looking house on the opposite side of the block. If what Sasha said was true and these guys were looting the unoccupied homes, I weighed up the chances of them finding their way to the house before we did. "What happened then?" I pressed.

"They were arguing about the stuff they'd stolen as they moved on to the next house and thumped on the front door pretending to be the police." She pointed to a house across the street with the front door standing wide open. "An old man answered the door, but he realized his mistake too late, and one of the guys blocked the door." She stared out past me at the faintly lit doorway, reliving the experience that had led her to seek shelter in the backseat of a car. "He shouldn't have answered the door. Why did he have to open the door?" She sobbed.

"Shh." I drew her against me and hugged her while she continued her story. "I think they killed him." She sniffled and wiped her nose across the back of her hand.

"What do you mean? Did you see them hurt him?"

"Yeah. They started yelling at the old man and pushing him around, and one of the guys swung a bat at him, and that's when I climbed in the car and hid. I figured they wouldn't bother searching such a dirty old bomb."

"You did the right thing hiding." I reassured her. I couldn't help feeling sorry for the man beaten to death by a gang of thieves.

Although I'd killed someone earlier in the day, the circumstances were entirely different. I'd only done it to end the man's suffering, and it was at his request. Brent was right. Without law and order, anarchy ruled. Thugs without a conscience would take the streets, looting and killing at will. We didn't stand a chance against an armed gang high on violence and bloodshed.

"We have to get moving. I don't want to be out here if those assholes reappear." I didn't mention that in my haste to find her, I'd left the knife and meat mallet behind, and we were unarmed and vulnerable. "How long ago did you see them? Do you think they might have moved on?"

Sasha considered the question and shrugged. "I'm not sure. It felt like I was crouched in the car for ages, but it might have only been fifteen minutes, maybe a bit longer."

"That's okay. We'll just have to take our chances."

I led Sasha back the way I'd come, intending to deposit her at the house on Park Street before retrieving Fiona and the kids. We'd almost reached the corner when I heard a car rumbling toward us, and I pulled my sister down behind a concrete water fountain in the middle of someone's lawn. I waited as it sped by with its high beams cutting through the dark like a glowing bull's eye, the driver not as savvy as the previous vehicle I'd seen with its headlights disabled.

Once the car had passed, I pulled Sasha to her feet, "Come on." We'd barely taken a few steps when a fireball lit up the sky opposite the park, followed by the telltale screech of rubber as someone hit the brakes. "Fuck. Back the other way. Now." I turned on my heel and dragged Sasha after me. "Hurry up," I urged, anxious to put as much distance between ourselves and the drone as we could.

Sasha pulled free of my grip. "We can't go that way. I saw the gang head in that direction." I was acutely aware of the seconds ticking by as we stood around debating the wisdom of following a group of murderous thugs when a drone had just turned a car into scrap metal less than three hundred yards away. "I understand that, but we don't have any choice. That drone will find us if we stick around much longer, and if it does, we're dead—no ifs, buts, or maybes. So stop crying, take my hand and run like your life depends on it, because if you want to help Fiona and her kids, we need to get the hell out of here before something bad happens. Got it?" She nodded unconvincingly, and I wasn't sure if my angry pep talk had gotten through to her, but she allowed me to take her hand and lead her down the sidewalk without further argument.

We set a brisk pace for a hundred yards or so. It felt like all I ever did anymore was run from death with a lump of fear in my throat so immense that I could barely breathe. If today was anything to go by, I couldn't imagine how we'd stand a chance trying to reach the cabin, especially if I had to watch out for a couple of toddlers and their clueless mom.

As we neared the other end of the block, I slowed to a walk. Sasha panted from the exertion, her preference for books and video games over physical activity taking its toll. "You should probably give the books a break and take up a sport," I suggested as we circled the streetlight on the corner. "Sorry I didn't brush up on my survival skills at bible study boot camp. I didn't realize the end of the world would come so soon," she replied.

"They have bible study boot camp?"

"No. I was being sarcastic," Sasha answered dryly. I tried not to smile. If she could still crack a joke, I figured she couldn't be too traumatized.

An automatic garage door whirred to life behind us, and I paused to check over my shoulder as a crack of light appeared from inside the garage of a house two doors down, revealing five pairs of feet shuffling about as the door slowly rose. Animated chatter drifted down the street interspersed with hearty guffawing, which felt grossly out of place considering the circumstances. Anyone capable of such unfettered humor when people were obliterated every other minute was someone I didn't want to stick around to meet. "Run," I told Sasha, and we took off down the street. Having already witnessed the unprovoked violence inflicted upon a defenseless old man, Sasha didn't need further encouragement. She sprinted along beside me, our feet barely touching the asphalt as we fled from the gang of murdering thieves.

I'd hoped we could escape unnoticed, but we were shit out of luck. High on adrenalin and blood lust, one of the thugs must have spotted us as soon as they ducked under the garage door because I could hear feet pounding along the road behind us accompanied by excited whooping and hollering. I guess they either didn't care if they attracted a drone or were too stupid to realize all the noise they were making was bound to get them killed. A quick look over my shoulder confirmed my fears. Five young men were pursuing us, each of them armed and rapidly closing the distance despite our best efforts to outrun them.

"Faster!" I urged my sister between ragged gasps as we passed the house with the friendly cat and the dead couple in the car out the front. I didn't like our chances of outrunning a group of young men that were bigger, stronger, and likely fitter than either of us. We pushed ourselves harder, finding that tiny bit extra in reserve that neither of us thought we had in us. I calculated how much further we had to go before reaching the house where Fiona was hiding with her kids.

Six houses. The gang was less than one hundred yards behind us. It was going to be close. In my desperation to find my sister, I'd left my lame-ass weapons back at the house with the dead baby in the backyard. If they caught up with us, we were fucked. My fists were no match for baseball bats and machetes.

Five houses. It felt like my feet couldn't move fast enough.

Four houses. Sasha was beginning to fade. "Keep going," I panted.

Three. They were closing in on us. We turned the corner. Almost there. I cut across the yard next door and clambered up the porch steps. I hammered on the front door, more scared of being clubbed to death by the assholes chasing us than attracting the attention of a drone. "Fiona, it's me. Open the fucking door!" I slammed my open palm against the door again. "Open the goddamn door," I half begged, half demanded. I pushed Sasha up against the door and turned to face our pursuers. I knew I didn't have a chance of fighting them off, but I'd die trying.

The first of them had reached the bottom of the porch steps when the door swung open. I thrust Sasha inside and rushed in after her. The guy at the front of the pack threw himself at the door. The force sent the door crashing into my face, and I staggered back. "You're mine, bitch," he growled through the gap, the stink of alcohol wafting from him, as I pushed back against the door. I knew I had to shut it before his bloodthirsty buddies reached the porch and forced their way inside.

Sasha joined me, and together, we pushed back against the swearing, machete toting guy on the other side. "Grab the kids and go to the garage," I yelled to Fiona over my shoulder. She remained by the stairs, watching helplessly as Sasha and I fought against our would-be attacker who had squeezed his arm through the opening, blindly waving a wicked-looking blade back and forth in the hope of finding its target. "Strap the kids into the SUV in the garage, and we'll meet you out there in a minute," I bellowed, my eyes never leaving the machete swiping dangerously close to my face. "Now!"

That spurred her to action. Thank fucking God. We were running out of time. Even if Sasha and I managed to secure the door, there was nothing to stop them from smashing their way through the floor-length windows. The machete blade swooshed close to my nose as I heard feet on the steps outside. Fuck. I threw all my weight against the door in a final attempt to close it against the snarling maniac swiping at me with the long curved blade. The edge of the door crushed his forearm against the door jam, and he released the machete with a pained howl.

I snatched the blade up off the floor and swung it down at his hand, which was still blocking the door. The machete's sharp edge, combined with the downward motion, easily sliced through flesh and bone, severing all four fingers of his right hand. He emitted a piercing shriek and jerked his bleeding stump out from the gap, allowing us to slam the door shut and turn the lock as his detached fingers rolled across the floor.

Sasha stood transfixed by the dismembered digits scattered on the floorboards like skinless cocktail frankfurters. I'd only just twisted the deadbolt when the group of youths flung themselves against the door, yelling obscenities while the guy I'd separated from his fingers continued to wail in the background. I turned to my sister with the machete still tightly gripped in my hand. "Quick, into the garage with Fiona."

"What about you?" she asked worriedly. "I'll be there in a minute. Just help Fiona get the kids in the car and strap everyone in."

Behind us, the narrow window beside the door shattered inward. "Hurry up and get out of here," I called sharply, raising the machete for round two. The fat end of a baseball bat tapped out the remaining fragments of glass before a hand reached inside and felt around for the deadbolt. "You'd better remove that hand if you don't want to end up like your howling buddy there," I threatened with as much menace as I could muster. I watched as the hand slowly released its grip on the lock and withdrew. "We're gonna fucking skin you alive, bitch." The owner of the baseball bat promised through gritted teeth. I didn't doubt it.

I'd bought myself precious moments, but it wouldn't be long before they overcame their trepidation at tackling a single machete-wielding woman. Ignoring the tirade directed at me, I crossed the entry and grabbed the car keys from a hook on the wall beside the door to the garage. Harry and Charlotte were already in the back seat of the SUV while Fiona wrestled with a baby seat, trying to remove the bolt, securing it so she could make room in the back of the car. "Forget it. There's no time, squeeze in with the kids, and we'll deal with it later. If there even is a later." I told her as I raced around the front of the vehicle.

I reefed the driver's door open and was about to climb inside when a young guy with a shaved head burst into the garage. He grinned triumphantly. "I got you now, bitch. And I'm gonna make you bleed." He wielded a Katana of all things, probably nabbed from a display cabinet of one of the homes he'd ransacked. I hoisted myself into the driver's seat and slammed the door shut as he skipped around the bonnet with the sword held aloft like some ancient feudal warrior. Too bad he was going up against a three-ton motor vehicle with central locking and enough horsepower to pull a small house.

I locked the car and thrust the key into the ignition as he pressed his face against the glass beside me. He couldn't have been more than eighteen or nineteen, and yet his face was twisted into the hateful snarl of a feral animal. It occurred to me that he and his buddies were most likely high on a dangerous cocktail of drugs and alcohol, which would go a long way to explaining their fearless, hyper-violent state. Sasha cried out as another guy entered the garage and walloped the bonnet with an aluminum bat, dragging it leisurely across the dented surface as he stared us down.

We had to leave before it was too late. The SUV rumbled to life, and I put my foot on the gas, revving the engine as two more attackers entered the garage. I buckled my belt and warned Fiona to hold on tight.

"What about the garage door?" Sasha asked aghast.

"Fuck the garage door." I thrust the gearstick into reverse and released the handbrake. The SUV shot backward, the tires squealing across the concrete floor at the same instant one of the thugs swung a bat at the windshield. The tip of the bat bounced off the glass as the rear of the SUV hurtled into the garage door. "Look out!" Sasha screamed and covered her face with her hands as the guy scrambled up onto the front of the vehicle and swung the bat a second time.

I panicked and slammed on the brakes, sending him rolling off the front of the bonnet, his face a comical mask of surprise as he disappeared in front of the vehicle. Someone grabbed the door handle on Sasha's side, and she shrank away. The guy I'd dislodged from the bonnet popped up with his bat swinging, and I jammed my foot down on the accelerator. Time slowed to a crawl as he registered what was happening. He looked up at me in terror before he disappeared beneath the front of the SUV, and we bounced around in our seats as we rolled over the top of him.

I thrust the SUV back into reverse and put my foot flat to the floor. The tires rolled over the lumpen mass on the floor, and Sasha cried, "What have you done?" Before I could answer, the SUV collided with the garage door, the metal panels crumpling outward as we burst out of the garage and hurtled down the driveway. I ran over the gutter as I reversed out into the street, and my sister's head thumped against the side of the vehicle when the front wheels dropped over the concrete lip. She gave me a dirty look as she rubbed the side of her head, which I did my best to ignore.

Unperturbed by our violent altercation and the thrashing they'd received, the remaining guys ran down the driveway after us, swearing and waving their weapons in the air. They had to be crazy high or stupid. Probably both. I'd just relieved one of their crew of his fingers using his own weapon and run another one over, most likely killing him in the process, and yet they kept coming after us. But now we were out in the street; they had no chance of catching us. I drove off, leaving them standing in the middle of the road, cursing.

Eight

I eased my foot off the accelerator as we approached the corner and glanced in the revision mirror. Fiona sat perched on the edge of the seat between Harry and Charlotte. She eyed me warily, no doubt questioning the wisdom of throwing her lot in with a callous killer. I glanced across at my sister. Her expression mirrored Fiona's. A hurtful combination of apprehension and dismay. At that moment, I was a stranger to her, someone dangerous and not to be trusted. Her misgivings hit me like a sucker punch. Didn't she realize I'd only done what was necessary to extricate us from a situation that would have ended very badly otherwise?

Before I could justify my actions or reassure them that I wasn't a psycho myself, the revision mirror lit up with a blinding flash of light as the street behind us was bombarded with a series of fireballs. "Oh fuck," I muttered dismally. I gunned it around the corner and pulled up alongside the curb behind a parked car a few houses down from the intersection. "What the heck are you doing?" Fiona cried. "We can't stop now."

I switched the car off and squeezed down beneath the steering wheel as best I could. "Everybody get down, and for fuck's sake, don't make a sound." To her credit, Fiona was smart enough not to argue with me. Following my directions, she unbuckled Harry and Charlotte's seat belts and pulled them down onto the floor, where they huddled together in silence. Sasha crouched down opposite me; her cheek pressed against the glove compartment. I heard the now-familiar whir of a drone, and I cautiously raised my head to peek out the window. I could just make out the insect-like shape of the approaching drone through the tinted glass. A small red light glowed on the underside of its body, and I wondered if it was some sort of laser sight.

We all held our breath as it drew closer to the vehicle. It hovered only yards away, seeming to sense our presence yet unable to pinpoint our exact location. Nobody dared move. Even the children remained frozen in place; their tiny bodies pressed hard against their mother. The drone eventually moved on, its small red light diminishing to nothing as it drifted off down the street, searching for a new target. I slowly counted to one hundred in my head before motioning for everyone to get back into their seats.

"That was fun. Can we play hide and seek again?" Harry asked his mother as she strapped him back into the seatbelt. Fiona smiled at her son and ruffled his hair. "Maybe later. I think we might need to play that game quite a bit. Do you think you could teach little Charlotte to play hide and seek as well as you do?" Harry nodded enthusiastically, seemingly oblivious to the dangerous situation we'd barely managed to escape from.

"You killed that guy back at the house," Sasha muttered. I turned to face her, tamping the irritation I felt at her accusation. Getting my back up wouldn't help matters. It was understandable that she would be distressed and need some sort of explanation. "Sasha, the guy that I ran over wasn't some innocent bystander that just happened to get in my way. He was chasing us with a baseball bat." I'd almost reached the end of my endurance, and I could hear a snarky edge creeping into my voice.

"You didn't have to run him over."

"Those guys beat a man to death. You saw them do it, and you told me they laughed while they killed a defenseless old man. Imagine what they would have done to a group of women and children. Think about what might have happened to Harry and Charlotte if they'd gotten hold of us."

"I don't know, Jess. I get that he wanted to hurt us, but killing him seems wrong," she said uncertainly.

I felt too edgy and tired to debate the new world order, but I didn't have any choice in the matter. Both Fiona and my sister looked set to flee into the night rather than remain in the SUV with someone capable of mowing down another human being. "You're right to think what I did seems harsh and brutal. Before today I'd never hurt another person, much less take someone's life. But everything is different now. The old rules don't apply. We have to reach the cabin where Brent is waiting for us. I don't want to be in a situation where I have to hurt anyone, but I will do whatever is necessary to make sure we get there safely, and I won't apologize for doing it. And if you want to keep on sucking in oxygen and have a hope of surviving this fucking mess, you'll need to accept that I'm gonna have to do some terrible things to keep us from getting killed."

I twisted around to face Fiona. "That goes for you too. If you plan on sticking with us, you need to understand that there will be times when we'll have to do things that don't sit comfortably. If you don't think you can deal with that, it might be best if you and the kids don't continue with us." Fiona looked from me to her children, weighing up her options. Running over that guy in the garage must have shaken her faith in me. I didn't know if her fear of being left alone would overcome her reservations about tagging along with a murderer. Because, regardless of my motives, two people were now dead due to my actions.

"I think we should stay with the tough lady. She gave us food and saved us from the bad guys." I looked across at Harry and winked. From the mouths of babes. Fiona squeezed her son's hand and nodded. "Alright. We'll stick with you. I don't think I could make it on my own out there. Not with the kids."

"I'm glad you're coming with us," Sasha replied with genuine warmth.

Not wanting to take any chances, I climbed out of the SUV and walked around to the front of the vehicle, and knocked out the headlights with the base of the machete's handle. I did the same to the tail and brake lights. Although I wasn't too keen on eliminating the option of using the lights if needed, I felt better knowing we couldn't accidentally attract a drone. With all the lights outside the vehicle taken care of, I climbed back into the driver's seat and removed the bulb from the interior light. I considered ripping out the fuse to disable the dash's soft glow, but I was kind of reluctant to go that far. I turned the key, and the engine quietly came to life. It was so quiet and unobtrusive it took me a second to realize it was even running. Give me my truck any day. At least when I was behind the wheel of that beast, I knew when the engine was running.

"I think we should try and make our way out of the city before daylight," I informed Sasha and Fiona. "It's not just the drones we have to worry about anymore. We got lucky back there. Those assholes only had baseball bats and machetes. Sooner or later, we're going to cross paths with someone packing some serious firepower, and when that happens, we'll be royally fucked. Excuse the language." My sister nodded in silent agreement. No doubt still mulling over my actions back at the house. "Okay," Fiona agreed meekly.

I checked the fuel gauge and was elated to discover the tank was almost full. I could have wept with relief. A full tank would get us nearly halfway to the cabin. Maybe further. If the needle had been near empty, I don't know what I would have done. The prospect of searching for a suitable vehicle at that moment after the day I'd had was unthinkable. Grateful that something was going our way, I checked the mirrors before pulling out into the street. We would have to cross downtown to reach the exit to the highway. Shit was messed up enough out here in suburbia. I hated to think about what it would be like when we eventually reached the heart of the city.

***

We'd been driving for over two hours. Any other time, a trip of that duration would have seen us well clear of the city and cruising along the highway with nothing but the occasional critter to watch out for. Not anymore. According to the readout on the dash, I'd only managed to drive an excruciating three and a quarter miles. It would have been faster on foot if we didn't have the kids. With no headlights and the streetlights blacked out on all but a few roads, our progress was slow. Throw in countless mangled wrecks blocking the way, forcing me to find an alternative route, only to be diverted yet again by a pile-up or downed power line lying across the road, and we had no chance of reaching the highway as I'd hoped.

By the time I noticed a subtle lightening of the sky to the east, we were only a mile or so from downtown. It was tempting to press on, but I knew it would be a mistake to try and reach the highway on-ramp during daylight. It didn't help that I was struggling to maintain my focus. The constant effort of watching the road in such hazardous conditions, coupled with the need to be on the lookout for any sign of a drone, had left me feeling brutally tired. My eyes felt gritty and dry and my neck and shoulders were aching. I checked the back seat. Both Harry and Charlotte were asleep, snuggled up against Fiona, who was still awake, though barely judging by the heavy droop of her eyelids.

Sasha had been my second set of eyes during our foray through the suburbs, diligently watching for drones or any other possible danger. Earlier, she'd spotted a person run out into the street seconds before I would have mowed them down. I managed to swerve around them, but it scared the shit out of me, and if it weren't for my sister, I wouldn't have seen them until it was too late. As it was, I narrowly avoided colliding with a parked car when I swerved around the idiot on the road, and I promised myself to be more vigilant in the future.

"I think we should get off the street and find somewhere to lay low for the day. I need to rest, and it's going to be daylight soon. It's harder for the drones to spot us in the dark, so I think we should travel at night even though it's a hell of a lot harder to find our way around without any lights."

Sasha stifled a yawn and asked, "Where are we going to stop?'

"I don't know, but we'll need to find somewhere soon. Dawn isn't far off. Look out for a place with a carport or a garage. Somewhere that will provide some cover." I wasn't sure how much luck we would have finding such a place. Most of the homes this close to downtown were built long before motor vehicles were commonplace. I yawned and gave Sasha a dirty look. But she just shrugged and continued to stare out the window. We'd traveled a couple of blocks when she yelled out for me to stop.

Thinking she'd spotted a drone, I slammed on the brakes. The seatbelt cut into my chest before my head ricocheted against the headrest. The kids woke up with startled whimpers, and Fiona fell forward between the front seats. "You need to reverse and turn right down the street we just passed."

I looked over at my sister. "You didn't see a drone?"

"Nope. You asked me to find somewhere for us to hide for the day, and I just found the perfect spot."

I craned my neck to look back at the street she was referring to, and sure enough, I'd driven straight through the intersection without even noticing. "There's a mall with a multi-level car park," she explained, "we could hide there without drawing any attention. Don't you think?"

I nodded in agreement and reversed down the road so that I could turn down the street to the mall. I couldn't quite remember the name of the shopping precinct, which was unsurprising considering I found a trip to the store as enjoyable as a urinary tract infection. It didn't matter, though. A mall was a mall. If you'd seen one, you'd seen them all-loads of run-of-the-mill stores selling fast fashion and useless gadgets that would be tossed in the trash a few months later.

"Do you think it's safe?" Fiona asked, startling me. She'd barely said a word since I'd smashed out the lights on the SUV hours earlier. The mall loomed up ahead, and I guided the vehicle into the turning lane, pausing for a moment to consider her question. The entrance to the car park was dark and ominous, nothing like the refuge we desperately needed. Someone must have gone around smashing the fluorescent bars that lit the parking bays, leaving the odd light intact to spread its sallow glow at random intervals. "I think we would be better off parked somewhere in there rather than remain exposed out here on the street," I finally replied. As if on cue, a succession of explosions that couldn't have been more than a block or two away shattered the pre-dawn silence. We all peered around anxiously, searching for the drone responsible for the attack.

"Maybe you're right," Fiona admitted fearfully. I crossed the abandoned intersection and entered the ground level of the car park. A thick blanket of darkness swallowed the SUV, making it almost impossible to see where I was driving. I kind of regretted smashing out the headlights as I inched forward. The tires squeaked noisily on the polished concrete as I navigated around the perimeter of the car park in search of the ramp to the next level. A surprising number of vehicles occupied the parking spots. Many had probably been abandoned by people who were shopping inside the mall when the drones first attacked. Others had become mobile refuges for the frightened folk hiding inside. I'd spotted more than a few anxious faces peering out at us as we passed, and I wondered how long they'd been cooped up inside their cars, too afraid to leave the mall and the cover it provided.

Once we reached the middle level, I circled until I found a space alongside one of the concrete support pillars and pulled up between the post and an abandoned minibus emblazoned with the garish logo of a local preschool. I killed the engine and unbuckled my seatbelt, signaling for the others to do the same. Sasha was squirming in her seat, and her face looked tense and uncomfortable. "Do you need to go to the bathroom?" She nodded vigorously and I felt bad for not even considering something as necessary as a restroom break. "How about we venture into the mall and use the restrooms? They're usually close to the exits anyway, and if it looks safe, we can try and find something to eat too."

Fiona gently shook the children awake. Charlotte looked around in sleepy confusion, and her mother smoothed her hair back from her face, reassuring the little girl that she was safe. Harry rubbed his eyes and asked where we were. "We're at a mall, honey. We'll stay here for the day and get some rest while we wait for it to get dark again." He was only five, and I wondered how much of the situation he understood. He looked over at me and asked, "Are we going to get something to eat? And I need to do a poo." Sasha snorted, and I quickly covered a twitching smile with my hand. "Um, sure. I'll try and find us something to eat after we use the restroom."

"Good. Can we go now? I don't want to poo my pants, 'cause these are the only ones I've got."

I looked out into the car park, trying not to giggle while I searched for the entrance. "Over there, next to the shopping cart return bay," Fiona said, pointing past Sasha's shoulder. Sure enough, when I looked out the front passenger window, I saw the familiar green exit sign glowing dimly above a set of automatic glass doors. "Okay, guys. We're going to stick together and quietly make our way over to the entrance. Fiona, if anything happens and we get separated, try and make your way back to the car as soon as it's safe to do so."

Everyone climbed out of the SUV, and I took a moment to stretch out the muscles in my legs and lower back. We'd only gone half a dozen steps when I turned and ran back to the SUV to retrieve the machete. Hopefully, our trip to the restroom would be uneventful, and I wouldn't need to use the large blade, but I'd prefer to take it as a precaution. We crossed the car park in a tight formation and reached the entrance to the mall unhindered. I raised my hand, signaling for the others to stop behind a vending machine positioned a meter or so from the sliding glass doors while I poked my head out to check the corridor.

"It's clear," I confirmed, and the others quickly joined me. We walked down the empty corridor, the sound of our footsteps bouncing off the walls in the unusually quiet shopping mall. Without mind-numbing music playing in the background to soften the sound of feet clip-clopping across the polished tile floor, every sound we made seemed to echo loudly along the corridor. If there were other people inside the mall (which I knew there had to be), they would have no trouble hearing our approach.

Once we reached the end of the corridor, Fiona held Harry and Charlotte back while I stepped out into the mall and looked around. According to a sign hanging overhead, the restrooms were down the other end of the mall along with Target and some coffee shop chain that I'd never heard of. I noticed a couple seated on a bench beside a large potted plant outside a nail salon, and I signaled for the others to wait while I cautiously approached the strangers. The man and woman huddled together, warily watching me as I walked over to them. From the familiar way they clung to each other, I assumed they knew each other intimately. Both wore wedding bands, although it didn't necessarily mean they were married to each other.

"Hi, I don't mean you any harm," I assured them, hiding the machete behind my back as I stopped at a respectful distance. "I've got some kids with me, and I want to know if it's safe to bring them inside the mall?" The man pushed his glasses higher up on his nose and raised his chin as he looked around for the children I'd mentioned. "I don't see any children," he challenged, his body language altering subtly, betraying his suspicions about me.

"I wanted to make sure it was safe first." I couldn't deal with any more drama right now, and I was about to give up and turn my back on the couple when the woman spoke up. "Paul, she only wants to know if it's okay to bring some children inside. There's no need to get defensive." She patted her husband's knee and smiled up at me. "It's been quiet in here. Other people are hiding around the place, and I've seen people come and take things from the stores before leaving again, but there hasn't been any trouble so far."

"Thanks. Do you know how far down the restrooms are?"

She pointed down toward a juice stand about halfway along the length of the mall. "If you walk down past that juice stand, the restrooms are down a corridor beside one of those stores selling scented candles. Tell us, what's it like outside? Have those machines stopped blowing people up? Paul said he thought he heard one earlier, but I didn't notice anything."

I saw the desperate hope on her face, and I hated having to be the one to tell her otherwise, but if she was expecting me to inform her that the machines were winding down and everything was going to be okay, she was shit out of luck. "The drones are still out there, and I don't think they'll stop killing people anytime soon. You should also think about finding somewhere less exposed to bunker down because it's not just drones you have to worry about anymore. There are people out there doing some terrible things." The woman nodded miserably, and her husband wrapped his arms around her protectively.

I turned away from the couple and thought they'd be lucky to survive another week if they continued to sit around clutching each other uselessly. Hating myself for being so casually cynical, I pushed the couple from my thoughts and focused on getting everyone to the restrooms before Harry went and pooped his pants. I waved the others over, and they wasted no time joining me. I could see by the panicked expression on Fiona's face that a fecal eruption was imminent. Killer drones and blood-thirsty thugs, I could handle. A five-year-old taking a dump in his duds was something else entirely. "Hurry," I urged everyone. "The restrooms are down past the juice stand." I led the way, jogging past the bemused couple with Sasha following close behind with Charlotte on her hip. The toddler giggled happily as my sister pretended to be an exuberant pony, snorting, and nickering playfully; the horrors of the previous night momentarily forgotten.

I ducked down the corridor beside the store selling a cloying array of candles and other pretty things designed to make a house a home, and held open the door to the restroom while Sasha trotted past with Charlotte. Fiona rushed in behind her and pushed Harry into the nearest cubicle. Disaster averted. We'd made it with only seconds to spare.

Although Harry did his best to stink us all out, it felt good to be able to go to the bathroom and, even better, to wash my hands afterward. I stood at one of the basins and splashed water on my face and armpits before lathering up with the sudsy handwash oozing from the dispenser on the wall. Sasha followed my lead and freshened up too. There was no telling how long it would be before we'd get another opportunity to wash.

Turning a critical eye to the face staring back at me under the harsh glare of the fluorescent lighting, I considered going out into the mall to find a toothbrush and some toothpaste. A clean set of clothes wouldn't go astray either. I'd been recycling the same pair of underwear for days, and I was starting to feel grubby. It didn't help that I was looking more and more like a crazy bag lady, with my stained singlet visible beneath the oversized plaid shirt I'd pilfered back at the house we'd been staying at.

After Fiona had finished helping the kids dry their hands on some paper towel, we stopped by the vending machine in the corridor, everyone crowding around to eyeball the contents longingly. It was all junk food, but nobody seemed to care. We were hungry after last night's violent adventure, and at that moment, food was food, no matter the fat and sugar content. Since none of us were carrying any money, I told everyone to step back and waited until Fiona had dragged Harry and Charlotte a safe distance away before swinging the machete. It hit the vending machine with a hollow thud and bounced off, the blow barely even marking the clear viewing window I'd just tried to break. "Huh?" I grunted, perplexed. Sasha giggled and informed me, "It's made of toughened glass Jess. They build them to withstand attempts to break them open. Otherwise, hungry idiots across the country would smash them open to steal the contents. I felt my cheeks flush with embarrassment. Of course. I knew that. I was just too damn tired and distracted to realize. "Are you calling me an idiot?"

Sasha grinned and shrugged. "That's what I said, didn't I?"

I shook my head and returned my attention to the treats inside the vending machine. "We could try tipping the machine forward to dislodge some of the candy bars. Then someone could reach up inside and grab them," my sister suggested helpfully.

"Good idea. At least someone is thinking straight." Sasha walked over and wrapped her arm around my waist. "You've gone above and beyond since those drones appeared. If it weren't for you and everything you've done, none of us would be here right now. Nobody expects you to do everything on your own. You aren't superman."

"Superwoman," I corrected her. "Come on. Let's see if we can shake some candy loose."

Fiona instructed Harry to keep his sister occupied while she helped us tip the vending machine. Once she was confident that Charlotte was engrossed in a simple hand-clapping game with her brother, Fiona came over and stood with Sasha on one side of the machine while I stood on the other. On the count of three, we pushed against it, trying to angle it forward enough to dislodge the contents inside. It didn't budge. "Shit, that's heavy," I huffed. "Try again. Put your back into it, but be careful. We don't want to knock it over."

Sasha and Fiona nodded in unison, and we tried again. I threw all my weight against it, and when I thought I was about to burst a blood vessel or something worse, the vending machine rocked forward onto its two front feet spilling candy and chips into the bottom of the machine. "Alright, ease it back," I directed. The vending machine dropped back onto all four feet, and I crouched down to retrieve the illicitly gained bounty. I shoved my hand into the opening at the bottom and pulled out a bunch of candy bars and nearly half a dozen bags of chips. What a score!

"Everybody wait here. I'll be back in a minute." I ran to the end of the corridor, crossed the mall, entered an abandoned kitchen supplies store, and found a stack of carry bags on a shelf beneath the counter. I returned to Sasha and the others, not in the least surprised to discover they'd cracked open a bag of chips and were greedily munching on the salty treats. "Throw everything in this, and we can sort it out later," I told my sister. She tossed everything in the bag except for some M&Ms. "I figure we could use a hit of sugar."

"Hell yeah. Crack those babies open," I told her, salivating at the thought of popping some of the candy-coated chocolate in my mouth.

The short walk back to the car was uneventful. I unlocked the doors to the SUV and hopped up into the driver's seat, waiting impatiently for Sasha to climb in beside me so that I could raid the bag of vending machine goodies. Once everyone was inside the car, my sister handed me a bag of pretzels before passing the shopping bag over to Fiona. We ate in silence, too tired and hungry to waste energy on small talk, and after I'd munched my way through the crunchy pretzels and a candy bar, I felt my eyes beginning to droop shut.

I'd reached the point where no amount of sugar or caffeine could prop me up. I noticed Sasha wasn't doing much better. Dark circles, the color of fresh bruises had developed beneath her eyes, and she seemed to be yawning every other second. I covered my mouth as my body mimicked hers, a colossal yawn stretching my jaw before I said, "Guys, I think we should try and get a few hours sleep while it's quiet. We should be safe here, but as a precaution, I want you all to stay inside the car and avoid making any unnecessary noise."

"I can keep watch if you like," Fiona offered. I shook my head. She had to be just as exhausted as I was, and she had two young kids to look after. Besides, I was confident nothing terrible would happen to us while we were parked in the mall. I hadn't seen any drones since we'd entered the multi-level parking garage, which put my mind at ease. "It's alright. Let's all try and get some rest before nightfall." I adjusted my seat, reclining at a comfortable angle, and allowed my eyelids to lower shut. The last thing I remembered before drifting off to sleep was the sound of Harry and Charlotte fussing in the back seat as Fiona tried to coax them to take a nap.

Nine

The car park was immersed in shadow when I woke to a thump on the back of my seat. Dazed and disorientated, I sat up and rubbed the sleep from my eyes. It took a few seconds to recall where I was and why I was there. I pressed the button on the dash to check the time. It was almost five in the afternoon. I'd slept for the entire day, and I wasn't the only one. Sasha was curled up with her back to me, snoring quietly. I twisted around to check on the kids in the back seat, and Harry grinned at me, clearly delighted to have woken me since his mom and sister were still sleeping.

"Hi, Harry. How long have you been awake?" I asked as though the five-year-old could supply me with a definitive answer. The boy shrugged and held up two TMNT figurines he'd taken from the Target store earlier. "I've been awake for a while. Everyone seemed tired, so I played with Donatello and Raphael while you all slept. Mommy was dribbling on herself before. There was a big wet patch on her shirt." I smiled at him and felt how dry and cracked my lips had become. Earlier, I'd been so focused on finding something to eat that it hadn't even occurred to me to grab some water while we were in the mall. Sleeping for almost eight hours left me feeling parched. I'd have to venture back into the mall and find something to drink before too long.

"Have you seen anybody outside while you've been playing?"

"Yes. Some people walked past just after I woke up. I was super quiet in case they were bad like those men that tried to hurt us before," he explained. I scanned the car park nervously, having no idea how long ago this had happened. "Do you remember how many there were?" Harry's face creased in concentration as he considered the question. He counted out three fingers on his hand and held them up for me.

"You saw three people?" I asked.

"Yep. Three. But I don't think they were bad. They just looked scared, and the lady was crying."

"Thanks for noticing that, Harry. You're a big help." His chest puffed out with pride, and he sat up straighter on the seat. "I don't know about you, but I'm damn thirsty." Harry's hand flew to his mouth to cover a startled chuckle.

"You said damn," he whispered in awe. Judging by his reaction, I guess he hadn't noticed the plethora of cuss words I'd said when we'd escaped from the gang of assholes back at the house.

"Sorry," I apologized, chastened by his shock at my colorful language. "I shouldn't say words like that. Are you thirsty too?"

"Yeah. I want a juice box."

"Mmmm. That does sound good," I agreed. "How about we wake everyone up so we can get some water and maybe even a juice box if you're lucky." I reached across and gently shook Sasha awake. She moaned and tried to swat my hand away, but

I persisted until she sat up and glared at me sourly. "I feel like I could sleep forever and still be tired," she complained.

"I know how you feel," I sympathized, "but it's already after five o'clock, and we need to get organized. Everybody probably needs to use the bathroom before we hit the road, and I need to go and find some bottles of water for the journey."

Sasha yawned, and I found myself doing the same. Determined to shake off the lethargy clinging to us like a heavy fog, I climbed out of the car and urged the others to do the same. Harry jumped out eagerly, turning to help his sister as she scrambled out after him. Fiona agreed to take the children to the restroom while Sasha and I ventured deeper into the mall to find a supermarket. We decided to meet back at the SUV no later than a quarter past six. That gave us around forty-five minutes to locate water, freshen up and do anything else that cropped up along the way. As a precaution, I'd hidden the car key in an empty potato chip packet and jammed it under the front wheel. Satisfied that it looked like some rubbish I'd driven over, I let Fiona know where it was in case something should happen to me, and she needed to leave with the children.

Sasha and I passed the bench where the couple had been sitting earlier in the day. It was empty now; the only reminder that they'd been there, an empty soda can abandoned on the floor beside one of the potted palms flanking the seat. It was eerie walking through the mall with nothing but the sound of our footsteps echoing around us. For a moment, it felt like we were the only people left in the world, although I knew it wasn't true. We'd seen several people wandering about before, and I could only assume they were still around. They were probably keeping out of sight for safety. I didn't blame them. If we didn't need to find bottled water for the road and maybe something to eat as well, I'd be keeping a low profile too. After our run-in with the group of thugs the previous night, my trust in other humans had diminished considerably.

Sasha ducked into a donut shop and made her way around the overturned chairs to search the refrigerators behind the counter, but they'd been picked clean. Nothing edible remained in the store, and since we didn't stand a chance of breaking down the door to the storage room, I told my sister to forget it. We didn't have time to mess around. "Come on. We'll head down to the ground floor and check out the food court." I led the way over to the escalator, my body momentarily disorientated when I stepped onto the stationary stairs.

When we reached the ground floor, I checked the overhead signs, my sense of direction non-existent inside the shopping complex. To our left was the street entrance to the mall, the wide corridor lined with clothing stores, a hairdresser, and a coffee shop. I would have killed for the earthy, slightly bitter taste of a freshly brewed long black. Sasha tugged at my arm, and I grudgingly returned my attention to our current situation. I swear I could taste the lightly roasted blend of coffee beans after I turned to follow my sister toward the expansive food court. "One day, things will return to normal. This situation won't last forever, Jess," Sasha said.

"Yeah, we just have to make sure we've still alive when that happens," I replied in an uncharacteristically gloomy tone. Sasha glanced at me worriedly before pointing up ahead. "Look, there's a whole bunch of people sitting around in the food court." She was right. Twenty or more people were scattered around the food court, hunched over their seats as they warily watched our approach. I wondered if Sasha and I wore the same shell-shocked expressions. It was doubtful. The people seated at the tables mostly resembled timid mice, ready to run at the merest hint of danger. Most of them had probably been hiding in the mall since the drones first appeared. Too afraid to venture out and find a safer alternative to a shopping mall where anyone or anything could easily attack them. And while I'd be the first one to bolt if a drone showed up, I wasn't about to let some random asshole dictate our future. We were only here to stock up on necessities and shelter from the drones during the daylight hours. Soon we'd be on our way to someplace less exposed.

"Jess, what's up with you?" Sasha asked. "You're going to scare these poor people if you keep eyeballing them like that." She was right, of course. I was acting like a bit of a nut case. Determined to dial it down, I forced myself to relax and soften the frown twisting my features. "Sorry. I guess I'm stressing about leaving tonight. I know we've got to keep moving, but it worries me being out in the open. We'll be so exposed."

"I trust you, Jess. You'll do your best to make sure nothing happens to us," Sasha assured me. It helped ease my fears a little. We made our way along the outer perimeter of the food court, passing the dizzying assortment of abandoned food outlets that were raided for anything edible. All that remained was the garish signage advertising the high-fat, carb-laden rubbish that passed for food and the disposable packaging littering the floor around us. Before the drones appeared, I would have gleefully stuffed myself with any of the fast-food offerings. But now, after a week of limited options, I'd happily sink my teeth into a raw stem of broccoli and devour the entire fucking thing.

As we made our way to the supermarket at the end of the food court, I was conscious of the scrutiny of twenty or more sets of eyes following our every step.

"Do you know if it's safe to leave yet?" A woman called out. She was standing beside a collection of carry bags, presumably the purchases she'd made before the attacks. Her carefully colored blond hair was beginning to exhibit signs of neglect, the dark roots showing, despite her efforts to remain neat and tidy. She watched me expectantly, undoubtedly hoping I'd tell her it was safe to return to her cushy middle-class life. "It isn't safe anywhere," I stated bluntly.

"So, those things are still out there?" she asked tentatively.

"Yes. There are drones everywhere, and they are still blasting people to hell." I had neither the time nor the inclination to sugarcoat it for her. I felt my sister bristle at the rough edge to my voice, but I wasn't about to coddle these people.

"Oh," The blond woman said, visibly deflating. She flopped back down onto her chair and wrung her hands.

A teenage boy seated with two other kids asked, "Do you know if the army is going to come to rescue us soon?" I shook my head, but before I could reply, the mall was plunged into near-complete darkness as the power went out. Sasha reached over and latched onto my arm, and I took her hand in mine and held tight. We heard footsteps thudding heavily on the tile floor as someone ran toward the food court. Behind them, someone screamed. And then the food court erupted in a blind panic as everyone scrambled up out of their seats, sending chairs and tables flying in every direction.

A deafening boom reverberated back near the mall entrance, accompanied by a momentary flash, and I tugged Sasha's hand, dragging her behind me as I felt my way along the countertops while my eyes adjusted to the dark. Some fucking idiot had led a drone inside the mall, obliterating our momentary refuge.

"Hurry, we've got to get the fuck out of here," I whispered. Too late. The food court lit up like a fireworks display. Orange balls of fire shot across the vast space, incinerating anything in its path—the drone targeting the bewildered people tripping on overturned chairs and tables in the chaos. Within seconds the mall filled with the familiar reek of burning flesh and agonized screams. Welcome to the new world order.

Something wet and warm and unspeakable landed on the back of my neck. A similar projectile must have hit Sasha. She shrieked in disgust and swiped at her cheek as we neared the entrance to the supermarket. "Quick, follow me and try not to make any noise," I told her as we slipped inside the store. None of the light from outside reached the supermarket's interior and it was nearly impossible to see my hand held out in front of me. Darkness was both a blessing and a curse. While it meant the drone wouldn't locate us as easily, it also left us stumbling around blindly.

"We need to find somewhere to hide while that thing's preoccupied with the people in the food court," Sasha suggested.

"Nice idea, but in case you haven't noticed, we can't see shit," I retorted, fear and frustration getting the better of me. "I'm sorry. You're right," I apologized. Being snarky when Sasha was only trying to be helpful was uncalled for, and she had a point. It wouldn't be long before the drone picked off everyone in the food court and came looking for new targets.

I felt my way between the checkouts and carefully navigated around an empty shopping cart. Sasha shuffled into it before I could warn her. The bump sent the cart rattling straight into a display at the end of one of the checkouts. Jars tumbled to the floor in a cacophony of breaking glass, the sharp, sour scent of pickled cucumbers stinging my nostrils as I took a faltering step back. We could kiss goodbye any chance of escaping unnoticed, thanks to that god-awful racket. We needed to get the fuck out of there and find somewhere safe to lay low.

"Come on. We gotta get out of here," I urged, stumbling over broken glass and vinegar as I pulled my sister along behind me. I accidentally booted a jar and sent it rolling across the floor. Fuck. It felt like the quieter we needed to be, the more noise we made. We retreated up one of the aisles and I felt slightly safer. At least we weren't standing out in the open anymore. If the drone wanted to cook us where we stood, it would have to come looking. Using the denuded shelves as a guide, Sasha and I crept down the aisle, distancing ourselves from the entrance and the carnage in the food court.

Before I could save myself, I felt my foot slip out from beneath me when I stepped in some syrupy goo, and I crashed to the floor, smacking the side of my head on one of the metal shelves as I went down. Sasha must have heard me fall because she was crouching beside me when I regained consciousness a few seconds later. I sucked in a ragged breath and reached up to gingerly touch my throbbing scalp. My fingers came away wet with blood.

"Jess. Are you alright?" my sister asked, slipping her arms around me to help drag me to my feet. "Shhh. It'll hear you," I told her between clenched teeth. Sasha hooked her arms beneath mine and lifted me off the floor.

"Thanks." A wave of dizziness passed over me, and I forced myself to count backward from ten, a trick I'd learned during my drinking days, which helped keep me from collapsing to the floor in an unconscious heap again. "Jess?" Sasha asked uncertainly. "I'm alright. I feel a bit woozy from the knock to my head but, I'll be fine. Just hold on to me for a minute until my head clears."

"Sure. But we don't have a minute," she muttered. "I think the drone just entered the supermarket. I saw a red blinking light down near the checkouts. I'm fairly sure it was following someone."

"Okay. That's good. If it's after someone else, that means we still have time to get away." I took a step and crumpled forward, my leg buckling when I tried to put weight on it. "What the fuck?" I gasped, pain radiating from my knee in excruciating waves. Sasha lifted me back up and helped me hobble to the end of the aisle, where we stopped to allow me to catch my breath.

"Look, there's an exit sign over there," Sasha pointed out. Sure enough, the universal green person glowed faintly only twenty yards away from where we stood. Thank you very much, fire and emergency safety codes. Exit signs were required by law to run off an independent power source for a minimum of one and a half hours in the event of an emergency. And I couldn't think of a greater crisis than this.

The exit sign had to lead out to the supermarket's storage area, which in turn would open out onto a loading dock for deliveries. All we had to do was reach the exit without drawing the drone's attention. It seemed easy enough, except for our inability to see much of anything in the near pitch-black supermarket. Throw in my inability to walk unaided while a ruthless death machine prowled the aisles, and the twenty yards felt more like two hundred. While I stood propped against the end of the aisle contemplating the odds of reaching the exit without being discovered, Sasha squatted down to feel along the lower shelves until her hand wrapped around an eight-ounce can. "Get ready to run for the exit."

"I'm not sure that I can make it," I admitted doubtfully.

"Just do it," she replied fiercely. "I'll help you, but we have to move quickly." I took a deep breath and focused on the exit sign. It was only twenty yards. Maybe less. Without warning, Sasha pitched the can down toward the checkouts at the other end of the aisle, where it landed with a loud clatter. "Run," my sister demanded as she pulled me away from the safety of the towering metal shelves. I limped along beside her, my injured leg slowing me down, but to her credit, Sasha dragged me along, her determination to find a way out of the supermarket compensating for my inability to put any weight on my busted knee. As we crossed the abyss, I wondered how much time Sasha's diversion would buy us.

Less than two yards from the doors beneath the exit sign, I got my answer. Flames scorched the floor behind us. Searing heat singed our backs and propelled us forward away from the drone. We practically tumbled through the swinging doors, and Sasha wasted no time hauling me behind a stack of pallets. Crouching behind the pallet loaded with packages of paper towels, daring not to breathe while we waited for the drone to blow the doors of their hinges, I felt the back of my head. Sure enough, there was a burnt patch, leaving me with a crispy bald spot the size of my fist.

Seconds ticked by, and nothing happened. I couldn't decide if the drone was waiting for us to make the first move (if it was even capable of such advanced thinking) or it had given up and gone in search of less troublesome prey. It was impossible to determine precisely how long we remained behind the pallet, but it must have been a while because my uninjured leg had gone to sleep by the time we crept out. Pins and needles tingled up and down my legs, and I couldn't feel my feet. I bent over and rubbed my lower legs, careful to avoid my injured knee.

"Let's find a way out. We can't wait around forever. There has to be a door at the other end of the storage area." Sasha took my arm and supported me as I hopped along beside her. We hurried between the pallets of groceries neatly stacked on either side of the walkway, which was wide enough to allow a loaded forklift through comfortably. As we neared the far end of the corridor, I noticed a sliver of silvery light spilling under a wide roller door directly in front of us. Beside it, another exit sign glowed softly above a door to the loading dock. Buoyed by the prospect of finding our way out of the mall, I surged forward, immediately regretting my enthusiasm when my knee gave way beneath me, and I crashed to the ground.

"Jess, are you alright?" Sasha asked, pulling me back up onto my feet.

"Yeah, I'm fine," I lied. "Let's get this door open so that we can get the hell out of here."

Before I could depress the bar running horizontally across the middle of the door, Sasha reached over and placed her hand over mine. "What if more drones are waiting out there?"

"Does it matter? We can't wait around here, hoping for a miracle. Fiona and the kids are out there somewhere, and we need to find them before something or someone else does." I could only hope Fiona had managed to return to the SUV before all hell broke loose in the mall. "We have to take the risk, but promise me, if a drone does find us, leave me. Don't try being a hero. Just run."

"I'm not leaving you, Jess. No matter what happens. So, don't try and get me to make some stupid promise." I considered arguing the point, but ultimately, I knew it would be pointless. I was the only family she had left. Of course, she wouldn't abandon me. "Okay. Let's do this." I braced myself for what could be waiting for us on the other side and pressed down on the bar. The lock clicked open, and I eased the door open a crack.

The loading dock was empty, the sky overhead a deep purplish-blue. Although twilight had settled over the city, compared to the supermarket's near pitch-black interior, the moonlight provided ample visibility. For once, it felt like luck was on our side. I herded my sister out onto the loading dock and pulled the door shut behind us. I paused at the top of the stairs, bracing myself for the descent, which I knew would be slow and painful. Even with the handrail on one side and Sasha on the other, I'm sure an eighty-year-old with a walking frame could have out-paced me.

Once we reached ground level, we made our way around the block, sticking close to the building and the uninspiring hedge that passed for landscaping around the perimeter of the mall. While the decorative grasses and neatly trimmed hedge wouldn't provide much cover if a drone appeared, it was preferable to being caught out in the open. When we finally reached the entrance to the car park, I was all but ready to give up. I fought back tears and slumped against the concrete wall beside the door to the stairwell and willed myself to toughen the fuck up. Parking on one of the higher levels didn't seem like such a bright idea now that I faced climbing a flight of stairs.

"Come on, Jess. I know you are hurting, but we're almost there." I nodded and tried to smile but only managed a half-hearted grimace. "Alright, just give me a minute," I said, delaying the inevitable. Out on the street, the roar of a truck hurtling along in the wrong gear caught our attention, and we watched in dismay as a garbage truck sped past, the tires squealing as it veered back and forth across the road erratically. "What's going on?" Sasha asked in dismay.

"I'm not sure. It's probably just some idiot who's never driven a heavy vehicle before," I postulated. Still, something about it unnerved me. In the wrong hands, a vehicle that size was capable of inflicting serious damage. The thought was all the motivation I needed to press on, and using my sister as a crutch, I hobbled into the stairwell. Once more, we were plunged into complete darkness, and Sasha clung to me tighter than was strictly necessary. Not that I could blame her, it would have been challenging enough navigating a flight of stairs sightless. Throw a cripple into the mix combined with the fear of the unknown, and the poor kid was practically shitting her pants.

The SUV was still parked where I'd left it, and Fiona and her children were nowhere in sight. Sasha retrieved the keys in silence and handed them to me. Neither of us wanted to acknowledge the likelihood that Fiona hadn't managed to return to the car before the drone followed some hapless fool inside the mall. I pressed the keyless entry remote and opened the door. While I labored to get in the car without further damaging my knee, Sasha walked around to the rear of the vehicle and opened the trunk.

After a moment or two, she gently closed the boot and hopped up onto the seat beside me. "They've been back to the car," she said. "There's a stash of clothes in the trunk with all the tags still attached. I think she must have raided Target after taking the kids to the bathroom."

"Then where the hell are they?" I asked in frustration. If they'd made it back to the SUV, why not just stay put and wait for us to return? They could be anywhere. We didn't have time to go looking for them, not that I was physically capable of running around searching for the missing mother and her kids. I exhaled loudly, overwhelmed by pain and fear and thirst.

"Should we go and look for them?" Sasha asked while scanning the car park for any sign of the missing trio. "Maybe Fiona thought of something we'd need for the drive and went back into the mall to find it."

'Yeah, that's plausible," I agreed. "But I don't think I can walk anymore. It took forever to get from the loading dock back to here. If I got into trouble, I'd be more helpless than Harry and Charlotte. At least they can run." After a long pause, Sasha said, "I can go look for them if you want me to."

"No, Sasha. I can't let you do that. We need to stick together."

"But they might need our help."

"It doesn't matter," I replied grimly. "There's nothing we can do for them. We should have left nearly an hour ago."

"Can we wait a little bit longer? What if they're hiding somewhere, waiting for the drone to leave? We can't abandon them now."

"They've got twenty minutes," I relented. It wasn't like I wanted to leave them behind, but we couldn't sit around waiting indefinitely. "If they haven't made it back to the car by then, we're leaving without them."

"Okay. Twenty minutes," Sasha repeated.

"I mean it." I checked the clock on the dash. "She has until seven-twenty-three. After that, we're out of here." I sat back, wincing a little when my head touched the headrest. I remembered the flames singing my hair and asked Sasha to inspect the damage. She tentatively felt the back of my scalp, and I tensed when her fingers found a small raw spot behind my left ear that I hadn't been aware of. "Sorry, Jess. I didn't mean to hurt you."

I shrugged dismissively. "My knee is so swollen; my jeans are probably going to split at the seams soon. A tiny burn isn't a big deal."

"Maybe not, but the chunk of hair that's missing might be a problem," Sasha said as she gently probed the crispy patch of hair at the back of my head. "I think you're going to have to cut it all off."

"Great. I'll put it on my list of things to do. First, we need to figure out the best route through downtown." The freeway on-ramp off Caldwell St would be the quickest option-assuming it wasn't blocked, and there was a clear run on the four-lane expressway. If not, we would have to navigate through the suburbs, using secondary roads until we got clear of the city. I wanted to avoid crossing the suburbs on the western side of the city if I could. Not only would it slow us down, but there was bound to be greater risks traveling through densely populated areas.

For now, I aimed to reach the Caldwell St ramp. That was by far our best chance of getting out of the city safely. I wasn't naive enough to think it would be easy. I'd seen the smoke billowing from the downtown area, but I was determined to find a way through somehow. I was calculating the fastest and potentially safest route to Caldwell St when Sasha squealed in excitement. "Look!" She jabbed the air, pointing across the car park to the entrance to the mall.

Fiona came running out of the doorway with a cardboard box clutched in one hand while she cradled Charlotte on her hip with the other. I stabbed the key into the ignition and started the SUV. Thank God it was an automatic. It would have been impossible to drive a manual with my knee all fucked up. I didn't know if they were in trouble, but it was fair to assume that they weren't running from the mall for the sheer joy of it. I sped across the near-empty parking bay. The tires squealed on the polished concrete when I braked a few spaces up from the doors to the travelator.

Fiona yanked the back door open and propelled Charlotte across the back seat. The box went in after her daughter, followed by Harry. Then she dived in behind him and slammed the door closed. "Go," she wheezed between ragged breaths. "There's a drone back in the mall. I'm not sure if it saw us or not." I pressed my foot down on the accelerator, and the SUV surged forward. "How far back was it?" I asked as I sped toward the exit.

"I don't know. It wasn't close. I guess it probably didn't see us. If it had..." Fiona didn't need to finish the sentence. Sasha and I knew she wouldn't be in the car with us if the drone had spotted the trio. Nevertheless, I found myself continually checking the revision mirror, just in case.

Ten

O nce we'd safely exited the car park, I looked back at Fiona angrily and asked, "What the hell were you doing back there?" Fiona was struggling to secure Charlotte's seatbelt. The buckle refused to lock into place, no matter how hard she jabbed it into the slot. "Try the other one," Sasha suggested, which quickly solved the problem. Now her daughter was secured safely in her seat, Fiona reluctantly looked over at me and shrugged guiltily. "The kids were hungry, and I didn't want to feed them any more candy."

"And?" I pressed.

"And I found some muffins in the cafe near the candle store."

"I didn't think there was anything left in there." I puzzled.

"They were hidden under a bag of ice in the freezer. I guess nobody bothered to look under the ice."

"I'm glad you found something for the kids to eat, but it wasn't worth the risk. We almost left without you."

Fiona looked aghast. "I had no idea a drone had gotten inside when I took the kids back into the mall. I would never have gone back if I'd known. What happened with you guys? Did you find any water?"

Sasha shook her head. "No. The drone followed us into the supermarket. We almost didn't make it out, and Jess fell and hurt herself."

"Shh," I hissed as I maneuvered around an abandoned Volvo left in the center of the road.

"Are you alright?" Fiona asked with genuine concern.

"I'm fine," I assured her.

"No, she isn't," Sasha interjected. "She did something to her knee and can't walk properly. Plus, she hit her head pretty hard. Oh, and a big chunk of her hair got burnt off."

"Gee, Sasha. Thanks for being so thorough in cataloging my list of misfortunes." My sister had the decency to turn away and peer out of the window sheepishly. I knew her heart was in the right place, but blabbing to the young mom would only make her worry unnecessarily.

I slowed down as we approached the four-lane we'd turned off hours earlier. The kids had started arguing on the back seat, and Fiona was trying unsuccessfully to convince Charlotte to stop poking her brother. After a quick check of the intersection, I started turning right. "Stop!" Sasha cried, and I jammed my foot on the brake. The SUV jerked to a whiplash-inducing stop moments before a police cruiser roared past us, followed closely by an ambulance. Like us, neither vehicle was using its headlights. I'd been too distracted by what was happening in the back seat to hear their approach. Another second or two, and we would have been t-boned by the cop car.

"We should follow them," Fiona suggested.

"Yeah. We'll be less likely to run into trouble if we stick close to the authorities," Sasha added.

"Maybe," I replied doubtfully. Without overthinking it, I pulled out behind the ambulance and gave chase. I gunned the engine, veering around a burnt-out car that was partially blocking the lane. Not wanting to lose sight of the emergency vehicles, I pressed my foot down a fraction harder. Driving so fast in the dark without headlights felt crazy and reckless. But at least it helped distract me from the excruciating pain in my knee.

"Where do you think they are going?" Fiona asked.

"I assume they're heading to one of the hospitals. Probably St. Bethany's since it's the closest."

"Watch out!" Sasha screamed. Up ahead, the rear of the ambulance exploded in a brilliant flash. I pressed the brakes. Careful to ease the SUV to a stop gently to avoid drawing attention to ourselves. I should have known three vehicles speeding along the deserted road would draw unwanted attention.

A paramedic jumped out of the back of the ambulance. Sections of his uniform were ablaze, the flames rapidly spreading across his body despite his frantic attempts to pat them out. Beside me, Sasha turned her face away from the human torch. Her hands were covering her ears to muffle his terrified screams. "Cover the kid's eyes," I told Fiona as I watched the drone close in on the paramedic.

Realizing we had to leave while the drone's attention was focused elsewhere, I threw the transmission into reverse. The SUV fishtailed wildly between the two lanes as I reversed down the road. "I can't see shit." I cried in frustration. Without the reversing lights, it felt like I was driving blind. "Sasha, there should be a street coming up on your left. I need you to check if it's clear to turn into it." My sister twisted in her seat to get a better look out of the window. "Yeah, it's all good. Just watch out for the motorcycle parked near the corner."

Fuck the motorcycle. I turned the steering wheel, and the SUV swerved across the opposite lanes. Another flash lit the night, putting an end to the paramedic. With no way of knowing if the drone had noticed us, I veered off the main road, clipping the motorcycle in my haste. The bike toppled over in a conspicuous clatter of metal and fiberglass. "I thought we were trying to be quiet," Sasha said.

"Thanks for pointing that out, captain obvious," I snapped. "You're welcome to drive if you think you can do a better job." I swung into a driveway, shifted the vehicle into drive, and sped off down the street. "It might be better if we avoid the main road for a bit," I said to no one in particular.

"That's probably a good idea," Fiona agreed.

"It might slow us down," I conceded, "but if it helps us steer clear of trouble like that, I think the delay will be worth it." I took the next right and continued slowly along a residential street that ran parallel to the four-lane we'd just left. Most of the homes along the road had avoided damage from either drones or looters. Only the lack of light behind the windows gave any indication that something was amiss. At the next t-intersection, I turned left, taking us further away from the main road.

"Do you know where you're going?" my sister asked. I took my eyes off the road to glance in her direction. The sullen set of her mouth spoke volumes. I'd managed to offend her with my childish outburst. An apology was quite possibly in order, but she would be waiting a while. My priority was to get us safely out of the city. Or, at least, closer to the exit ramp downtown. Until then, she could suck it up.

"I have a rough idea. There's a strip mall a few blocks over where I used to work at a bar when Mom was still alive." I had to guide the SUV up over the curb and across someone's lawn to bypass a head-on collision blocking the road. As we continued along the street, the residential homes slowly gave way to an assortment of businesses. Some were barricaded shut with metal bars or roller doors across the storefronts, while others hadn't faired so well. Looters had trashed more than a third of the stores. Their windows smashed in, and the doors forcibly opened. I wasn't in a position to judge. I'd done much the same thing out in suburbia, except I hadn't been so senselessly destructive about it. I couldn't help wondering if it had been strictly necessary to plunder a bridal boutique. Try as I might, I just couldn't picture a pretty gown or a costly veil being a requirement for survival.

We pulled into the abandoned parking lot outside the strip mall, and I removed my seatbelt. "Why are we stopping here?" Fiona asked as she peered uneasily out at the strip of abandoned stores. "I'm going to see if I can find a way inside that drugstore and get my hands on some painkillers."

"You should let me go in," Fiona replied. I turned in my seat, ignoring the white-hot flare of pain it sent up my leg, and asked,

"Why would you want to do that? It looks like it's locked up tight anyway."

"I'm a nurse's aide, or at least I was before I had the kids. So, I probably have a better idea of what to look for than you. Plus, I can get some antiseptic cream for your burns." What she said made sense. Although, I had to wonder how long she'd worked as a nurse's aide since she looked younger than me and had been caring for Harry and Charlotte for nearly five years. Since the thought of even attempting to put any weight on my knee made me want to puke, I agreed to let her go. I'd parked out the front of the drugstore. The car beside us had had all its windows smashed in by some industrious little shit. "If it looks sketchy out there, get your ass back to the car. Understand?"

"Understood. I promise I'll be super careful." She reached over and kissed Harry and Charlotte on the forehead before locking eyes with me for a moment. "Thank you," I said before she opened the door and hopped out onto the asphalt. Sasha and I watched as she ran over to the door and tried the handle.

As I'd expected, the door was locked, the blinds drawn against prying eyes. Fiona rattled the handle again, more in frustration than in any hope that it would magically open. Scouting the ground for something suitable to lob at the glass, she jumped back when a face suddenly appeared around the edge of the blind. Startled, I leaped from the car without thinking. My swollen knee refused to support my weight, and I only just managed to reach out and grab the driver's door to stop myself from collapsing onto the ground beside the SUV. Sasha made to jump out and assist me, but I shook my head. "Stay there," I whispered between gritted teeth.

"What the hell do you think you're doing?" A gruff male voice called out. Fiona raised her hands to show she was unarmed and replied, "My friend is hurt and needs some painkillers." The man inside the drugstore eyed her with disdain. "Sure, they do. Just like every other strung-out junkie desperate for a fix." Shaking her head emphatically, Fiona said, "No, it's not like that. We're not looking for drugs. I've got two little kids in the car. The woman who rescued us fell over while running from a drone. All we need is some Tylenol and maybe some muscle rub to help with the pain."

The man seemed to consider her plea before pushing his glasses up on his nose and unlocking the door. "You'd better not be fucking with me," he warned as he stepped outside. My breath caught when I saw the shotgun he had aimed at the ground in front of Fiona. "Fiona, forget it. Let's go," I uttered. Fiona motioned for me to be quiet and returned her attention to the man and his shotgun. "I'm not messing with you. I promise. That's my friend over by the car. Go check for yourself if you don't believe me."

"Alright then," he agreed before taking a set of keys from his pocket and securing the door to the drugstore. He wasn't messing around. Nobody was getting inside that place without his permission. Not wanting to appear weak and vulnerable, I straightened as best I could, watching warily as the bald man approached. He stopped a few feet away and took a moment to check for any signs of danger, but the sky around us was empty.

When he was satisfied that the most dangerous thing inside the SUV was a couple of kids with muffin crumbs in their laps, he turned his attention to me.

"Your friend tells me you've hurt yourself. Mind if I check you out to make sure you're legit?"

"If that's what it takes," I reluctantly agreed.

"That's what it takes if you want my help," he assured me.

"I don't want your help. I just need something to dull the pain so that we can continue on our way."

"Expecting me to hand over medication *is* asking for help. And, I'd prefer not to stand around in the open, debating the matter."

Realizing I'd have to comply if I wanted a lousy bottle of Tylenol, I took a faltering step toward him.

"I'm going to crouch down and have a look at your leg." I nodded and watched as he dropped down in front of me. He mumbled something I didn't quite catch, and I asked him to repeat it. He glanced up at me and shook his head. "There is significant swelling in your knee. Can you put any weight on it?"

"Not really. I think it's pretty fucked up," I admitted.

"Right. I'm going to take a better look if you don't have any objections." He poked and prodded my knee, his fingers digging into the swollen flesh as he rotated my kneecap. I stifled a scream and fell back against the car as a wave of pain worse than anything I'd ever experienced before overwhelmed me.

"I'm sorry, I didn't mean to hurt you," he said.

I took a steadying breath and nodded. "It's alright. I'll be okay in a minute." He reached out and felt the cut on the side of my head. "You've been through the wringer, haven't you? At least the bleeding has stopped, although you have a sizable lump on your head."

"Yeah, I know. But that's the least of my concerns at the moment."

"Maybe. You probably have a concussion, so you shouldn't be driving. At least for the next twenty-four hours." He continued to catalog my injuries with the indifference of a veterinarian examining livestock. When he accidentally touched the burn on the back of my scalp, he apologized. "Sorry. That's why I opted to become a pharmacist instead of a doctor. I've been told more than once that my bedside manner leaves a lot to be desired."

"There's certainly room for improvement," I agreed. He chuckled and took a step back out of my personal space.

"Fair call. As I mentioned, I'm a pharmacist, not a doctor. But I'm also an avid bodybuilder, and I'm studying for a degree in sports science. I have a good working knowledge of anatomy, and my guess is you've dislocated your knee."

"Don't say that. What am I supposed to do with a dislocated knee?"

"I'd suggest you find a doctor. Maybe try and reach the hospital because you need treatment."

"We saw an ambulance blown to bits on our way here. Do you think trying to reach a hospital is a good idea?"

"I don't know what else to tell you," he admitted.

"Tell me you can fix it. I have to get these people out of the city. And I can't do that if I can't fucking walk," I half sobbed. The pharmacist considered my plea while looking around uncomfortably. We'd been standing around in the open for too long, and I could tell he was starting to feel cagey. "Look, I can try popping it back into the socket for you, but it's not something I've ever done before, and I'm no emergency room doctor."

I took a moment to consider the offer. Having no other viable option, I was quick to agree. "Alright. If you're willing to give it a shot, I'll be your guinea pig."

"Jess, we don't know anything about this guy," Sasha cried incredulously.

The pharmacist grinned. "Smart kid," he said.

"Too smart for her own good, sometimes."

Sasha wasn't about to let up. "I'm serious, Jess. This is crazy."

I understood her concern, but if we couldn't fix my leg, we had no chance of reaching Brent and the sanctuary of the cabin. "My leg's fucked. We have to try, at least."

"If you seriously want to do this, y'all better follow me inside." Fiona stepped in close to me and hooked her arm around my waist. I wanted to shoo her away, but I needed help more than I needed my dignity. "Bring Harry and Charlotte inside," I said over my shoulder to Sasha. I could feel her disapproval as I pushed the car door shut and hobbled over to the drugstore. Fiona propped me against the glass storefront and returned to help my sister wrangle the children. My bald companion took the keys attached to a chain, which in turn was secured to his trousers, and unlocked the door. He propped the door open with his foot and helped me inside.

Using the wall for support, I shuffled further into the store while he ushered the others in and secured the door behind them. A faint light glowing at the back of the store provided sufficient illumination to allow us to navigate between the aisles without tripping over anything. When we reached the back counter, Fiona directed Sasha and the children to sit on the chairs positioned in two neat rows for customers waiting to have their prescriptions filled. The pharmacist, whose name I was yet to learn, grabbed a bag of jellybeans from a stand beside the counter and tossed it to Sasha. "Here. Share them with the little ones. It might help keep them occupied while I try and fix your mom's leg." Sasha snickered, and if she'd been within arm's length, I would have clipped her up the side of the head.

"She's my sister," Sasha corrected him and ripped open the bag of jellybeans. She deposited a handful of the colorful treats into each of the kid's upturned hands. The pharmacist turned to me and apologized. "I hope I didn't offend you. I just assumed since you have that whole protective mother thing going on that she was yours."

"It's alright," I shrugged. "Our mom died a while back, so I guess I'm the closest thing she has to a mother now."

"You must be doing an alright job since she's still alive despite everything that's been happening. Now, I'm going to give you something to help dull the pain because it's going to feel damn rough when I start moving your leg around. If you want to take a seat, I'll be back in a minute."

He disappeared behind the counter, and I hoped he was finding me something nice and strong. Preferably something that would knock me on my ass because for all my bravado, I wasn't looking forward to having the burley pharmacist attempt to reassemble my broken body. A few minutes later, he returned with two small pills and a paper cup half-filled with water.- "Here, take these." He dropped the pills into my palm and watched as I gulped them down with the water. "Now, we just have to wait until they kick in, and then I can examine you and figure out what we're dealing with."

"Okay. That sounds easy enough," I replied. The pharmacist looked down at me and shook his head doubtfully. "I'll get you to lie down on the floor, and you can let me know when the painkillers start to take effect." He helped me off the chair, lowering me to the floor with little effort. "Pop this under your head." He gently positioned a u-shaped travel pillow beneath my head, being careful not to irritate the burn. I couldn't be sure, but I thought I saw pity reflected in his eyes before he turned away to go and confer with Fiona. That couldn't be good. While I watched Fiona and the pharmacist discussing what I presumed was my upcoming 'procedure,' the drugs began to work. The pain seemed to melt into the background, replaced by a floaty relaxed state. For the first time since that fateful Sunday morning when the sky filled with murderous machines, I felt the tightness in my chest loosen.

Suddenly Fiona was kneeling beside me, her hands pressing against my shoulders while the pharmacist took to my jeans with a pair of scissors. "Hey! What are you doing?" I asked groggily. "They're my only pair of jeans. I don't want to tackle the end of the world in some skimpy ass daisy dukes." The pharmacist shook his head and smiled as he carefully cut away the denim covering my grotesquely swollen knee. "Yeah, it looks like it's dislocated," he confirmed. Thankfully, the painkillers he'd dosed me with made his poking and prodding feel a lot like the playful caress of an eight-week-old kitten.

Fiona shifted her weight so that she was leaning over me, and I could see right up her nostrils. I giggled like a little kid and tried to stick my finger in her nose. She swatted my hand aside and returned her attention to the big bald beast of a man kneeling beside my legs. "No matter what she says or does, make sure you hold her still. She might seem giddy and chilled out now, but that won't last." I didn't like the sound of that, and I told him so. He ran a hand over his scalp and sniffed. "I can't give you anything stronger without risking an overdose. So, I need you to tough it out." That was easy for him to say. He wasn't the one lying on the dirty floor of a drugstore waiting to have some random person attempt to do the job of a highly trained physician.

He reached down and removed my boot before straddling my leg. I swallowed nervously as he gently pushed my good leg out of the way. "I know this is going to hurt, but try not to scream. We don't want to draw unnecessary attention to ourselves." I nodded slowly and felt tears run down my face as I realized what was about to happen. Fiona must have felt me tense up because she pressed her full weight on my shoulders, pinning me to the floor. The pharmacist gave me an appraising look before hopping up and disappearing down one of the aisles. When he returned, he was holding a fat roll of bandage. He crouched beside me and removed the plastic wrapper. "Open your mouth and bite down on this. Hopefully, it will help muffle your cries." I opened my jaws and allowed him to stuff the dry, icky tasting bandage between my teeth.

Then he moved back down my body and knelt with a leg on either side of my melon-sized knee. I swallowed nervously and tried unsuccessfully to convince myself that it wouldn't be so bad. I'd taken some painkillers, and I was feeling disconnected from everything, so maybe it wouldn't hurt as much as he'd warned it would.

Nope. It was even worse than the pharmacist had led me to believe. I know he'd urged me not to scream, but when his hands locked around my damaged knee, I couldn't stop myself from howling into the roll of bandage stuffed inside my mouth. I bucked beneath Fiona's weight, desperate to free myself from the white-hot pain radiating from my knee. My vision grew hazy as the burly pharmacist manipulated the dislocated joint, and the last thing I remember before passing out was the worried expression on Sasha's face as she hovered in the background.

Eleven

I slowly became aware of muffled, dream-like voices somewhere nearby. I strained to hear what they were talking about, but I couldn't make out the words. For some reason, I thought I was snuggled up in bed at Brent's place, waiting for him to bring me a cup of coffee and his signature dish of eggs and bacon with some greasy hash browns on the side. I tried flinging the covers back to go help in the kitchen, but my arm felt like it was glued to my side. "Brent, come give me a hand, would you?" I called out. I forced my eyelids apart, fighting the urge to sink back into sleep's comforting embrace. And I probably would have drifted off again if Harry hadn't wandered over. Seeing me blinking up at him in confusion, he called over his shoulder to his mom. "The scary lady is awake," he informed her while keeping a wary eye on me.

The scary lady. That might have been hurtful under different circumstances. As it stood, I could kind of understand where he was coming from. The first time the kid had seen me, I was splattered with the blood of a man I'd just bludgeoned to death. And things hadn't improved much since that initial introduction.

Harry had witnessed me wield a machete like a maniac, run someone down with a car, and generally act like a raging psycho.

It took my sluggish brain a moment to realize I wasn't in Brent's bed, and he wasn't in the kitchen, making me something to eat. Instead, I was lying on the floor with a jacket draped over me to provide some semblance of comfort while I slept on the itchy commercial carpet. My eyes fluttered shut as I tried to figure out why I was lying on the floor of a gloomy drugstore. The lure of sleep pulling me back under. Then Fiona was crouching beside me, rudely shaking me awake. "Jess. Come on. It's time to wake up." Fighting the urge to shake her off, I pushed through the lethargy and focused on her face.

A frown creased the skin between her eyebrows as she encouraged me to return to the land of the living. I couldn't tell if her concern was for me or our circumstances in general. "How long have I been asleep?" I managed to croak from between dry, cracked lips. I remembered we'd entered the drugstore when it was night. Even with the shades drawn, I could tell it was light outside. "You've been asleep for over eighteen hours," she informed me.

"What the fuck?" I pushed myself up into a sitting position and immediately regretted it when I was overwhelmed by a wave of dizziness. Fiona reached out and steadied me until it passed, and I clung to her like she was a lone buoy in choppy water. "Between the painkillers we've been feeding you and the fact you've been lying down for a long time, it might be a good idea to take it easy."

"It might be a good idea if I go use the bathroom."

"Of course. You must be busting. I'll get Phil to help you up."

"Phil?" I asked.

Fiona shrugged. "Yeah, Phil - the big bald guy that dispenses the medicine. He didn't get a chance to introduce himself before. But we've had plenty of time to chat while you were unconscious."

Before I could respond, Phil appeared and took hold of me under the arms. "It's good to have you back with us."

"Yeah. Sorry about sleeping for as long as I did. You probably didn't plan on being stuck with us for nearly twenty-four hours."

"It's okay. You were exhausted, and your body needed time to heal. Fiona and your sister told me about what you've all been through." Phil scooped me up, keeping hold of me as I gingerly tested my injured leg. Although it hurt to put weight on it, my knee was now capable of supporting me once more. My body sagged with relief. There was still a chance I'd get to see Brent again. Sasha could ride out the end of the world safely secluded in the mountains without the fear of being hunted down by killer machines.

"You can let me go now. I'm alright." I told Phil.

"Even though I was able to pop your knee back into the socket, you will still need to be careful. And it's going to hurt for a few more weeks, maybe longer if you don't give it a chance to heal properly."

"I could be dead in a couple of weeks," I responded. Phil inhaled slowly, my words touching a nerve, although why he'd be bothered was lost on me. It wasn't like we knew each other. Perhaps he felt some sort of connection after hearing about me from Fiona and my sister. "Nevertheless, it's going to be difficult for you to get around unassisted until the inflammation subsides."

"Have you got any drugs here that will help with that?" I asked. Phil studied me, presumably searching for any sign that I might be convinced to rest up while our chances of escape dwindled. Eventually, he replied, "I've got something I can give you to make it bearable. And it might help to use a crutch. If that's really what you want."

"What do you mean? Of course, that's what I want. As soon as it gets dark, we'll be out of here. I'm grateful for everything that you've done for us, but we have somewhere to be."

"Sasha told me about the cabin in the mountains. She said your boyfriend is waiting there for you."

"That's right. We've already experienced too many delays."

Phil glanced over at Fiona and the children huddled on the floor, flipping through trashy magazines before returning his attention to me. "What?" I prompted. The guy obviously had something more to say. And if Fiona's cagey expression was anything to go by, I wasn't going to like it.

"We've been discussing it while you were asleep, and we think it might be better to stay put for the time being."

"You think it might be better?" I slowly repeated while my eyes locked on Fiona. This was the same woman I'd found wandering the streets in broad daylight with two hungry and terrified children in tow, seemingly oblivious to the danger they were in. I'd taken them in, promising them refuge at the cabin if we managed to get there, and the minute an armed man flexed his biceps, she was ready to jump ship. Her betrayal felt like a punch in the guts.

"You've been making plans while I was asleep? How fucking delightful. Since none of you need my input, I'll leave you to it." I shrugged free of Phil's steadying grip, straightening my back and squaring my shoulders. Fiona's face crumpled, and she looked from Sasha to Phil and shook her head in dismay. "It's not like that. Please don't be angry, Jess. We've all been sick with worry about you."

"You don't have to worry about me. I'm fucking fine." I turned away, limping toward the door marked staff only. Sasha jumped up and left Charlotte to doodle on a notepad by herself. "Wait up, Jess," she said, taking me by the elbow and guiding me through the doorway. She led me along the narrow corridor to the cramped bathroom. "I'll take it from here," I told her more harshly than I'd intended.

"She's scared, Jess. We all are. You shouldn't be so hard on her. She feels safe here with Phil. He seems like a decent guy, and she's trying to do what's best for Harry and Charlotte."

I shuffled around so that I could look at my sister. "Staying in the city is a stupid idea. The place is crawling with drones. It's only going to get more dangerous."

"I know that. But after everything that's happened out there, it's hard to give up somewhere that feels safe."

"Just because the guy has a gun, it doesn't automatically make him Rambo. The diet shakes and jellybeans will eventually run out. Then what? It'll be ten times worse out there, and there will be nowhere left to go."

Sasha chuckled. "You've got Phil all wrong. Leaving the city makes sense, but I don't think Fiona has been outside the state. She finds the idea of traveling hundreds of miles to a cabin in the mountains overwhelming. And she's never met Brent. She doesn't know if he's a good guy or not.

"That's a pretty succinct analysis of the situation," I told her, and she grinned. "I'm top of my class for a reason."

"Obviously. Now let me go pee before I do it in my pants." I pushed the door shut and unbuttoned my jeans, which were now a disturbingly short pair of cutoffs. As I sat down on the toilet, I thought how much Brent would enjoy seeing me in a pair of itsy-bitsy denim shorts. Thinking about my boyfriend was bittersweet. I missed him terribly. Reaching the cabin and burying my face against his expansive chest was all that kept me going sometimes. But knowing how unlikely it was that I'd ever see him again hurt so much that I couldn't afford to let him creep into my thoughts.

Instead, I focused on what Sasha had said about Fiona. It made sense, and once I had a chance to cool off, I could understand Fiona's concern. However, I still believed our best chance of survival was in the mountains with Brent. Far from built-up areas that drew the drones like flies on shit. It was now a matter of convincing her that she should stick with us and take the risk. I only had three or four hours to plead my case (and apologize for being a total jerk). After that, it would be dark, and Sasha and I would be leaving with or without Fiona and her kids.

When we rejoined the others, I noticed Fiona had her back to me with Charlotte nestled in her lap. The little girl had given up on drawing and had her thumb firmly planted in her mouth as she snuggled against her mother. Harry was happily playing with what looked suspiciously like a rubber enema bag. In this crazy new world, fun was where you found it.

Phil called me over to the small kitchenette hidden at the back of the dispensary. "You need to have something to eat. The painkillers have probably dulled your appetite, but you need to push through it," he advised when I finally hobbled over to his side. "They don't taste great, but they'll do in a pinch," Phil explained, dropping a variety of weightloss shake sachets onto the counter beside the sink. I read the labels without much enthusiasm. Dutch chocolate, Summertime Strawberry, Honeycomb, and Vanilla Bean flavor. They all sounded so delectable, but I knew that they all tasted like rubbish. They were a weight-loss aid, after all. If they were too good, the people trying to melt away the pounds would guzzle them down like the sugary soda they craved.

"If you drink a shake, I'll share one of these with you." He placed a protein bar on the counter in front of him, and I eyed it enviously. I reached out to take it, and he whisked it away. "After you have a shake," he insisted. "And once you've eaten, I'll give you something to help with the inflammation." I tried staring him down, hoping he'd cave in and give me the protein bar and the pills without the watery shake, but he dealt with more challenging people than me working in the drugstore. "Fine," I sighed. "I'll have the honeycomb flavor."

"Good choice." He took a shaker from an overhead cupboard and sprinkled the sachet in with some water from the tap. After a vigorous shake, he handed it to me and patiently waited for me to drink the low-calorie concoction. I felt like a stubborn toddler refusing to eat her greens. "Jesus Christ!" I cried in dismay after I took a tentative sip. No wonder people are so fucking fat. It tastes like ass." Phil chuckled, crossing his arms over his chest and rocking back on his heels. "It's not that bad," he said. I cocked an eyebrow in his direction and gulped down the remaining liquid.

After I handed over the empty shaker, Phil snapped the protein bar in half and handed me my share. I took a bite, savoring the chewy texture. When I'd finished, I said in a voice loud enough for everyone to hear, "I'm sorry for being such a raging psycho before. I seriously over-reacted."

"That's okay," Fiona replied, avoiding my gaze. Somehow, I doubted the young mom was genuinely ready to forgive me. At least not yet. I still had a few hours to work on her before nightfall. Hopefully, she would be more receptive to my apology with the benefit of time.

"Here." The pharmacist interrupted my thoughts, thrusting a collection of pills in my direction. " These should help you get through the next week or so. Follow the instructions on the label, and you shouldn't run into any problems."

"Thanks," I said, checking out the collection of drugs he'd given me.

"Be careful with the painkillers. They pack a hefty punch, but you'll probably need them if you insist on pushing your body to its limits."

"Duly noted. Anything else I need to know?"

He shook his head and sighed. "Nothing that you want to hear."

"We'd be fools to stay here any longer, despite what you might think."

"You're a fool if you think you can navigate hundreds of miles with that leg of yours while dodging killers and flying insects that shoot fire out of their asses."

"Thanks so much for your vote of confidence," I replied sarcastically.

"I'm simply presenting the facts."

"Yeah, I know. It's a long shot, but I'm still going to try."

There was an uncomfortable silence as I pondered our limited options for survival. Phil probably thought I was mad for wanting to leave, while I thought he was equally bonkers for believing staying put was a viable option. A tremendous bang at the rear of the store jolted me from my thoughts.

Phil reached behind the counter to retrieve the shotgun, the harsh set of his mouth, leaving me with little doubt of his intentions. He would shoot anyone that tried to force their way inside the drugstore. He motioned for Fiona and the kids to join him behind the counter, and the trio rushed over fearfully. "I want you and the children to hide under the counter. Keep quiet and don't come out until I tell you it's safe to do so." Fiona pushed Harry and Charlotte under the counter and crawled into the cramped space after them. "You too, Sasha." I urged my sister.

"No. What about you?"

"There isn't time to argue. Squeeze in with Fiona and wait until I come back for you." The banging continued as someone battered at the back door. I grabbed the crutch Phil had propped against the wall and hobbled after him. He quietly opened the door to the back hallway and shook his head when he caught sight of me. "Go wait with the others," he said.

"No chance," I told him with a fatalistic grin. He stepped into the narrow passageway with a shake of his bald head, and I followed close behind, pulling the door shut after me. As we drew closer to the exit, it sounded like a giant hammering against the door. "It's reinforced with steel, so they'll have a devil of a time breaking it down," Phil explained.

"Are you sure?" I asked doubtfully. Whoever was on the other side was fiercely determined to break into the drugstore.

"There was a burglary a few years back. Someone stole a bunch of drugs, and the cops suggested we increase security to avoid a repeat. That door won't budge."

"What about the glass insert?"

"It's protected by a metal grill. Even if they manage to smash the glass, they can't squeeze between the bars."

"Maybe not, but with all that noise they're making, it won't be long before a drone shows up."

"True," he agreed. Phil approached the door with the shotgun raised and ready. "You need to quit banging on the door and get the hell out of here," he calmly addressed the would-be attacker.

"Fuck you, pops! Either give us the Oxy, or we'll break this motherfucker down."

I wanted to press my face to the glass panel and look out at the idiots threatening to bust their way inside. But I had no way of knowing if they were armed, and I didn't fancy a bullet in the head.

"That's not happening, pal," Phil growled, and I took a cautious step back, unnerved by his aggressive tone. They continued to beat on the door. A pair of steel-capped boots joining in by the sound of it. I hoped Phil was correct about the door being impervious to the frenzied attack of a bunch of strung-out junkies. Their hunger for the potent painkiller outweighed any instincts for self-preservation.

"Let us in, you fucking pig!" someone screamed, followed in quick succession by the end of a crowbar smashing against the glass insert. A fine spiderweb of cracks spread across the glass before one of the assailants used the crowbar to tap the broken glass out of the frame. A face twisted with rage and desperation pressed against the metal bars. One bulging, bloodshot eye locked onto mine, and a shiver rippled through me. The guy wasn't functioning with a full deck. Withdrawals had stripped him of his sense of humanity, and all that was left was a burning need for drugs.

"I'm going to bash your fucking head in until your brains leak out your ears," he warned.

Phil stepped between us, pointing the shotgun barrel at the junkie's face. "Step back from the door, or I'll pull the trigger, and it will be your brains splattered on the ground." Fuck yeah, Phil.

The strung-out drug addict ducked out of sight for a moment before returning with a battered trash can raised above his head. Litter cascaded down onto his shoulders, and one of his cronies cheered him on raucously, clapping and stomping his feet like an excited monkey. He lobbed the bin at the door, and I instinctively ducked. "Oh shit," Phil groaned. He skipped backward away from the window and grabbed me by the arm, dragging me down the hallway after him. The sudden movement set my knee off, and I gritted my teeth against the white-hot pain jolting up my leg with every unsteady step I took.

Outside, a series of blasts shook the rear of the store. Hot, dry air puffed down the hallway through the window, ruffling my patchy scorched hair. Phil dragged me inside the toilet cubicle and slammed the door closed, muffling the junkie's death screams. I sank onto the toilet seat and clapped my hands over my ears. Phil stood in front of me. He held the shotgun across his body while we waited for the drone to blast its way inside. Seconds ticked by, and nothing happened. Eventually, when the screams had ceased, and no further attacks were forthcoming, I pushed up off the toilet and squeezed around Phil. "Do you think that's a good idea?" he asked when I eased open the door and risked a peek out into the hallway. "We'll soon find out," I shrugged and limped down to the door at the end of the hall.

I cautiously peered between the metal bars running vertically across the window and immediately regretted my curiosity. The guy that had threatened to bash my brains out only minutes ago was lying face down on the asphalt. Most of his shirt was burnt away, and his legs were two charred stumps. All that remained of his companion were some greasy globs of meat scattered across the ground. A flap of skin clung to the cement path that ran along the back of the stores. It took me a second to realize I was staring at a pale set of lips and a large, broad nose. I swallowed bile and turned away, willing myself not to puke.

Phil stepped over to the window and surveyed the damage outside before assisting me as I made my way along the hallway. "I told the idiot to back off. Why the hell didn't he listen?" Phil lamented.

"Don't waste your time feeling guilty. They made their choices. Nobody forced them to bang and holler the way they did."

"Still," he shook his head sadly and held my crutch as I lowered myself into one of the chairs in the waiting area.

"I must have twisted my knee when we were running for cover. Damn thing hurts like hell."

"Stay put, and I'll get you something for the pain. But first, I'd best let Fiona and your sister know that it's safe to come out now."

"Yeah, they must be going crazy, all squished together under there."

A few seconds later, Sasha ran over to my side and wrapped her arms around me. "I didn't know if I was ever going to see you again. What happened?" I allowed her to cling to me for a bit longer before shaking her off and explaining, "Some drug addicts were looking to score, and I guess they weren't thinking very clearly. All the noise they made attracted a drone, and you can figure out the rest." Phil returned minus the shotgun and handed me some water and a pain pill. "Just the one?" I asked dubiously. I popped the tablet in my mouth and washed it down with a swig of water.

"I thought it might be best to start with one and see how you go. If you plan on heading off at sunset, you don't want to be slow-witted from opioids."

"Good point," I agreed. Phil excused himself, and when he was out of earshot, Sasha crouched beside me and admitted, "You were right. We can't stay here." Her eyes kept flicking back to the door to the back passageway. Our run-in with the addicts had unsettled her. "People are getting desperate. It makes them dangerous. Hopefully, we can convince Fiona to come with us."

I squeezed her hand. "Hopefully."

Twelve

Nobody talked much during the next couple of hours as the afternoon crept toward evening. I tried approaching Fiona, hoping to change her mind about remaining at the drugstore with Phil. She hadn't forgiven me for my nasty outburst earlier, and when she saw me approach, she shifted slightly, so her back was to me while she told Charlotte a story. So much for convincing her to come with us. Acting like a vicious crackhead had ensured it would only be Sasha and myself heading out at sunset.

Accepting my newfound status as an outcast among our mismatched group, I dragged a chair down one of the aisles. It was no easy task, thanks to my lack of skill with a crutch. Positioning the chair near the front door to guard the expansive glass storefront, I sank into the chair to wait for the sun to set. It was by sheer luck (or stupidity) that the junkies had tried breaking in via the back door. If they'd thought to come around the front, a fist-sized rock lobbed at the window would have been all it took for them to gain access to the store. I couldn't understand how Fiona failed to see how vulnerable they'd be if they stuck around.

Once the afternoon shadows had deepened, I pushed myself up out of the chair and went to the door to peek around the blind. Although it wasn't fully dark outside just yet, it would be by the time we got ourselves organized and said our farewells. I was relieved to discover the SUV was still parked where we'd left it. When I turned to find Sasha, I was startled by a presence lingering near the end of the aisle displaying a dizzying array of adult diapers. Apparently, incontinence was something I had to look forward to if I made it to old age. Phil must have noticed the shock on my face because he immediately apologized for frightening me. I shrugged it off, more embarrassed by my lack of awareness than anything else.

"Do you still plan on leaving tonight?" he asked.

"Yep. I'm about to find Sasha, and then we'll head off. I appreciate everything you've done for us. Without your intervention, I can't even imagine what would have happened to us. Me especially. But you're on borrowed time in this place, and I don't want to be here when the next asshole smashes their way inside, looking for their next fix."

"I understand. Until today I hadn't fully realized what a beacon for trouble this place is. When you guys showed up the other night, I thought if this is as bad as it gets, then I can easily ride it out inside the drugstore."

I chuckled. "Helping defenseless women and children isn't quite the same as fending off desperate drug addicts or enterprising criminals."

"Agreed. Except from what I've heard, you're not entirely defenseless." We stared at each other for a long moment, and

I wondered how much Fiona had told him about me before I replied. "I've done my best to keep us all alive. Although it looks like it's your turn to do what's necessary to protect Fiona and the kids."

He grimaced and said, "I'll do whatever I can, but since those junkies tried to break in, I'm not so sure I can keep them safe."

"At least you've got a gun. All I've got is a machete stolen from some prick who tried to use it on me. And even though it looks badass, it can't compete with a bullet."

"Yeah, you should probably upgrade your weapon," Phil agreed.

"You think? God knows I've tried. That was one of the first things my boyfriend told me to do when the shit hit the fan, but I'll be damned if any of the houses I've been in have so much as a baseball bat for self-defense."

"Your boyfriend sounds like a smart and resourceful guy. I can see why you're so eager to join him."

"He knows his stuff. If anyone can survive the end of the world, it's Brent."

"It must be difficult for you to be so far apart."

I felt myself tearing up and admitted, "I miss him so much, and I wish I could tell him how much he means to me. I've never really talked to him about how I feel, and now I might not get the chance."

"Hopefully, you'll see him again," Phil said kindly, and I nodded. The touchy-feely moment passed, and we headed to the back of the store where the others were playing cards. Charlotte was too young to grasp the concept and smacked her chubby hand down onto the pile whenever someone laid a card out, much to her brother's frustration. "It's time to go, Sasha," I spoke up, reluctant to spoil their game.

Since I didn't know when we'd have another chance to use a bathroom, I encouraged Sasha to freshen up before leaving. After she'd vacated the tiny washroom, I took her place inside the room, leaning the crutch up against the closed door while I scrubbed my face with the harsh antiseptic soap until my skin was shiny and tight. I gave my armpits the same treatment and made a mental note to swipe a can of antiperspirant on my way out. It might be the end of the world, but it didn't mean I had to stink like a hobo.

When I opened the bathroom door, Phil was waiting in the hallway with a plastic carry bag. He held it out, and I took it from him. "What's this?" I asked, prodding the contents curiously.

"I threw together a few things that I thought you'd need if you plan on reaching your boyfriend in the mountains. There's a first aid kit, some of those diet shakes you like so much, and, umm..." He seemed embarrassed suddenly, and when I dug around in the bag some more, I understood his discomfort. Sanitary products. I had to hand it to him; the guy was thorough. "Thanks. I can't imagine too many people would even register a thing like that. In another week or so, I'll be thanking you for considering my reproductive cycle," I smiled.

"It comes with the job. I hope you don't mind," Phil said, and I shook my head.

"Nah, it's all good. You've been so helpful; I honestly can't thank you enough."

"That's okay. I figure I must do what I can. Otherwise, I risk ending up like those savages that tried to break in earlier."

"That might be true." I sighed, bracing myself for what was to come. "It's time we got moving. How far do you think it is to the overpass?" I asked Phil, wondering how far our detour to the drugstore had taken us from Caldwell St.

"I'd say you're looking at close to two miles. Maybe more if you have to find an alternative route around a traffic accident."

Less than two miles. That didn't sound so bad— a ten-minute drive in favorable conditions. With pyromaniac drones patrolling the skies, heinous traffic snarls, and God only knew what else prowling the streets; it could take us half the night to reach the Caldwell St ramp. Still, even at that pace, we should be well out of the city by dawn. "Sasha, it's time to go. Say goodbye to Harry and Charlotte."

Sasha walked over to where the kids were playing and crouched down between them. She drew the pair in close and hugged them tightly. Again, I found myself wondering if I should be leaving them behind. Not that I had a say in the matter. Fiona was their mother, and it was up to her to do what she thought was best. And she believed staying with the pharmacist was preferable to heading out on the road with Sasha and me. I'd hoped the incident with the rampaging dope fiends might have changed her mind, but she was still committed to sticking with Phil even if she had only known him for less than forty-eight hours.

"Don't go, Sasha," Harry implored my sister. He clung to her unabashedly. His tiny hands wrapped tightly around her arm.

"I'm sorry, Harry, but I have to go with Jess. We're going to meet our friend who is waiting for us in the mountains. He said there weren't many drones there, and we'd be safe in the cabin."

"There really won't be any of those wasps that spit fire?" the boy asked in wonder.

"I hope not."

"Why can't we come with you? I haven't been to the mountains before."

"I'd like you to come with us, Harry, but your mom thinks it would be better if you stayed here with Phil."

"No!" the little boy wailed. His impassioned cry startled Charlotte, and she burst into tears. Both children bawled against Sasha, wet stains spreading across her t-shirt. Fiona ran over and tried to pry them off my sister, but they were determined not to be left behind and clung to her with all their might, resisting their mother's attempts to detach them from their new friend.

Understanding resistance would only exacerbate the problem; Sasha continued to hug the children. Their hysterical crying quickly diminished, replaced by hitching sobs that left my sister drenched in a revolting combination of snot and tears. Fiona stepped away from the distraught trio, her face taut with anguish. She glanced uncertainly from me to Phil and then back to the children. I stood resting on the crutch, waiting impatiently for the maudlin goodbyes to be over. While I felt sympathy for Harry and Charlotte, the need to get moving overrode any sentimentality.

Fiona's attention returned to me, and I matched her gaze. Whatever she was thinking about, it was creating a fair amount of internal conflict. Her face fluttered through a multitude of expressions before she finally found her voice. "I've changed my mind." She announced uncertainly. "We're coming with you."

"What?" I asked, surprised by her change of heart. "I'm confused. What made you reconsider?"

She looked over at Phil apologetically. "After what happened before, I don't feel that it's safe to stay here anymore. People are going crazy, and I'm not sure staying in the city is the best thing for the kids."

I agreed with her sentiments, but I also felt it was vital for her to understand the danger we faced. There was no certainty in this violent new world, and I couldn't guarantee her safety. "Fiona, I honestly believe that reaching the cabin is our best chance of survival. But it's going to be dangerous. We might not even make it."

"I know there are no guarantees."

"Alright," I shrugged. "If you're willing to take the chance, let's get this show on the road." Fiona nodded and went over to the children to explain the change of plans. Harry and Charlotte stopped crying immediately and began cheering instead. I limped over to Phil, ignoring my throbbing knee. "Are you okay with this new development?" I asked. He studied the children intently before returning his attention to me. "The shit is going to hit the fan sooner rather than later. If you can get those children to a less populated area before that happens, they might have a chance of growing to adulthood."

"It would be a tight squeeze, but there's room in the SUV if you want to join us." I was mildly surprised to hear the words come out of my mouth. I hadn't even been considering asking him to join us. Judging by his startled expression, Phil hadn't seen it coming either. He raked his hands over the stubble on his face and groaned. "I don't know. I'd planned on sticking around here until the situation is resolved. I'd hoped my boyfriend would find his way here, but it's been a while, and if he were going to show up, I think it would have happened by now."

"I'm sorry. I didn't realize you were trying to find someone too. Have you had any contact with your boyfriend since the drones appeared?"

Phil gave an almost imperceptible shake of his head. "He was out of town on business when it happened. I haven't heard from him, and I know it's unlikely he survived."

I didn't know what to say. The poor guy was hoping to be reunited with a ghost. His partner had probably been reduced to a mass of rotting meat while catching a cab to some characterless motel in a neighboring city. "Look, it probably won't end well no matter what you decide, but at least if you come with us, you won't be alone."

"Yeah, alright. Count me in," he agreed. I smiled. It would be helpful to have someone proficient with a gun along for the ride. Plus, Phil was starting to grow on me.

Twenty minutes later, everyone was finally ready to leave. I peeked behind the blinds, watching the erratic flashes of light exploding across the skyline in the distance. None appeared too close. For the moment, it was all clear in the immediate vicinity outside the strip mall. Fiona squatted in front of her children and took one of their hands in each of her own. "Remember to be very quiet when we leave the drugstore."

Sasha added in a theatrical whisper, "How about we pretend we're mice? Mice are quick and quiet. Nobody even notices when they scurry past. Do you think you can be like a mouse?" Harry and Charlotte nodded enthusiastically, intrigued by the prospect of becoming a twitchy rodent. Fiona mouthed a silent thank you to my sister and allowed her to take Charlotte's hand.

I pressed the unlock button on the key and heard the familiar thunk of the locks disengaging before Phil slipped out onto the concrete walk outside the store. Satisfied that we were alone, he held the door open while we filed out of the drugstore and hurried over to the SUV. I was the last one to reach the vehicle, and Phil asked if I was okay to get behind the wheel. "I'm fine. It's been a few hours since I took anything for the pain. If it gets too much for me, I'll let you know." I wasn't ready to give up control. Besides, I figured Phil would be more efficient with the shotgun since he was familiar with handling the weapon.

I recoiled when a blast rocked the night less than a block away. Fuck. I passed Phil the crutch and hopped up behind the steering wheel. "Let's get the hell out of here before that thing finds us." I checked the fuel gauge. We still had enough gas to get us out of the city and then some. Hopefully, we'd get lucky and find a gas station along the way that was still functioning. But that was a problem for the future. I couldn't get caught up thinking about that now.

A second blast, closer than the previous one, jolted me to action. I started the car and carefully reversed out of the parking space. I crossed the pothole-riddled parking lot and turned out onto the street. We sped away from the stretch of empty stores, only slowing when I spied a T-intersection up ahead. "Turn right," Phil advised, and I followed his instructions. Between his medical knowledge, his comfortable handling of a firearm, and his Google Maps style confidence, I was beginning to wonder how we'd ever managed without him.

I assumed Phil was guiding us back to the main arterial road we'd fled days ago when the drone attacked the ambulance ahead of us. A car traveling along the opposite lane startled me, and I slammed my foot on the brake instinctively. Everyone was jolted by the seat belts locking against the violent motion of their bodies continuing forward despite the SUV's sudden stop. I giggled nervously and apologized when I realized my error. Of course, there would be other cars on the road. I reminded myself that we wouldn't be the only ones daring to navigate the streets, and I should probably dial the paranoia down a notch if I wanted to maintain my sanity.

"Is everyone alright? I didn't mean to react like that." Fiona and my sister assured me everyone was okay. Phil glanced at me questioningly, and I felt heat rush to my cheeks. Maybe he was right. Perhaps the pain meds were affecting me more than I thought.

"Before you say anything, I'm fine. I just let my nerves get the better of me. A few days holed up in the drugstore, and I've gone soft. I won't let it happen again."

"Sure. It took me by surprise too. Don't worry about it." Damn. I was beginning to wonder if Phil could be the world's most perfect human. Even when I was clearly in the wrong, he didn't call me out on it. His patient acceptance made me even more determined to prove that I could drive us to the Caldwell St ramp and beyond.

Up ahead, the streetlights lining the four-lane arterial road flickered brightly. I was surprised when Phil told me to slow down. "Huh?" I asked in confusion.

"There's a one-way lane coming on my left that runs parallel to the main road. If it isn't blocked off, we should be able to follow it down to the Hilton and Combs Street intersection." Hilton and Combs were the two major roads that met in the center of the five-block downtown area. You could spend twenty minutes trying to cross the intersection during peak-hour. Although current events had most likely snuffed out waiting times at the traffic lights, and we wouldn't have to worry about trying to stay calm while the minutes ticked by with little forward momentum. "Slow down, or you'll miss the turn. It's on the other side of that apartment block." He pointed to a squat three-story building a few houses down.

Following the pharmacist's advice, I slowed the SUV to a crawl and peered up at the apartment block, surprised to discover slivers of light spilling out from behind some of the windows on the upper floor. He hadn't been exaggerating when he said I'd miss the turn. The lane was narrow, and even knowing it was coming up didn't stop me from overshooting the turn. A car parked close to the corner prevented us from being able to squeeze past, and I had to reverse the SUV a short distance before climbing the gutter to avoid scraping the side of the sedan taking up half of the lane.

It was pitch black in the laneway. Without streetlights, shadows cast by the multi-story buildings swallowed any feeble moonlight that reached the narrow strip. I was virtually driving blind. A dog shot out from scavenging in an overturned garbage can, and my heart constricted, fearing I'd run it over. Instead, the dog hurried out of the way seconds before the front of the SUV clipped the bin and sent it rolling against a cinder block wall with a boisterous clatter. Phil and I glanced at each other nervously, hoping the noise wouldn't alert a drone to our whereabouts.

We reached the end of the block, and I slowed down to check for hazards before turning onto the main road. "Fucking hell," Phil muttered.

"What is it?" I asked uneasily.

"Look," he pointed in the direction of downtown. Only then did I notice the ominous orange glow in the distance. Thick tendrils of smoke rose into the sky, creating a dense cloud that hung over the entire downtown area. "Half of downtown must be on fire."

"It looks that way," Phil agreed. Fiona leaned forward, squeezing between the front seats so that she could peer out the windscreen. "Oh, no. That's not good. How are we going to reach the highway now?" I could detect the rising panic in her voice, and so could Phil. "It will be alright," he assured her. "It probably looks worse than it is. I think we should continue as planned and assess the situation once we get a bit closer."

"I agree. Let's not freak out before we know what we're dealing with," I said and drove toward the carnage, ignoring the anxiety building in my chest.

A few minutes later, we reached the end of the lane without spotting a single drone. Someone dashed across our path as I edged my way forward, and I tapped the brakes to avoid clipping them as they disappeared down a narrow driveway. They were the first person we had seen since entering the back alley, and it was starting to feel like we were the only people left so close to the heart of the city.

It was short-lived.

I pulled out onto Drummond Boulevard. Cars littered our path. Some were scorched wrecks; others left abandoned in the middle of the road, the driver's long gone. The streetlights along this section of the road were blacked out, making visibility difficult. I drove forward slowly, navigating around a station wagon parked at an angle across the street. An auto shop smoldering on the opposite side of the boulevard distracted me, and there was a thump as the tires rolled over something large enough to bounce us around the SUV. I slammed on the brakes.

"What are you doing?" Fiona asked.

"I'm going to check what that was. Maybe I hit an animal," I answered and unbuckled my belt.

"Are you crazy? Forget about it."

I had opened the door a crack when Sasha hissed, "Drone. I saw it near that building that's on fire."

Phil reached across me and gently pulled the door shut. "Nobody move."

I looked out at the auto shop, trying to locate the drone. Maybe Sasha was mistaken.

"Shit," Phil muttered. "It's right in front of us. Can you see it?"

I looked out the windshield, and sure enough, there was the drone, hovering in the air a short distance from the vehicle. I slowly reached out and switched off the engine, afraid the sound of the idling car had drawn it to us. We watched in terror as the drone slowly circled the SUV.

Charlotte began to fidget. "Be very still, honey bun. We don't want the metal wasp to find us," Fiona whispered. That was an understatement. The drone returned to the front of the vehicle and remained suspended above us, seemingly waiting for us to move or make a sound. I doubted it would have to wait much longer. Despite Fiona's plea for Charlotte to remain still, the little girl was growing increasingly agitated.

Luck was on our side. A motorcycle roared past, its headlight illuminating the road as it zig-zagged around the wreckages. The drone lingered above us a moment longer before taking off after the kamikaze motorcyclist. We let out a collective sigh, and I started the engine. It could only get worse the closer we got to the burning heart of the city.

"Sasha, climb into the back and look out for that drone. If it comes back our way, I want to know about it."

Thirteen

My nerves were shot, and we hadn't even reached the six blocks that made up the downtown area. There was a massive pileup of mangled cars blocking the road. I mounted the curb and navigated around an overturned stroller. I pointedly avoided looking too closely in case there was a child strapped inside.

The air was thick with smoke, and Phil switched the air-conditioner to recirculate, but it didn't help much. There were too many people in the car, and the smoke had already infiltrated the interior. "Dear God," Phil moaned. "It looks like we're about to enter the inner circle of hell." I had never seen the inner circle of hell, but I could easily imagine that it would look awfully like the blackened and burning buildings ahead of us. Flames engulfed some of the older buildings built before the introduction of fire-resistant materials, thick black smoke billowing from the burning structures.

The streets were deserted. I'd expected to see more people in the downtown area, but they must have fled to the suburbs. A body hung out of the window of an abandoned deli. A group of cats had gathered around the corpse and chewed greedily at the arms dangling down. I dragged my eyes away from the feasting felines a moment too late.

"Watch out!" Phil yelled as we entered the intersection. I slammed on the brakes, but the Jeep was traveling way too fast. The vehicles collided in a piercing screech of metal. The Jeep's grill connected with the SUV on the front passenger side, and the two cars careened across the intersection, locked together by the force of the impact. The airbags deployed, and the violently inflating safety device punched me in the face. My head ricocheted against the headrest. I felt like I was trapped on a malfunctioning fairground ride as the vehicles spun across the intersection.

Once we came to a stop, I pushed the deflating airbag away and gingerly felt my throbbing face. Blood trickled from my nose, and I dabbed it with the tail of my shirt. The kids were crying in the backseat, and someone in the Jeep was screaming uncontrollably. Beside me, Phil's head lolled to the side. His eyes were shut, and his arms hung limply in his lap. The passenger door was badly crumpled in, having taken the worst of the impact. The nose of the Jeep was practically inside our vehicle crushing the right side of Phil's body.

I reached across and nudged him. "Phil? Can you hear me?" He didn't respond. I couldn't tell if he was dead or alive. "Check his pulse," Fiona prompted as she unclipped her seatbelt and inspected Harry and Charlotte for injuries. I nodded and felt around his neck until I found a faint and thready pulse. "He's alive," I said, my shoulders sagging with relief. "Sasha, are you okay back there?" I asked over my shoulder as I tried to assess

Phil's injuries. The screaming from the other car continued unabated and I looked through the shattered passenger window at the Jeep's crumpled bonnet. The driver was dead, their face obliterated in the crash. Beside the deceased driver, the pudgy middle-aged passenger continued to wail. Before I could snap at them to shut the hell up, I saw a drone approaching from an alley on the other side of the street. "Drone!" I bellowed, "Everybody, get down!" I grabbed Phil's arm and pulled him toward me as I slithered down into the floor space beneath the steering wheel.

A wave of searing hot air rolled over the SUV as the drone blasted the screaming man out of existence. I squeezed my eyes shut as I waited to be incinerated, knowing my lapse of concentration was the reason we were all going to die. If only I hadn't been so easily distracted by the cats eating the deli guy.

Time seemed to grind to a halt.

I wondered if I was already dead and quickly dismissed the idea. My knee was throbbing unbearably from being cramped up in the leg space, and it seemed unlikely that I'd be concerned with such a minor injury if I'd just roasted to death. I'd barely had time to ponder why the SUV hadn't been torched when the third-story window of a building nearby erupted in flames. I could only assume some poor schmuck had been lured to the window by the sound of the crash and inadvertently exposed themselves to the drone.

I cautiously poked my head up from beneath the steering wheel and peeked between the front seats. It was an immense relief to see my sister staring back at me. Fiona was still curled protectively over Harry and Charlotte. Assured that they were uninjured, I turned my attention back to Phil, acutely aware of the need to get moving before the drone returned. It was obvious that Phil was gone. I choked back a sob as I gently pushed his body back up into an upright position. The right side of his body was raw and blistered where the flames had rolled across his body. I checked his pulse anyway. Thirty seconds passed before I gave up.

He was dead.

"Jess."

Phil had gone out of his way to save me, and what had I done for him in return? I'd promised him a fighting chance at riding out this blood-soaked nightmare and the hope of finding sanctuary in the mountains. And what had I managed to deliver? A brutal death mere hours after joining our desperate group of survivors. His body would be left to rot in the car like the countless others we had passed along the way.

"Jess. What are we going to do?" Sasha said, interrupting my pity party. She didn't bother asking if Phil was alright. She already knew the answer. I fought down the emotions twisting my guts, and forced my eyes away from Phil's blistered face. I had to pull myself together.

I dragged myself up into the seat and tried starting the engine. The motor coughed and sputtered as I pumped the accelerator. "Come on," I implored the wretched vehicle, but it was no use. The crash had caused too much damage. The SUV was a wreck, and we were stranded in the middle of the intersection while the buildings around us burned, and drones prowled the sky. "Fuck!"

I hammered my fist against the steering wheel in frustration. Charlotte started crying, and Harry took her chubby hand in his.

"I'm sorry for swearing. I didn't mean to sound so angry," I apologized. "The car won't start. We're going to have to try and find somewhere safe to hide while we figure out a new plan."

"You mean somewhere safe like the drugstore?" Fiona asked, not bothering to hide the bitterness in her voice. I opened my mouth to reply, and Sasha glared at me and shook her head. There wasn't time to get into a fight about it. I scanned the surrounding area, searching for somewhere suitable to hide. Our best option was an overturned bus lying diagonally across the road just beyond the intersection. "We need to make a run for that bus over near the old post office building," I told them.

"Do you mean the bus lying on its side with a hole blasted through the roof?" Fiona scoffed, wrapping her arms tightly around Charlotte.

"That's the bus I'm talking about." I took a noisy breath, trying to diffuse the anger boiling inside me.

"Are we going to make a mad dash all together or try to sneak across one at a time?" Sasha interrupted. I took a moment to consider the question. If we made a run for it as a group, we risked making ourselves a larger target, and if we tried running for the bus one at a time, we were in danger of being separated if the drone returned. Either option was fraught with danger. "I think we should probably go together," I said, my body tensing as a series of gunshots cut through the night. They were close. "We need to move. Now."

I slipped out of the car and silently dropped to the ground. The air around us was thick with smoke that smelt strongly of melting plastic and other chemicals. I stifled a cough and helped Sasha out of the back of the SUV. Harry was next. I popped him on the ground beside Sasha, and she took his hand and pulled him in close. I scooped up little Charlotte and held her against my chest while I watched out for the drone. Fiona climbed out of the car and snatched Charlotte out of my arms with a scowl.

"Is everyone ready?" I whispered. Sasha and Fiona nodded. "Okay. We need to run as fast as we can for the hole in the roof of the bus. When you get there, don't fuck around. Climb straight inside and find somewhere to hide."

"What if we can't make it?" Sasha asked.

"You have to make it. But if something happens, try and take cover in that car over there." I pointed to a car with its door standing open midway between the bus and our position huddled against the SUV. "Let's go." Sasha hoisted Harry onto her hip, and after I urged her on, she ran toward the bus. Fiona followed closely behind, Charlotte's head bobbing over her mother's shoulder. I limped along after them, only remembering the crutch when I was midway between the SUV and the car. It was too late to turn back now. Pain gnawed at my knee like a hungry animal chewing a carcass, and I had to stop at the abandoned vehicle to give my leg a break. I counted to ten and then pushed away from the car.

Fiona and my sister were huddled against the overturned bus watching for drones as I limped over to them, and I wondered why the fuck they had not climbed inside yet. When I reached the bus, I thought I understood their reluctance to enter. The stench of decaying flesh was an invisible barrier halting me in my tracks. My hand went to my nose, and I instinctively turned my face away from the offensive odor. "Jesus Christ." I couldn't begin to imagine what it would be like inside the bus. Was it safe to breathe such fetid air? Or would we be at risk of catching some dreadful airborne disease?

"The drone is back," Sasha whispered beside me. "It's across the street. I don't think it has seen us yet." I slowly turned to look behind us. My eyes eventually locked onto the drone hovering amongst the flickering shadows cast by the burning buildings. An icy finger of fear traced a path along my spine, all concerns about the stench inside the bus forgotten. I eased my left leg through the hole, which was roughly the size of a small refrigerator being careful not to catch myself on the sharp, jagged metal edges. It was very dark inside the bus, and I grabbed hold of a seat to steady myself.

Sasha passed Harry through the hole, and I placed him on the floor behind me. Glass from the broken windows crunched underfoot as I whispered for him to be careful. He nodded while gagging and quickly buried his face in the crook of his arm. Smart kid. The smell was intolerable.

When Sasha tried to push Fiona and Charlotte through, I reached out and grabbed hold of her wrist. "No. You're next." She tried to pull away from me, but my grip was firm, and I quickly dragged her through the opening. Once my sister was safely inside, I took Charlotte from Fiona and passed the child to Sasha.

By now, the drone was hovering around a newsstand on the opposite corner. "Climb through very slowly," I whispered. "No sudden movements, just smooth and slow." I helped her inside the bus, my eyes never leaving the drone lingering across the street. Some of the tension drained away once we were all inside the bus, but we were by no means safe. We used the back of the seats for support as we shuffled further along the bus away from the holes blasted through the roof. It was disorientating trying to navigate along the overturned bus, and I caught my foot on the metal window frames more than once.

There was a dark and reeking mound blocking our path. I turned to the others. "Watch out for the body. It's rather ripe. We'll need to step over it." Sasha hoisted Harry up onto her hip and carefully hopped over the body. For once, I was thankful that we couldn't see very well in the dark. If the horrendous stench of spoiled meat was anything to go by, we didn't want a closeup of the dead commuter at our feet. "Walk further down away from the smell while I help Fiona," I told my sister. She nodded, placed Harry on the floor, and took Charlotte from me. The trio continued toward the front of the bus.

Fiona hesitated. "It's okay," I encouraged her. "Take my hand."

She shook her head. Her eyes riveted to the bloated corpse at her feet. "No, I can't. It's too gross." She retched and turned her face away from the body. My patience was wearing thin. "Fiona, my knee is fucking killing me, Phil's dead, and there's a drone lurking across the street. Quit it with the theatrics and step the fuck over the body." She slowly turned back to me. I reached out to help, but she ignored the offer.

"I should never have let you convince me to leave the drugstore," she mumbled harshly.

"Maybe you're right," I admitted. She probably didn't hear my apology because a blast that was way too close for comfort shook the bus. I ducked between two seats and waited while Fiona tried to jump over the body to join me. I don't know if her foot caught on something or she slipped, but she landed heavily on the bloated mass of flesh. An enormous fart sound erupted from the corpse's orifices as Fiona's weight expelled the gas that had built up inside the body. She thrashed around, slipping in the noxious liquid that had pooled beneath the remains.

I forced myself out from my hiding place and tried to drag Fiona off the body, but she shrugged me off. "Don't touch me!" she hissed as she slithered around in the reeking goo. I took a step back, unnerved by her anger, and watched in silence as she scrabbled to her feet and stumbled toward me. "Oh, my God! I'm covered in stinky dead person juice. I think I'm gonna be sick," she wailed. She bent over and threw up, her body heaving long after her stomach was empty. Eventually, the retching subsided, and she was able to stand up. She reached up to wipe her mouth but remembered her hand was covered in unthinkable gore and dropped it to her side.

"We'll get you cleaned up as soon as it's safe to leave the bus," I said.

"Just take me to my kids," she replied.

We found Sasha and the children hunkered down further along in the open area for wheelchairs or parents with kids in strollers. If the drone didn't discover us, we would be safe for a couple of hours while I figured out our next move. Fiona squatted down beside Harry, but he wriggled closer to my sister. "Mommy, you stink. Get away from us," Charlotte said.

Fiona choked back a sob and sank onto the floor as far from the others as she could. I crouched down in front of her, gritting my teeth against the pain that flared in my knee. "I'm sorry, Fiona. This situation is messed up, but I promise you that I'm going to do whatever it takes to find a way out." She wouldn't even look at me, not that it was easy to see much in the dark. "We're probably going to be stuck here for a while. Why don't you take off that dirty t-shirt?" She finally dragged her eyes up to meet mine.

"Am I supposed to run around topless now? Is that part of your great plan?"

I sighed. Fiona was determined to make this difficult for me. "No, of course not. I thought you could change into my shirt. I can get by with just a tank top." I waited while she considered the offer.

"Alright," she agreed and peeled off the offensive t-shirt. I passed her my shirt, and she quickly slipped it on, buttoning it up as she drew Harry and Charlotte away from my sister. I limped over to Sasha and eased down beside her. She took my hand in hers and asked, "Are you alright? Maybe you should take one of those pills Phil gave you."

"Fuck!" I cried in frustration.

"What's the matter?"

"I left the fucking backpack in the SUV along with the gun." I wanted to scream. Or tear out what remained of my hair. I couldn't believe I'd been so stupid. It was bad enough I'd left the backpack behind containing the first aid kit Phil had put together for us, but forgetting the shotgun was something else entirely.

We were utterly defenseless.

I couldn't see any way around it. I'd have to go back for the gun. I pushed myself up off the floor with a grunt.

"What are you doing?" Sasha asked.

"I have to go back and get the gun. We don't stand a chance without it."

"Are you kidding? We nearly died in that accident. You can't go back now."

"I don't have a choice."

"Jess, you can't run on that leg. If the drone notices you, you won't stand a chance."

"Sasha, right now, we have nothing. If some asshole decides to attack us, we are screwed. You have to remember, not everyone out there wants to be your friend."

"Okay," she agreed. "I'll go instead."

"Like hell, you will!" I couldn't believe my ears. Did she honestly think I would allow her to run out into the open on her own to retrieve the gun and some painkillers?

"You're injured, and you aren't as quick on your feet as me. It makes sense for me to do it," she explained. I shook my head vehemently. "No way. I don't care if I'm slow. I can't let you do it. It's too dangerous."

Sasha waved her hands in the air and said, "Look around, sis, I'm in danger no matter what. We all are."

Damn her sensible logic. I knew she was right, but I couldn't bring myself to allow her to expose herself like that. She must have realized what I was thinking because she leaned across and pecked me on the cheek. "I love you, Jess." She stepped out of reach before I could grab her and whispered over her shoulder, "I'll be back soon."

I knew I'd never reach her before she managed to climb out of the ragged hole in the side of the bus, but that didn't stop me from trying. By the time I reached the twisted metal opening, it was too late. Sasha sprinted toward the abandoned car between the bus and the SUV containing Phil's body. I frantically searched the sky for drones, hoping to find none—no such luck.

The flames from the burning buildings illuminated a drone stalking an overweight woman a few hundred yards from the overturned bus. She screamed as she thundered down the sidewalk after an equally corpulent man. I didn't know where they came from. Maybe they'd fled one of the blazing apartments. Perhaps like us, they'd lost their wheels. Either way, it didn't matter. Their noisy, attention-grabbing attempt to outrun the metal murder machine allowed Sasha to reach the car unnoticed. I watched on helplessly as she ducked down beside the car, checking that it was safe to continue before dashing out into the open once more.

Halfway down the block, the fat lady was silenced in a flash of flames and fried flesh. It felt like a giant fist was squeezing my heart as I watched Sasha look over her shoulder at the drone hovering above the charred remains of the woman. She quickly calculated the odds of making it to the SUV and pressed on. She closed the gap between herself and the SUV, and I was finally able to breathe when she reached the open driver's door and climbed inside the mangled vehicle.

Thick dirty smoke billowed from the burning interior of the car that had hit us, and it wouldn't be long before the SUV caught alight. I tried not to think of Phil's body consumed by flames. It was a terrible way to go, and he deserved better. I had to remind myself that he was dead, and it didn't matter what happened to his body.

I kept my eyes locked on the SUV as my sister searched for the backpack containing my pain meds. Time was ticking away. The fat woman's companion still occupied the drone, but it wouldn't be distracted for much longer. Sasha needed to hurry the hell up and get her ass back to the bus. It was a relief when she climbed down from the SUV with the backpack slung over her shoulder and the shotgun clutched tightly in her hands.

Sasha took a moment to adjust the backpack's strap before stepping away from the SUV. A movement behind the wrecks caught my attention. I was so focused on the drone lurking nearby that I hadn't even considered the possibility of human threats. "Sasha! Behind you!" I called out. I realized too late that I'd made a mistake. Not only had I risked drawing attention to us with my outburst, but I'd also put Sasha at risk by distracting her.

I climbed out of the hole in the bus and started running toward my sister. I willed my traitorous legs to move faster, but even if I'd been fighting fit, I could never have reached her in time. "Run, Sasha!" I screamed too late. My sister turned back and saw the woman charging at her with a tire iron raised above her head. The woman was considerably taller than my sister and quickly closed the distance between them. Another couple of strides and the crazed bitch would be within swinging range of my little sister.

"Shoot her!" I screamed in desperation. "Turn around and fucking shoot her." We locked eyes for a split second, and I knew her terror was mirrored on my face. "Do it," I urged, and she spun around, aiming the shotgun up at her assailant. The woman's face twisted into a hateful snarl, and she surged forward, swinging the tire iron. Sasha blocked the blow with the barrel of the shotgun. The tire iron flew out of the woman's hand and clattered to the ground a short distance from the pair.

The woman grabbed hold of the barrel and tried to jerk the gun out of my sister's hands. She must have outweighed Sasha by at least fifty pounds, but my sister held on tight. They tussled over the weapon, and the crazed attacker dragged Sasha back and forth as she tried to steal the gun.

I was only a few limping steps from them when the woman noticed my approach. She thrust the gun forward with a vicious snarl. The shotgun stock struck Sasha in the stomach, and she doubled over with a grunt. "Get away from my sister, you dirty fucking bitch," I roared as I reached the pair and snatched the gun from Sasha. The woman snarled at me, baring rotted teeth. Madness filled her eyes, radiating from her like murderous death rays.

She spat profanities in my direction. I released the safety on the gun and pulled the trigger. There was a brief flash accompanied by an enormous boom, and the woman hurtled backward. She landed on the road a few feet away from us. She groped at the ugly wound in her belly and screamed in pain. I should have felt sorry for her, but all I could manage was contempt. I fought the urge to smash her head with the butt of the gun to shut her up.

Sasha reached out and dragged me away before I could act on the impulse. "Leave her, Jess. We need to get away before the drone shows up." I followed my sister back toward the car, ducking instinctively when a ball of fire hit the road a short distance from the screaming woman I'd shot in the gut. We dropped down beside the car and wriggled underneath it. It was a tight fit, and gravel dug into my elbows and knees. If we survived the night, I was confident that my belly would be grazed and raw from forcing my way under the car. There was a second blast that silenced the wounded woman, and I squeezed my eyes shut as a wave of heat raced toward us.

We lay frozen beneath the car, not daring to move in case the drone was toying with us. The possibility that it might be hovering above the car, waiting to vaporize my sister and me when we crawled out into the open, left me paralyzed with fear. Sasha's fingers brushed against mine, and I squeezed her hand, reassured by her touch. It wasn't much, but the contact helped keep me from flipping out.

Time seemed to slow down while we waited for the drone to move on. I counted the minutes as I breathed in the sickly stench of the burned woman. At the ten-minute mark, I decided it was time to check if it was safe for us to return to the bus. Sasha held tight to my hand, her fingers digging into my palm. I understood her concern, but the longer we lay under the car, the harder it would be to overcome the terror gripping us.

"We can't stay here forever," I told her quietly. "You were brave enough to go get the gun on your own, so I know you can pick yourself up and run back to the bus. Fiona and the kids must be worried sick about you."

Sasha took a deep breath and nodded. She slowly released her grip on my hand. I swallowed hard and dragged myself out from beneath the car, hoping my head wouldn't be obliterated the second I emerged. When nothing happened, I let out a massive sigh and used the open door for support as I stood up. The intersection was clear. I crouched back down and motioned for Sasha to join me.

Fourteen

I woke up feeling groggy and disorientated. I sat up and rubbed my eyes while I got my bearings. "I don't remember falling asleep," I admitted when Fiona crawled over and joined me. "It's those pills Phil gave you. They're no joke. You took two when you and Sasha made it back a few hours ago. I swear, within ten minutes, you were out cold. You were snoring so loud Harry and Charlotte laughed until they had tears in their eyes. Harry didn't know women could snore just as loud as men."

I smoothed my hair into a fresh ponytail, wincing as my hand passed across the blistered bald patch. Fiona handed me a bottle of water, and I gulped it down greedily. "I didn't know if you and Sasha were going to make it back to the bus. I don't know what I'd do without you," Fiona admitted.

"It got a bit sketchy for a moment, but you don't have to worry."

"I can't help it. I'm scared. We're trapped in this stinking bus with rotting bodies and drones flying around outside, waiting to kill us. I don't see how we are going to get out of here."

"I told you earlier. We'll find another car. We're only a block or two from the overpass. We can be out of the city by daybreak."

Fiona looked over her shoulder anxiously. Harry and Charlotte were curled up asleep with Sasha, who was also dozing. "How do you plan on finding a car? There are drones everywhere, and all the cars are either smashed up or burnt out."

"I'll find us a car," I assured her. "I didn't say it would be easy or without risk, but what other choice do we have?"

It wasn't like I wanted to venture back out into the streets. Truthfully, I could have happily curled up and gone back to sleep, but that wasn't an option. The bus was only a temporary refuge. We had to keep moving. I had to remind myself that Brent was waiting for us at the cabin. There had already been so many delays. If we took too much longer, he might lose hope that we were still coming.

It cut me to the core to imagine how difficult it must be for my boyfriend to sit around, waiting for us to show up. He wasn't the type of guy to step back and let someone else get their hands dirty when he was more than capable of getting the job done himself. He was a survivor, a bare-knuckled brawler, my soft and cuddly teddy bear. I could only hope he had enough faith in me to wait a little while longer.

Despite all the obstacles stacked against us, I forced myself to rally. It had been me selling everyone the mountain escape when the others would have preferred to bunker down in an abandoned house somewhere and wait for the nightmare to end. It was too late for me to give up now. We had come too far and lost too much. I wasn't giving up; I'd just reached my physical and emotional limits. It was one terrifying experience after another, and between the constant fear and the effects of the painkillers, I was at a low ebb.

Sensing my gloom, Sasha left the children and hugged me tightly. "I thought you were sleeping," I said.

"Nah. I was just resting my eyes," she smiled. The warmth and reassurance of human contact revived me, and when we eventually separated, I felt much better. "I need some ammunition for the shotgun," I told my sister.

"Okay." Sasha passed me a handful of shotgun shells and the penlight she found at the bottom of the backpack. I reloaded the shotgun and stuffed the extra ammunition in the pockets of my jeans shorts. "I suppose I'd better get moving. I'm not sure how long it will take to find another vehicle, so try not to freak out if it takes me a while."

"What do we do if you don't make it back?" Fiona asked anxiously.

"I don't plan on dying out there, but if something does happen, I think you should still try and make your way out of the city." I gave Fiona a quick hug, hoping to reassure her as I knew the prospect of continuing alone was freaking her out. As I made my way along the bus, being careful to avoid tripping on a decomposed body, I noticed Sasha following behind me. "What do you think you are doing?" I asked more sharply than I intended.

"I'm coming with you," she replied defensively.

"No, you're not. Stay here with Fiona. She needs you."

"You need me too. I'm coming with you. End of story."

This new, willful side of my sister was going to take some getting used to. I sighed and continued down to the hole in the bus. I helped Sasha climb through before following her out into the night. I pointed across the intersection at Lincoln St. "There's a parking station halfway down the next block. We should be able to find something drivable there," I whispered.

"Won't it be on fire like everything else around here?"

I shook my head, "Probably not. It's concrete, so I doubt it would catch alight easily."

"Okay. Let's do it," she agreed doubtfully.

I jogged across the intersection, glad for the painkiller's numbing effects. It was unnerving entering Lincoln Street. The air was hot and difficult to breathe. Sasha coughed into the crook of her arm and pointed at a car up ahead. As we got closer, I realized it wouldn't be going anywhere. It was a blackened wreck, containing the charred remains of what had once been a family. We hurried on, not wanting to think about the small twisted bodies in the back seat.

There was a taxi parked outside The Realto Hotel. I grabbed the door handle to check if the keys had been left inside, but the door was locked. "Fuck," I muttered in frustration and cupped my hands against the window to look inside. With flames from the office building behind us flickering in the reflection, I struggled to see the interior of the taxi. "I don't think the keys are inside," I told Sasha. It wasn't worth smashing the window in and risk drawing attention to ourselves when it was doubtful that we'd even be able to start the thing. "Come on. The parking station isn't far. We're bound to find something there."

We reached the multi-story parking station, and I removed the penlight from my pocket. "Are you sure this is a good idea?" Sasha asked, her eyes locked on the dark entrance. It looked like a bleak and ominous cave. Or maybe a mouth hungrily stretched open, waiting to devour us. "Let's just get in there and get this over and done with; we've only got a few more hours until daylight," I said, pushing aside my reservations about entering the building. "Here, you can take the torch. I can't hold both it and the shotgun." I passed her the torch, hoping its tiny beam of light would help assuage her unease.

My desire to be out of the city by daybreak gave me the motivation needed to overcome my reluctance to enter the building. I led the way up the ramp, the pitiful circle of light from the torch the only source of illumination inside the building. The sound of our feet echoing off the concrete walls as we climbed the ramp was very loud, and I suddenly regretted all the zombie movies I'd watched snuggled against Brent's formidable chest. Although I knew I had nothing to fear from the dead, I had no idea who or what waited for us in the dark.

"The valet booth should be up ahead on your right. I'll go first, but try and shine the light in front of me so I can see where I'm going." I stepped over the yellow lane divider and passed the boom gates, which lay broken on the ground. Someone must have objected to paying for the privilege of secure parking when the drones showed up and started killing everyone. "Point the light up a little," I said. She raised the torch, and I noticed a random spatter of blood in the corner of the valet box's sliding glass window. "Pass me the torch."

"Why?" Sasha asked.

"Just hand it over. I want you to wait here while I check inside." She sighed and handed me the torch. It was unclear if she had seen the blood splattered across the glass. I was hopeful it had gone unnoticed. My sister had already witnessed far too much violence.

With the shotgun raised in front of me, I edged my way around to the open doorway. I swung the light inside the small room and lowered the gun. I had to step over the body of the young parking attendant sprawled across the floor. My heart ached for the young man that had died an ugly death in such a cold and impersonal space. Someone had beaten the shit out of him before sticking him with a knife multiple times.

Time and the heat of summer had been unkind. His body was grossly bloated and discolored. Anger boiled inside me. The poor guy had been working a shithouse job for minimum wage, and it hadn't even been a drone that killed him. Instead, he was taken out by some sick fuck that no longer felt compelled to play by the rules of polite society. I had to breathe through my mouth inside the tiny box-like room. The stench of decay was overwhelming, but I tried to hide my repulsion since I didn't want Sasha to get curious about what was inside.

All I could think about at that moment was Brent. I longed for his strong embrace, far from pyromaniac drones and blood-thirsty humans, safe from all the horrors I'd seen thus far. But that was just an excruciating fantasy. I wasn't anywhere near being reunited with my boyfriend. If I were honest with myself, we'd probably never see each other again. If one of those wasp-like drones didn't burn me to a cinder, some blood-thirsty asshole would probably finish me off.

"Jess. What are you doing?"

I looked out the window at my sister. "Gimme a minute," I mouthed. I took a hi-vis vest from a hook on the wall and draped it over the dead parking attendant's face. It wasn't much, but it was all I could do for him. My attention returned to the task at hand, and I crouched down to sift through bunches of keys strewn across the floor. There was no way of knowing what sort of vehicle belonged to each set of keys beyond the branded insignia. All I wanted was to find a car and return to Fiona and the kids. Why the hell did everything have to be so damn complicated? I wondered as I squatted to collect keys from around the attendant's body.

Getting back up was a struggle. My knee protested painfully, and it was a moment before I could convince my leg to cooperate and carry me out of the parking attendant's makeshift mausoleum. I closed the door behind me in respect for the dead guy inside and to shield Sasha from the sight.

"Did you find what you need?" Sasha asked, hopefully.

"I've got a bunch of keys. Now we've just gotta find which car each of them belongs to," I replied and handed the torch back to her. We searched for a suitable car, moving deeper into the cavernous heart of the parking station.

"There aren't many cars up here," Sasha said quietly as the torch illuminated the empty parking spaces around us. She was right. It was practically empty. There mustn't have been much demand for parking on that fateful Sunday morning when the drones first appeared in the sky. That or everyone had fled, not realizing the folly of trying to outrun the murder machines in broad daylight. "It will be alright. I've got at least half a dozen sets of keys here. One of them has to belong to a car that will get us the hell out of this place."

We jogged over to a collection of vehicles parked near the entrance to the stairwell. I pressed the unlock button on the VW remote. There was a flash of light and the familiar click of a vehicle automatically unlocking behind a banged-up people mover. I raced around the van and repeatedly swore when I discovered one of those hideous remakes of the iconic VW beetle. I threw the keys across the car park in a fit of frustration.

"We could have squeezed inside the beetle. Harry and Charlotte don't take up much room, you know."

"Yeah, and if we get in another crash, I guarantee none of us will be walking away. That thing will be crumpled like a soda can underfoot."

None of the remaining keys matched the other cars parked nearby. "I know it doesn't look too flash, but that old people mover would fit us all, and it looks a lot tougher than the beetle," Sasha suggested.

It was a good idea. If the van were mechanically sound, it would do the job. "I'll have to go back and see if I can find the keys. Wait here and don't move. I won't be gone long."

Footsteps echoed behind me, and I spun around, my finger on the shotgun's trigger. Two shadows emerged from behind a concrete pillar. "Get your hands up where I can see them, and don't even think of moving another step closer," I growled. Sasha pointed the torch at them. "Jess, it's okay. They aren't going to hurt us," she tried to convince me. The young couple stood frozen to the spot, holding tight to each other's hand as I kept the shotgun pointed at them. "Bullshit," I replied quietly. "Why else would they try sneaking up on us while my back was turned?"

The young male, who I estimated to be nineteen or twenty at most, spoke up. He swallowed nervously before explaining, "We were scared. We saw you had a gun and didn't want to end up like the parking attendant."

I motioned for Sasha to move away from the van and get behind me. Once she was safely away from the couple, I asked them what they knew about the parking attendant. The girl cleared her throat and explained in a shy voice, "We've been trapped here in the parking station since the beginning. At first, we thought it was as good a place as any to hide from the drones, but then the buildings around us started to burn, and we realized we needed to get out before it was too late."

"We were getting ready to make a run for it when these thugs showed up," the guy continued. "We were hiding in the stairwell when we heard shouting. I opened the door wide enough to peek out and saw a group of guys in baseball caps with bandanna's covering the lower half of their faces. The power was still on back then, and I could see them beating up the parking attendant. I wanted to run over and help him," he said.

"But you didn't," I said. It sounded harsh, even to my ears.

"I wouldn't let him go," the girl was quick to interject. "They would have done the same thing to Dylan. They outnumbered us, were armed with knives, and I think one of them even had a gun." She leaned closer to Dylan, clinging tight to his arm as she relived the incident. "At first, we couldn't understand why they wanted to hurt him like that, not when drones filled the sky and were hunting down people in the streets."

"Go on," I encouraged the pair, the gun still pointed at them.

"After they killed the parking attendant, they stole a couple of cars from the top level. One was a Lexus, and the other was a BMW convertible. It all seemed pointless, considering everything that's been happening. Once they left, we ran over to check on the parking attendant, but he was dead." The girl was visibly distressed by the memory, and I wondered how she would react to the horrors outside the parking station.

"Yeah, they did a real number on the poor guy," Dylan added. "I can't understand why they would kill someone over a few stupid cars."

I shrugged and lowered the gun. "Welcome to the brave new world. Nothing makes much sense anymore."

"How long ago did that happen?" Sasha asked from behind me.

"It might have been a week ago, maybe longer. I think the parking attendant thought he could wait it out like us, but the drones kept killing people, and then we ate everything in the vending machines."

"Been there, done that," I said, remembering the snacks we had feasted on from the vending machine in the mall.

"Then we saw you and thought you might take us with you when you find the keys to the van. It belongs to the dead guy, by the way." Dylan said, hopefully.

"No chance," I scoffed. Sasha had different ideas because she jabbed me in the ribs and told them we would try and help them if we could.

"Like hell," I retorted. The couple's faces crumpled in despair, but I held firm. "We already have Fiona and the kids to look out for," I reminded my sister.

Sasha grabbed my arm and dragged me away from the frightened couple so they couldn't overhear us, arguing in hushed voices. "We can't leave them here," she said. "They've got no food, and the buildings are burning down around them."

"That's not my problem." I was getting impatient. The minutes were ticking by, and dawn would catch up to us if we didn't move things along.

"Don't you care even just a little bit about what happens to them?"

"Not really. They are strangers. We know nothing about them. Why would I risk our safety to help them?" I said while keeping my eyes on the duo huddled together a short distance away.

"Jess, we can't turn our backs on them. Have you forgotten Phil?"

"Of course, I haven't forgotten Phil," I shot back.

"He risked his safety to help us, to help you, especially."

"I'm aware of that, but look where it got him. In case you have forgotten, Phil is dead and is slowly burning in the wreck back at the intersection." The words were out of my mouth before I could stop them. I'd gone too far, and I didn't need to see the shocked expression on Sasha's face to know it.

"What's happening to you?" she asked in disgust. "You are getting colder and harder and more suspicious every day that this nightmare drags on. Sometimes I think you would rather hurt people than help them, and that's not the Jess I know. Mom would be so disappointed if she could see you now."

Her words felt like a punch to the gut. A deep sense of shame washed over me. Sasha couldn't know how badly her words hurt me. My father had been a violent and abusive man. His temper was short, and his fists fast and brutal. As a small child, I had watched my warm and loving mother retreat into herself whenever my father was around. Her very essence seemed to evaporate the moment he walked through the door.

She had stayed with him far too long. His vicious tongue and violent attacks an accepted part of our lives for years. It wasn't until he lashed out at me when I was seven years old, flinging me across the room like a rag doll because I dared to make too much noise while he was watching the television, that my mother finally decided enough was enough. We packed our things and left town the next day. Sometimes, during my darker moments, I still enjoy imagining the perplexed and furious expression on his face when he came home to an empty house.

It had never occurred to me that I could be like him until now. I felt physically ill at the prospect. I tried to convince myself that everything I'd done since that fateful Sunday morning had been in self-defense. Mostly it was true. I'd had to be cold and ruthless to survive. But maybe our desperate circumstances had allowed a tiny violent part of me to blossom—a dark and unwanted gift from my absent father.

"You're right. We should help them if we can," I conceded.

Sasha beamed with happiness. "I knew you would do the right thing."

"We'll help them get out of the city, and then they are on their own. Deal?"

"Deal," she nodded. "But maybe you will change your mind by then," she added hopefully.

"Don't bet on it. Come on. We need to hurry. The sun will be rising soon."

We returned to the young couple who were watching us with hopeful expressions. "You can come with us," Sasha announced happily. They physically sagged with relief and took a moment to hug each other. I walked over and, in a lowered voice, said, " I'm doing this for my sister. But make no mistake-if either of you try anything, I won't hesitate to kill you both. Do you understand?" They vigorously nodded as I stepped back to join Sasha. "Are you okay to wait by the van with the girl while I go find the keys?"

"Yeah, I can do that."

"Dylan, is it?" I asked the guy. I kept thinking he looked so young, but I was probably only five or six years older than him. "You can come and help me find the keys while your girlfriend stays with my sister."

"Her name is Bec," he informed me, rather bravely, I thought, considering I'd just threatened to kill him. Perhaps there was hope for him yet.

I turned my attention to his girlfriend, keeping my face neutral despite the smile that threatened to split my carefully constructed facade. "Bec, can I trust you to wait with my sister while Dylan and I go find the keys to the van?"

She glanced at the shotgun pointed at the ground, then looked me in the eye. "Absolutely. We won't move an inch. I promise."

I looked at Sasha to confirm that she was comfortable being left alone in the dark with the girl. Although she nodded her acceptance of the idea, I lingered, reluctant to let her out of my sight. "Go," she insisted. "I'll be fine. You need to hurry up and find those keys. Fiona is going to think we abandoned her."

She was right, as usual. I had to let go of the constant fear I felt for my sister and get on with it. I reluctantly removed the torch from Sasha's hand, knowing how terrifying it would be for her standing in the dark, the only source of light, the distant glow of the burning buildings.

"Let's go," I told Dylan and turned away from my sister. With any luck, it wouldn't be the last time I saw her alive. I made my way back to the valet box, careful not to allow my boots to squeak on the polished concrete. When we reached the cramped room, I directed the beam of light on the door and told Dylan to open it. He looked back at me fearfully, his hand hovering inches from the handle. I tried to hide my annoyance. "Go ahead," I whispered. "It's not the dead guy inside that you have to worry about." His eyes widened in fear as he digested my words, and I realized too late how my comment might be misconstrued. "Relax," I assured him, "I just meant he is dead. He can't hurt you. It's the living that is dangerous. And the drones," I added unnecessarily.

He didn't seem very reassured by my pep talk. If anything, he looked like he was about to do a runner. "Here. You can hold the torch while I go inside and find the keys."

"Okay. I can do that," Dylan nodded nervously. I passed him the torch and opened the door. A puff of air ripe with the stink of decay caused him to turn his face away with a grimace. As I crouched beside the parking attendant, I wondered how many bodies Dylan had seen up close since the drones had appeared. If his stricken expression was anything to go by, the dead guy at my feet was probably his first.

Ignoring the revulsion curdling my stomach, I reached inside the parking attendant's trouser pocket. My fingers traced the outline of a stick of gum, a tattered billfold, and finally wrapped around a keyring. "Yes!" I cried with more enthusiasm than was strictly warranted. "Let's get the fuck out of here," I said, rising to my feet. I dangled the keys in front of Dylan and slapped him on the shoulder. He looked at me in surprise, clearly taken aback by my act of camaraderie. He wasn't alone.

We hurried back to the van, and I was relieved to discover Sasha still standing beside the vehicle with Bec nearby. My shoulders relaxed in relief when I saw she was safe. I gave her hand a quick squeeze before unlocking the doors. "Have either of you ever handled a gun before?" I asked as we piled inside the stale interior of the van. Dylan shook his head in the negative.

"I know how to shoot a handgun. I've never used a shotgun, though," Bec replied. I don't know who looked more surprised- her boyfriend or me. My money was on Dylan. His jaw was practically resting on his chest.

"My dad used to take me to the shooting range." She glanced across at her boyfriend sheepishly. "We only ever practiced with handguns," she offered in the way of an explanation. I couldn't tell if Dylan was in awe of this newfound knowledge of his girlfriend or if he was disturbed by it.

"Okay. You sit up the front with me. Be careful of the kickback. It's probably a lot more powerful than anything you have handled before." I handed her the shotgun, hoping my trust wasn't misplaced. Bec looked down at the gun doubtfully and walked around the van to the front passenger door.

"Will you be okay in the back with Dylan?" Sasha gave him a quick once over and assured me she would be fine. She slid open the door and climbed inside. "It smells funny in here," she said, wrinkling her nose in distaste. Dylan hopped in beside her and pulled the door shut.

Sasha was right-the van did smell. It was the unmistakable odor of dirty feet, fast-food wrappers, and weed. One of those stupid troll dolls from the nineties stood in the middle of the dash, and I reached forward to stroke the tuft of fluffy neon hair sprouting from the top of the plastic head. I felt a pang of grief for the dead parking attendant and his efforts to personalize his stinky van.

Shaking off the melancholy threatening to settle over me, I thrust the key in the ignition and managed to crack a smile when the engine started on the first try. There was a fraction under a third of a tank of gas. It wasn't ideal, but it would at least get us out of the city and then some. "Belts on people. This shit is about to get wild." I put the van in gear and switched on the headlights, knowing it was risky but unable to see where I was going without them. "Let's go get Fiona and the kids."

Fifteen

A s we descended the ramp, I killed the headlights and eased the van to a stop at the exit. The smoking remains of a body lay on the sidewalk on the opposite side of the street. It hadn't been there when we entered the parking station. "Look sharp. There must be a drone nearby. I want everyone watching for trouble. And Bec-try not to blow our heads off."

Dodging the burnt and abandoned wrecks, avoiding running over any bodies, and watching for drones felt akin to navigating one of those extreme obstacle courses on a reality show. A streak of movement up ahead caused me to hit the brakes, but it was only some other suicidal nut job driving by without their lights on. We emitted a collective sigh of relief before I crossed the intersection and pulled up beside the hole in the bus.

It took a second to convince myself to trust Bec and Dylan enough to leave them in the people mover with my sister while I went looking for Fiona. I put the van in park but left the engine running. "I'm going to get Fiona and the kids. I won't be long, but if something happens, shoot first and ask questions later." I slipped out of the van and gently pushed the door shut behind me.

Once I'd climbed through the hole in the overturned bus, I waited for my eyes to adjust before venturing further. "Fiona, it's Jess. I found a van for us." I stepped over the leaking body that Fiona had slipped on earlier and headed towards the other end of the bus, where I'd left the trio.

They were gone.

"Fiona," I called in as loud a whisper as I dared. I checked between the seats in case they had fallen asleep, but all I found was a pair of bodies slumped against each other near the back row. Panic clawed at my chest, and I silently berated myself for leaving them alone. What had I been thinking? We should have stayed together. There wasn't time to wait around, hoping they would return. If we didn't leave now, there was no way we could exit the city before sunrise.

"Harry? Charlotte?" I whispered in desperation.

"Jess, be careful," Harry cried.

I heard the shuffling footsteps a second too late. I spun around as some big stinky fucker launched himself at me. I flew backward, hitting the floor hard as my assailant landed on top of me. They reeked of sweat and festering wounds, and I gagged as powerful hands locked around my throat. As I clawed at the hands throttling me, Fiona's silence made sense. She hadn't run away. She had been hiding from the maniac who was squeezing the life out of me.

He was immensely heavy, his weight crushing my spine against the metal window frame beneath me. I tried to prise his fingers from around my neck, but they wouldn't budge. Oxygen deprivation was kicking in. I gasped and bucked beneath his weight, but I couldn't dislodge him. I was running out of time. Any second now, I would sink into oblivion, and Sasha would be left to fend for herself. In a last-ditch effort to save myself, I reached down and forced my fingers beneath my attacker, digging into my pocket for the knife. My hand locked around the handle, and I pulled it free. I pressed the button, and the blade flicked out.

As unconsciousness swooped in to take me, I plunged the blade into my attacker's throat. He loosened his grip on me, and I inhaled sharply as a hot stream of blood squirted me in the face. I stuck the knife in him again with a savage cry and wriggled out from beneath him as he sprang back. Blood gushed from the punctures, and he collapsed beside me with a gurgled cry.

I lay beside him, breathing heavily as I recovered from the surprise attack. I wiped at the coppery-smelling blood coating my face and stifled a sob. "Fiona," I croaked. "Fiona, we gotta go." I sucked in putrid air from inside the bus and thought I'd never inhaled anything so sweet. Fiona appeared beside me and took my hands, pulling me to my feet. "I'm sorry, Jess. I should have warned you, but I was just so scared he'd get the kids. Are you okay?" She held my arms, steadying me while I pulled myself together. "Aside from almost being strangled to death, I'm fine," I assured her. Once I was confident that I could stand on my own, I shook her off. "We need to get going."

While she gathered up Harry and Charlotte, I asked, "Where the hell did he come from?"

"I don't know. He showed up shortly after you left. At first, I thought it was you, but then I heard him huffing and puffing as he climbed through the opening, and I knew we were in trouble. He was mumbling to himself and stumbling, so I hid up the front of the bus with Harry and Charlotte."

"He didn't come looking for you?"

"I don't think he knew anyone else was inside the bus. He was just looking for shelter. He might have passed out for a bit because he went quiet for a while. I think you startled him."

That made sense. The stranger must have woken when I was calling out to Fiona. In his pain and confusion, I must have seemed like a threat. I sighed. There was another body to add to the steadily growing list. Fuck. What sort of person had I become? Or had this been who I was all along? I dismally wondered if Brent would understand my body count. I hoped he would accept my actions as those of a person determined to survive instead of the blood lust of a stone-cold killer. It was becoming increasingly difficult to know which one I was. And that scared the hell out of me.

When we reached the bus's jagged opening, I was shocked to see how much lighter the sky had become. In another thirty minutes, it would be too dangerous to travel. Fiona passed Harry out to me, and I quickly loaded him into the van. Suddenly, I became aware of six pairs of eyes staring out at me in horror.

"What?"

Dylan leaned out of the van and pointed at the side mirror. "You should probably take a look at yourself," he suggested. I shook my head irritably. I bent over and was taken aback by the ghoulish face that peered back at me in the dim light. I looked like a survivor from a cheap slasher movie. My face and chest were slick with my attacker's blood. It seemed to be a reoccurring theme, but I couldn't afford to waste time cleaning myself up. "I'll deal with it later," I said, "right now we gotta go. I can't deal with any more crazies or killer drones."

Once we were all safely inside the van, I circled the overturned bus and headed for the freeway. It was only a short drive, and the streets were relatively clear. We reached the on-ramp sooner than I expected. I had to maneuver around a shopping cart lying on its side near the entrance. As we neared the access to the freeway, I noticed a snarl of vehicles blocking our path. "Goddamn it," I cursed. Dylan popped his head between the front seats to see what the problem was. Unable to continue, I pressed the brakes. Before I could protest, Dylan jumped out of the van and jogged up the ramp to investigate.

Beside me, his girlfriend watched tensely, and I questioned my decision to arm her with the shotgun. "Bec," I said. She dragged her eyes away from the sky long enough to look across at me. "Remember to breathe."

She nodded and inhaled deeply while she watched her boyfriend jog around the van to the driver's window. I think we can squeeze through the gap if you help me move that overturned motorcycle."

"Okay," I agreed. I unbuckled my belt and hopped out of the van. Bec followed me, and I turned to face her. "What are you doing?"

"You guys need someone to keep a lookout while you move the bike," she informed me. I inhaled sharply, resisting the urge to argue. "Fine," I conceded. "Stay close and watch for trouble."

Dylan led us up the ramp and pointed to a spot between a station wagon with a crumpled bonnet and a mangled SUV. "Do you think we can get through?"

"Maybe," I agreed. It would be tight, but what other choice did we have?

I bent down to help Dylan lift the bike. It was a custom job-a beast of a machine that must have been its owner's pride and joy. Its owner lay pinned beneath the bike, left to rot in the elements. I forced myself to ignore the stink of burnt rubber and singed skin. Behind me, Bec gagged noisily. I tried not to hold it against her.

Dylan and I lifted the motorcycle. As I expected, it wasn't easy. I grunted with the effort, grappling with the cumbersome bike. My feet struggled to find a grip in the puddle of human grease around the motorcycle, and I hoped I wouldn't slip over and land on my ass.

As we cleared a path for the van, the shotgun went off behind me, and I instinctively ducked. There was a brief flash of light overhead before burning debris showered down around us. Dylan and I dropped the bike and crouched down, shielding ourselves from the fallout as best we could. I felt the sting of molten metal hit my shoulders and shook it off in a panic, afraid my clothes would catch alight.

The next thing I knew, Bec was beside me, urging me to hurry up and move the bike. I looked around in confusion. "Did you just shoot one of those things out of the sky?" I asked.

Bec grinned nervously. "Yep. I don't even know where it came from. I pointed, pulled the trigger, and BAM."

"No shit," I marveled.

"Your dad taught you well," Dylan added as he stood up and brushed himself off.

"Yeah, well, let's not tempt fate. All that noise will probably draw more of them. We need to shift that bike and get the hell out of here."

I counted to three, and together, Dylan and I managed to get the bike upright once more. One of the tires had melted away, making it difficult to move. Once we managed to half drag half push it out of the way, we ran back to the dead biker. The van probably could have run over the top of him, but I didn't want to risk it. I gripped him around the ankles and pulled. Fuck. The dude was glued to the road. "Dylan, give me a hand. This guy doesn't want to budge." Dylan grabbed hold of one of the biker's ankles while I held tight to the other, and we managed to shift him out of the way.

With the path now clear, we ran back to the van, Bec jogging beside me as I hobbled along. We climbed inside the vehicle, and I quickly started the engine. I guided the van through the narrow opening we had created at the top of the ramp. I barely touched the accelerator as I squeezed between the scrap metal remains of the station wagon and SUV.

The gap between the two vehicles was even narrower than I'd anticipated. Metal scraped against metal with a ghastly squeal that was sure to attract unwanted attention.

"Maybe you should go back," Fiona suggested.

"It's too late for that. We can't stop now." I continued along the narrow gap, and the van's passenger mirror connected with the SUV. There was a brief cracking sound as the mirror tore away from the van. Then we were free of the snarl, and I allowed myself to relax enough to take a breath. We had to weave across all four lanes, snaking between the cars blocking the way. It was slow going, and I wondered if we would ever escape the city.

Twenty minutes later, we were driving through open country, and for the first time in weeks, the air was clear. The sun was peeking over the horizon, and we'd have to find somewhere to lay low for the day or face spending the daylight hours cramped together in the van. We had already stopped twice when Bec and Sasha spotted drones in the distance. During those brief pauses, with the van packed to capacity, it was excruciating trying to keep everyone quiet and comfortable as we waited for the drones to leave the area. I couldn't imagine an entire day cooped up in the heat with six other people.

"It's getting too dangerous to continue. We need to find somewhere to stop for the day," I said to nobody in particular. We continued along the empty blacktop, having exited the freeway a couple of miles back to head north-west along the lesser-used route. I was beginning to wonder if I had made a mistake opting to use the back roads. Houses were few and far between, and the next town was at least sixty miles away.

"Over there!" Bec cried out excitedly. Her sudden outburst was more than my frayed nerves could handle. "What the hell?" I growled after the back of my head smacked against the headrest when I jammed my foot on the brakes. Bec smiled sheepishly and pointed out a driveway up ahead and to the right. Trees lined the lengthy driveway, concealing the farmhouse and barn from the road. "Nice work Bec, but do you think you could dial down the enthusiasm next time. You gave me a mini heart attack."

"And I think I've got a mild case of whiplash," Sasha added, rubbing her neck for emphasis. Dylan snickered and quickly looked out the window at the farm entrance when Bec glared over her shoulder at him.

"Let's go check it out." We continued up the road, and I turned into the entrance to the property, waiting while Dylan hopped out of the van to unlatch the gate. Once Dylan had secured the gate behind us, we continued up the long tree-studded driveway. The early morning light filtered through the overhanging foliage, casting dreamy shadows across the windshield, and I could almost forget we were fleeing an apocalyptic horror show. Almost.

The driveway ended in a clearing between the rear of the two-story farmhouse and the barn. Both buildings were well-maintained. Cheerfully planted garden beds ran the length of the back porch, the petals of the red and purple petunias starting to show the first signs of wilting. The lawn around the house was untidy. It probably hadn't been cut in weeks. Somehow, I doubted lawn maintenance was a priority during the apocalypse.

I pulled up outside the barn and left the van running while I climbed out to help Dylan open the large sliding doors. I walked around to the passenger side window. "Give me the gun." Bec carefully passed the shotgun through the opening, and I pointed it at the barn as I motioned for Dylan to slide one of the doors open. He shielded himself behind the heavy door as he dragged it back.

As Dylan eased the door open, I kept my finger poised beside the trigger. "It's clear," he said, and I sagged with relief. I'd had about all the excitement I could take, and all I could think about was finding somewhere quiet to curl up and go to sleep. Preferably for at least ten hours. Maybe if I hadn't been so exhausted, I would have thought to wonder about the people that owned the farm. Those colorful petunias hadn't survived the heat of summer without regular watering. But as it was, my focus was to find a safe place to hide from the threat of drones.

"Hey, Dylan, do me a favor and reverse the van inside the barn while I have a look around." He nodded and made his way back outside to the others. I glanced around the barn's interior, noting the meticulously organized workshop set up along one wall. An old red tractor stood beside a battered pickup that had seen better days. Someone must have been working on the truck when the drones attacked. The hood was raised, and there was an oil-stained rag on the ground beside one of the front tires.

I hobbled out of the way as Dylan carefully reversed the van in, stopping short of the tractor by a few inches. I should have gone over to the barn doors and pulled them shut behind us, but all the strength went out of my legs. I sank onto a bale of hay, unable to support myself any longer. Sasha jumped out of the van and rushed over. "Jess, are you okay?"

"Yeah. I'm only tired," I replied, smiling weakly. Bec and Dylan joined us, and I felt obligated to make some sort of speech. "We should be safe here as long as we keep quiet and don't do anything to draw attention to ourselves. Let's try and get some sleep while we can."

Fiona and the kids were piling out of the van when one of the barn doors slid open to reveal an older man in a worn pair of overalls. He was armed, and the rifle was pointed directly at us. At me specifically.

"What the heck do y'all think you're doing trespassing on my farm?"

The shotgun lay across my lap, and I left it there. There was no need to inflame the situation by getting into an armed standoff with my sister and Fiona's kids stuck between us. Luckily, Bec and Dylan had the good sense to remain silent. The pair stood motionless nearby, watching the scene unfold from beneath lowered eyes.

"I asked you a question, and I expect an answer," he said, directing his gaze at me.

"We mean you no harm," I tried to assure him. He frowned suspiciously, the furrows deepening in his weathered face. "That doesn't mean too much considering you are covered from head to foot in blood and have a gun draped across your knees like it's the most natural thing in the world."

The man had a valid point. If our roles were reversed, I would have felt the same way. Actually, I probably wouldn't have been so calm if I had discovered some blood-soaked, gun-toting weirdo and her merry band of misfits trespassing on my property. Somehow, I had to convince him to let us camp out in his barn for the day. Considering my words carefully, I said, " I know I look threatening, but we honestly aren't here to cause trouble. We've just made it out of the city, and we need refuge for the day. As soon as night falls, we'll be on our way."

"What she says is true," Bec added quietly. "This woman rescued my boyfriend and me from a parking station downtown. It was hell, and we probably wouldn't have made it out alive if she hadn't helped us."

Dylan nodded in agreement. "We were unarmed. She could have easily killed us or left us behind, but she didn't."

The farmer looked hard at Bec and Dylan before returning his attention to me. I could tell he wasn't going to be an easy nut to crack. "We need somewhere safe to hide from the drones, but we can leave. We'll get back in the van, and you can watch us go." I hated the thought of driving out into the open once more and exposing everyone to attack, but it was better than being shot for trespassing.

"That won't be necessary," a woman said as she stepped through the gap between the barn doors. "Bill, can you please lower the gun so that we can talk this through without the threat of violence tainting things."

Bill shook his head. "Nope, I can't do that. That ghoulish looking one sitting on the hay is armed."

The woman took a moment to examine us all. "They're mostly women and children. When did you start pointing your gun at little kids?" she asked gently.

"When fire started raining down on innocent folks, and savage killers like this one here decided to make themselves at home on my property, I figured it was time to do what's necessary to keep us safe," he replied.

"He's right," I admitted. "I am a killer. I've taken more than one life since those machines appeared in the sky. I've had to do it to protect myself and the people you see here. Still, I don't expect that to ease your mind." I slowly stood up, keeping the shotgun pointed at the ground. My knee felt like it was stuffed with rusty nails. I wanted my pain pills and somewhere safe to sleep. Neither seemed likely to happen anytime soon.

I waited while the couple whispered back and forth, occasionally pausing to glance in my direction. Eventually, their argument ended, and Bill returned his attention to me, albeit with the gun lowered now. "Today is your lucky day. My wife believes we should be charitable and help y'all out. And while I still have reservations, I'm willing to listen to her on this matter-providing you agree to give up your weapons while you're on our land."

Fiona looked over at me questioningly. So did Sasha. I didn't know what they were expecting, but I was too darn tired to put up a fight. I slowly lowered the shotgun to the ground, choosing to believe the couple genuinely wanted to help us. Was that a hint of disapproval on my sister's face? It had been too fleeting to tell, and besides, it didn't matter anyway. I could only do what I thought was best for the group, and right now, that meant staying on the farm until nightfall. If I had to relinquish the shotgun-so be it.

"Okay. Take a step back while I collect the gun," Bill said while watching me closely as I took an unsteady step backward. He walked over and quickly crouched down to grab the weapon. For a brief second, I experienced a moment of terror when I thought he would turn the gun on me and shoot us all. But he did no such thing. Instead, he assured me, "You can have it back when you leave. Until then, it's going into the gun safe."

"Why don't y'all follow me over to the house, and I'll fix everyone some breakfast." Bill's wife offered.

"Ma'am, that sounds amazing," Dylan grinned, clearly delighted by the prospect of a nourishing meal. The woman smiled and motioned for us to follow her. "Call me Ruth. We haven't seen a drone since yesterday morning, but you should still be careful, although I probably don't need to remind you of that." Fiona shook Ruth's hand and introduced herself. The older woman lifted Charlotte and deposited the girl onto her generous hip before leading the group out of the barn.

Sasha hung back and offered her arm for support. I waved her off, "I'm fine. I don't need any help," I told her. Bill walked over and stopped in front of us.

"This is my sister Sasha. She's just looking out for me," I explained.

"Morning, Sasha. You head over to the house with the others and have some breakfast. I'm going to have a quick chat with your sister, and then we'll join you."

Sasha's eyes narrowed suspiciously. "Why do you need to get her on her own just to talk to her? That doesn't sound right to me."

A slow smile spread across Bill's face as he looked from my sister to me. "Your sister seems like a smart girl."

I agreed with him.

"Well?" Sasha prompted him. She wasn't about to let it go.

"All I want is to find out a bit of background information about your group before my wife goes and pulls out the good china for y'all. There's nothing nefarious going on. That means..."

"I know what it means. I'm a spelling bee champion. I have medals to prove it," Sasha informed him.

"I have no idea what it means," I admitted sheepishly.

Sasha rolled her eyes-that moody teenage attitude creeping over her once again. "I suppose it's okay as long as Jess doesn't mind."

"We won't be long, Sasha. I'll give Bill a quick rundown on what's happened to us, and then I'll join you. Make sure you save me a plate-I'm hungry as hell."

Sasha stared up at Bill before reluctantly leaving us behind, and it was all I could do not to laugh. She was so cute when she was staring down a six-foot-tall man armed with a rifle.

We watched her duck across to the house, using the overhanging tree branches as cover. Once she had climbed the porch steps and slipped inside, Bill turned his attention to me.

"Follow me around the side of the barn."

"Why?" I asked, immediately suspicious.

He studied me for an uncomfortable length of time before saying, "It must be worse out there than I thought."

"It's been tough," I conceded. "After the first day or two, I knew what to expect from the drones, or whatever they are. If they see you- they turn you into BBQ. But it's the people that have been the real problem. Without law and order to keep people in check, there's no way of knowing who will try and stick a knife in your belly or blow your brains out for the can of beans in your backpack. It feels like everyone wants to kill us, and for some damn reason, instead of only having to look after my sister, I'm responsible for Fiona and her kids, and now I've got Dylan and Bec tagging along too."

"It sounds to me like Bec and Dylan found someone that they felt they could trust when they crossed paths with you. You strike me as a survivor. Tough and, I suspect, ruthless when the situation calls for it. Some people thrive in chaotic conditions like these. Perhaps you're like that."

I shook my head. He was cracked in the head if he thought the apocalypse was my playground. "I cut people's lawns before those metal monsters appeared and started blowing people up."

"And now you're taking care of a group of desperate people unable to protect themselves. If what they say is true, you've kept them together and guided them out of the city with little thought for yourself."

"We haven't all made it. I tried to keep us all safe, but I failed. You have no idea how bad it was in the city. I'm hoping it will get easier now we're out."

Bill took a deep breath and looked out at the bright, clear sky. "I hope it gets easier for you and your group now that you're away from the urban areas, but there are bad people everywhere. It would be a mistake to think otherwise. Now, follow me around the side of the barn. There's a faucet you can use to clean yourself up before going inside."

Relieved that he wasn't trying to lure me somewhere more private so he could put a bullet in my skull, I followed him outside. The faucet was against the wall of the barn, next to a bench littered with gardening tools. "I'll keep watch while you clean some of that gore off your face. I don't suppose you have a change of clothes in the van. All that blood is liable to set my dogs on edge."

I splashed my face with water, relishing the cold feeling as it dissolved the filth coating my skin. Only a steaming hot shower and loads of soap would remove the worst of it, but even a slight improvement was better than nothing. "I didn't hear any barking when we pulled up," I said, puzzled.

Bill scoffed at my ignorance. "They only bark if I let them. However, inviting a stranger inside who looks and smells like they've been rolling around a slaughterhouse killing floor might test their obedience."

I sniffed myself and grimaced. I stank like old roadkill. "Fair enough. Although, you do realize a splash of water on my face isn't going to solve the problem?"

"You can take a shower after breakfast, but for now, that will do. At least I can see what you look like now." He tossed me a clean rag, and I wiped my face dry.

"Yeah? And what do I look like?"

"Human. It was hard to tell before."

I cracked a smile. "I think I forgot to introduce myself in all the excitement. I'm Jess. And I'm *really* grateful for your hospitality."

"Under different circumstances, our hospitality wouldn't involve being escorted with a loaded weapon. We should head over to the house. I think I can smell Ruth's famous pancakes."

Just the mention of pancakes made my stomach rumble loud enough for Bill to notice. "Let's hope they haven't eaten them all. It sounds like you could do with a good feed."

As we climbed the porch steps, the cooking smells became stronger, and so did my hunger. I followed Bill inside, and a pair of curious Border Collie dogs greeted us. Although they were alert and watching me intently, they didn't show any signs of aggression. Bill bent over and ruffled each of their heads, seemingly signaling that I was okay and they could relax. "You can pat them. They won't hurt you," Bill assured me. "The black and white one is Buster, and the one with the blue eye is Pope."

I reached down and let the dogs sniff my hand before patting them. They enjoyed the attention and trotted after me as Bill led me through to the kitchen. Everyone was seated around the table in the middle of the room. Nobody was talking. They were all too focused on filling their bellies to waste time on words.

Ruth removed an egg from the frypan and placed it on a plate with some strips of bacon. "This is for you," she said, handing me the plate. There are pancakes on the table."

How she managed to whip up enough food to feed us all in such a short time was a mystery. Hunger trumped good manners, and I greedily snatched up the last two pancakes from the plate in the middle of the table and smothered them in maple syrup. Ignoring the cutlery set out beside a pile of paper napkins, I stuffed food into my mouth as quickly as I could chew it. I couldn't remember a fried egg ever tasting so good. Gooey egg yolk dribbled down my chin, and Bec looked over at me, horrified. "What?" I shrugged before biting down on a crispy piece of bacon. I knew I'd make myself sick if I kept it up, but I couldn't seem to stop myself.

Bill walked over and handed me a mug of tea. "Drink this." The tea was hot and sweet, and I sipped it gratefully. Sasha finished her pancakes and stood up. "Jess, I'm finished eating. Take my seat."

I opened my mouth to tell her that it wasn't necessary, but it kind of was. I took my plate and mug of tea and sat down. It was only after I'd polished off the last of my breakfast that my knee started to bother me. Sasha must have noticed me wince because she stopped smothering the dogs in cuddles and leaned over beside me. "Do you want me to go and get those pills Phil gave you? You look like you need them," she asked quietly so the others wouldn't hear.

I nodded and squeezed her hand. "That's probably a good idea."

Sasha skipped around the table and was heading for the back door when Bill intercepted her. I felt myself tense up as they exchanged words, my hand instinctively reaching for the cutlery in the middle of the table. Bill was squatting beside me before I could wrap my fingers around one of the bread and butter knives. Not that I could have done much with it anyway. He was crazy if he thought I wouldn't put up a fight. I knew it had been too good to be true. Why would anyone open their home to someone who had confessed to unspeakable acts of violence?

He might have looked country simple, but Bill was sharper than most. "You don't need to get defensive. I'm not trying to take advantage of your vulnerability."

"I'm not vulnerable," I said with more venom than was necessary. Bec and Dylan looked across the table at me, alarmed.

"Sasha said you needed some medication that's out in the van. I just offered to go with her to make sure she's alright. Although we haven't seen one of those drones for a while, I don't want to take any chances. She's only a kid."

Around me, the others looked relaxed and happy for the first time since I'd met them. Now that they had eaten, they were talking amongst themselves. Ruth helped Charlotte drink from a tall glass and quickly dabbed the girl's chin with a napkin when milk spilled over. Nobody else was on edge except me.

"What do you say?" Bill asked, interrupting my thoughts.

"Alright. That's a kind of you to offer. I shouldn't have snapped then. I'm just so tired and on edge."

"That's perfectly understandable."

Sasha came over and lay a hand on my shoulder. "We won't be long. Sit back and enjoy your cup of tea."

I drank a mouthful of the beverage and thought about Brent and the miles separating us. I longed for the reassuring bulk of his arms wrapped around me. More than anything, I wanted the constant feeling of impending doom to dissolve away, and I felt like that would happen once I reached the cabin and saw Brent. He had always had a calming effect on me, smoothing out my grumpy moods and tempering my impulsive behavior.

Bill startled me out of my reverie when he sank into the chair beside me and rattled the bottle of painkillers. I reached out to take them, but he moved them beyond my reach. "These pills are no joke. I had to take them years ago when I broke my ankle.

They're highly addictive." He took a fresh pancake from the stack and bit off half in one hit.

"A pharmacist gave them to me after I dislocated my knee. I only take them when the pain becomes unbearable because they slow me down and make me feel drowsy."

"Alright. I was just checking that you're not some crazed junkie."

"Wow. Is that how I come across?"

Bill shrugged and popped the rest of the pancake in his mouth. "You can't blame me for wondering. First impressions count and showing up here the way you did raises all sorts of questions. I wanted to make sure you are functioning with all your faculties intact since you're in charge of a group of people relying on you to keep them alive."

"Right now, Bill, I'd be lucky if I've got two functioning brain cells in my head. I'm dog tired and could fall asleep right here at the table."

Bill slapped the table and chuckled. "Fair enough." He passed me the painkillers before turning to his wife. She was filling the sink while Bec stacked dishes ready to be washed. "Ruth, can you take Jess upstairs to the spare room? She's exhausted. If we keep her awake much longer, I'll have to carry her up there myself."

Ruth left Bec at the sink and dried her hands in the folds of her skirt before gently placing them on my shoulders and guiding me away from the table. "Follow me. I'll put you in the room with a single bed. That way, the young lady with the little ones can share the double bed."

"Yeah, that's fine with me," I agreed as I hobbled up the narrow staircase behind her. At the top of the stairs, Ruth led me along a narrow hallway, past the bathroom, and opened the door to a small room that was big enough to fit a single bed, a set of drawers, and a narrow desk positioned under the window. It felt like a five-star hotel. I sighed and sank onto the bed.

"I'll go get you a towel and a fresh set of clothes so you can freshen up before you go to sleep. I'll be back in a minute."

"Thanks, Ruth," I said drowsily. The painkillers were kicking in, and a warm disconnected feeling spread through me, turning my already exhausted limbs to jelly. I lay back, my head sinking into the soft pillows, and closed my eyes.

Sixteen

When I awoke, it was dark inside the room except for a thin sliver of light spilling under the closed door. It took a moment of fumbling before my fingers found the switch to the lamp, and the low wattage bulb dimly lit the room. I rubbed the sleep from my eyes and yawned. My mouth tasted like a garbage can, and my body smelled even worse.

Ruth must have returned after I passed out and left a towel and a floral sundress circa 1992 for me to change into. It wasn't exactly my style. I couldn't even remember the last time I'd worn a dress, but I wasn't able to pick and choose. I gathered up the towel and change of clothes and slipped out into the narrow hallway. The murmur of voices drifted up the stairs, and I contemplated going down to find out what had been happening while I was asleep.

My desire for a hot shower and clean clothes won out. The bathroom door clicked shut behind me, and I couldn't peel my filthy cutoffs and singlet off fast enough. While I waited for the hot water to come through, I caught sight of my naked body in the mirror above the basin. I'd always been lean and muscular. Partly due to genetics, the rest, thanks to the physical nature of my job. But the hardships of the past few weeks had had a startling effect on my body. I'd gone from being lean and wiry to scary heroin chic. The numerous cuts and bruises didn't help much. No wonder Bill had been so wary.

I climbed under the spray and soaped myself from head to foot at least three times. When I no longer stank and the water ran clear, I grudgingly turned off the shower and toweled myself dry. The dress felt soft and deliciously fresh against my pink skin. Ruth had thoughtfully provided underwear, but they were at least three sizes too big, so I had no choice but to go commando. Since the dress fell to my knees, I figured nobody would notice if I had a bare backside.

I gathered up my reeking clothes and made my way downstairs. Bec and Dylan were curled up together on the couch asleep, while Fiona and the kids were nowhere in sight. I found Sasha seated at the kitchen table, her nose in a book. She smiled when she saw me and quickly marked her place in the book before jumping up to hug me. "You slept through dinner, but Ruth saved you a plate."

"Sorry about that. I guess I was even more tired than I thought. Where are Fiona and the kids?"

"They already went to bed. Harry and Charlotte were getting grumpy, so Ruth helped Fiona bath them."

"Okay. What about Ruth and Bill?"

Sasha shrugged. "I think they are out on the front porch."

"Is that safe?"

"I guess so. Do you want me to heat your dinner?'

"That would be great. I'll just check in with Ruth and Bill, and I'll be back in a minute."

I turned away, and Sasha called after me.

"Yeah, what?" I asked, stopping to look at her over my shoulder.

"It's a nice dress you're wearing. I bet Brent would love to see you in it," she said, sassing me.

I smiled. "I didn't think you would even notice."

"Of course, I noticed. I'm pretty sure it's the first time I've seen you in a dress. Like, ever."

I rolled my eyes and left Sasha to heat my dinner while I went to find Ruth and Bill. They were sitting on the screened-in porch, sharing a pitcher of iced tea. Even though mature trees surrounded the house, providing ample cover, I thought they were taking an unnecessary risk exposing themselves to a potential attack, but I kept it to myself.

"You're awake at last," Bill said.

Ruth turned to me and smiled. "We thought it best to let you sleep. I hope you don't mind," she said quietly.

"What time is it?" I asked.

"After ten," Bill answered.

"I'll change the sheets before you go back to bed. I'll wash them with your dirty clothes, although I'm not sure I'll be able to remove all the stains," Ruth said doubtfully.

"Thank you for offering, but we really can't stick around. I've already overslept. We'll need to get going soon."

One of the dogs stood up and padded over to me. His moist nose snuffled around my feet before he licked my toes. I reached down and patted him to divert his attention from my bare feet.

"Do you think it's a good idea to drag poor little Harry and Charlotte out of bed?" Ruth asked.

"Ruth's right," Bill agreed. "It's too late to leave now. Stay another day. Get some more rest, and then you can go after sunset tomorrow.

My desire to reach Brent and the cabin's safety and seclusion made it difficult to see their point of view. The prospect of further delays made me want to tear out what remained of my hair. Bill must have sensed my reluctance because he said, "That fella waiting for you up in the mountains will wait another day. Isn't it better that you are all properly fed and rested before continuing?"

"Besides," Ruth added. "We've been lonely out here by ourselves for the past few weeks. It's a nice change to have some company."

It was hard to argue with their logic.

"The pair of you can be persuasive; you know that?"

"We make a good team," Bill agreed and reached across to squeeze his wife's hand.

"Now that's settled, take those filthy clothes and pop them in the laundry tub before you eat your dinner. I'll be in shortly to help change the sheets on your bed."

I'd filled up on a simple yet immensely satisfying meal of spicy rice and beans and was flicking through an old Reader's Digest I'd found lying around when I heard the all too familiar sound of an explosion nearby. I leaped out of my chair; the momentary sense of peace shattered. It was a timely reminder that nowhere was safe.

Bec and Dylan sat up, woken by the noise. I motioned for them to stay put as I quietly crept over to the living room window. I couldn't see much. The trees surrounding the house blocked the view, which with any luck would work in our favor. But it didn't help me figure out what the hell was going on. I eased the curtain back into place as Bill strode down the hallway and entered the room. "Did you see what happened out there?" I asked.

He nodded. "It looks like a car got hit out on the road. We should turn off the lights. There's no need to draw unwanted attention."

"I agree."

Dylan switched off the lamp in the living room and went out to the kitchen to do the same. Sasha joined us, and I sent her to sit with Bec. A pained voice crying for help carried across the night.

"Shit. Someone's still alive out there, and they are making one hell of a racket. I hate to sound callous, but if they keep hollering like that, there's no way the drone will move on."

"I'll go check it out. See if I can do anything for them," Bill said.

"Let me grab my boots, and I'll come with you." I could hardly let him go on his own. The man and his wife had opened their home to us when we needed someplace to stay. The least I could do was accompany him when he went to investigate.

"That isn't necessary. I can go alone."

"Look, there isn't time to argue about it," I said. "I'm coming with you. End of story."

"Fine. Let's go."

I quickly jammed my bare feet into my boots and laced them up while Bill grabbed his gun.

"Aren't you forgetting something?" I asked as I stood up. Bill stared at me with a blank expression. "I can't go out there unarmed," I clarified.

Precious seconds ticked by as he considered my request. In the background, the injured person out on the road continued to howl. I was surprised the drone hadn't silenced them already.

"Fine." He went and retrieved the shotgun he'd confiscated from me earlier in the day and grudgingly handed it over. I told Bec and Dylan to watch over the others while we were gone, though neither would be much use in a hostile situation.

Bill and I crept out onto the porch, and he slowly opened the screen door, wincing as the hinges creaked loudly. Bill shook his head as he held the door open for me. "I've been meaning to oil the darn thing for months."

We crossed the yard, darting between the garden beds and ducking beneath drooping branches. As we ran along the grass strip flanking the long driveway, the rice and beans felt like a heavy ball in my stomach. Despite being over twice my age and on the heavy side, Bill was surprisingly fast on his feet. He stopped when he reached the gated entrance to the property and waited for me to catch up. He looked kind of smug, and I had to resist the temptation to tell him to try running around without a bra or socks to protect his feet. But I realized it was childish to feel defensive over such a trivial matter. And besides, we had more pressing issues to attend to.

The burning car was a distance down the road, and the injured occupant was still making an awful lot of noise. It made me nervous, not knowing where the drone was. Why hadn't it stuck around to take care of the screaming guy? "I don't like this," I whispered. Bill didn't seem too keen either, but we couldn't stand around forever.

"We should use the fence for cover until we get closer to the car," he suggested.

"I'm not sure the fence will do much to conceal our approach, but okay."

Bill lumbered off, keeping close to the post and rail fence, and I followed him. As we drew closer to the burning car, I thought I saw movement on the far side of the road. "Bill, I think I saw someone."

He dropped down behind a thick timber fence post and scanned the road. "I don't see anything."

"Over by the car. I thought I saw someone stumbling away from the wreck." When we couldn't see anyone moving about, we climbed between the rails and crossed the grassy shoulder beside the road. We circled the car with our weapons raised.

The hood was a mangled crater with the windshield blown in. Glass crunched under my boots as I edged around to the driver's door. Acrid smoke hung in the air around the car, toxic fumes from the burning interior clogging my throat.

"Please help me," the injured driver pleaded when I looked in through the window. His face resembled a steak that had been left on the grill too long- his skin charred and cracked. Pieces of glass from the windshield protruded from his ruined features, reminding me of a nightmarish porcupine. He hadn't been wearing a seatbelt either. His arms hung limp at his sides, his lap filling with blood.

There was no saving him.

"It hurts so bad," he cried.

"I know. I'm sorry," I said lamely. I had no idea what to do. We couldn't help him. Only a team of emergency room surgeons would have a chance at repairing his ruined body. And that wasn't ever going to be an option. But we couldn't leave him as he was. He was suffering terribly, and all the noise he was making would bring unwanted attention.

"You have to be quiet," I told the injured man, feeling like the world's worst person for trying to silence him.

He was in too much pain to listen. I glanced around to check Bill's attention was elsewhere. He was still searching along the roadside for the elusive figure I thought I'd seen. I bent down and removed the knife I kept hidden in my boot. "I'm so sorry," I whispered as I reached inside the car and plunged the blade between his ribs. The knife pierced his heart, and he had enough time to look up at me in surprise before his head slumped to the side. He was dead. His agonized cries wouldn't be a problem for us anymore.

I quickly wiped the blade clean and slipped the knife back in my boot as Bill walked around to join me. "I can't see anyone else. Are you sure you saw someone?" he asked.

I shrugged. "I don't know. I thought I saw someone crouch down in the grass, but I could be mistaken," I admitted.

Bill looked in through the window at the dead driver. I held my breath as he reached inside the car and checked for a pulse. "He's dead," Bill stated as he noticed the blood staining the driver's grubby t-shirt. My breath caught when he fingered the stab wound. He turned to me with narrowed eyes. "He's been stabbed." I could tell by his troubled expression that he knew I had silenced the injured man.

"He couldn't be saved. I had to think of everyone back at the house. We couldn't risk having the drone return."

Bill quickly looked around before peering at me with an intensity that made me squirm uncomfortably. "I was right about you," he said flatly.

"What do you mean?" I asked.

There was a lengthy pause before he finally answered. "When I saw you in my barn, covered in someone else's blood, I knew you would do anything to survive."

I felt a deep sense of shame wash over me. Not so much by his words, but more by his wary and somewhat disgusted expression. "I'll do anything to protect my sister," I admitted. "Can you honestly say you wouldn't do the same for Ruth?"

To his credit, he took the time to consider my question before answering. "I guess I would. But that doesn't mean I'm comfortable with your actions."

"I understand," I admitted grudgingly. "We should head back to the house. We've already spent too much time out here. And as soon as the sun sets tomorrow, we'll move on."

"Alright," Bill said, turning away from the car. We didn't talk as we made our way back to the farmhouse.

When I woke up the following afternoon, Sasha was sitting downstairs in one of the armchairs. Buster was asleep at her feet. She placed a scrap of paper to mark her place in the book she was reading before looking up at me with a smile. "Hey Jess. I was wondering if you would ever wake up."

I smiled as I pulled my hair back into a bun. "It's been a rough couple of weeks. I guess I needed the rest. We're going to leave once it's dark, so make sure you're ready to go."

Ruth must have been in the kitchen and overheard us talking. She walked over and stood beside Sasha, placing a hand on my sister's shoulder. "We wish you would reconsider. Surely after last night, you can see how dangerous it is out there."

"We can't stay here forever. I have someone waiting for us, and besides, you can't support all the extra people indefinitely."

"We'll find a way to make it work. It doesn't seem right sending three young children out into such an unsafe situation."

"Ruth, I am so grateful for your kindness and hospitality during such trying circumstances, but we will be leaving tonight." Ruth looked down at my sister sadly and smoothed her hair back from her face. "I guess I'll go fix y'all something to eat before you leave since I can't change your mind."

I slumped onto the couch, feeling uncertain about my motives for dragging everyone away from the safety of the farm.

"Hey Jess, can Dylan and I talk to you about something?" Bec asked, poking her head into the room meekly.

"Sure. What's up?" I asked, although I had a reasonably good idea what she wanted to say. The couple joined me on the couch, and Dylan took Bec's hand in his. He swallowed nervously. "Well? What did you want to talk to me about?" I finally asked when neither of them said anything.

Bec cleared her throat and glanced at her boyfriend before saying, "Dylan and I have decided to stay here on the farm. We think it's too risky continuing to the mountains. I mean, you don't even know if your boyfriend is still..."She didn't finish the sentence. She didn't have to. What she said was true. It was a massive risk to press on, and I couldn't say with any certainty that Brent would still be there if we made it. But that didn't make it any easier for me to hear. Their decision to stay behind blindsided me. Although they'd only joined our group a few days earlier, I'd come to accept that they would be with us for the rest of the journey.

Sensing my feelings of hurt and betrayal, Dylan weighed in. "Bec and I can never thank you enough for saving us from that parking garage. If it weren't for you, we probably wouldn't still be alive. You did right by us even though we were total strangers."

"And yet, you would rather stay here," I added. "I get it. You feel safe here on the farm."

"We do feel safe here with Ruth and Bill. And we can't face the prospect of going back to feeling terrified every second of the day," Bec admitted.

"You might have been scared, but you still managed to shoot one of those things out of the sky."

Bec allowed herself a small, satisfied smile. "That's true, but I can't guarantee that I'd be able to do it again. I can't be out there wondering if I'll be able to pull the trigger when the time comes. I'm sorry, but it's just too much. I can't do it."

I sat quietly for a moment, processing everything. "I understand. Ruth and Bill are good people, and I'm sure they will do everything they can to protect you both." I quickly excused myself and left the room.

Later, when the sky had darkened, Bill took me aside while Ruth generously packed us some food for the road.

"Since we can't convince you to stay, Ruth and I want you to take Buster. He's taken a real shine to Sasha, and he's a good guard dog." Bill said.

"I'm not taking one of your dogs. The last thing I need is another mouth to feed. Besides, what if he barks when he shouldn't and lets a drone know where we are?"

"He'll only bark when you need to hear it. He can help protect the children. Ruth and I would feel much better if you agree to take him."

I took a second to consider the offer. The only pet I'd ever been responsible for was a goldfish, and it had died soon after I received it as a tenth birthday present. The prospect of caring for someone else's dog unnerved me. But it wouldn't hurt to know I wasn't the only one looking out for everyone.

"Look, if you think it's a good idea, we'll take him with us," I agreed.

Bill smiled and clapped me on the shoulder. "Excellent. I've placed a twenty-pound bag of kibble in the van. It should last a good while if you ration it out."

"Of course, you have," I replied. He'd had no intention of letting me leave without the damn dog.

"You can return him when all of this craziness subsides."

After we had said our goodbyes to Ruth and the others, Bill accompanied us out to the barn. Buster trotted along beside him, the picture of obedience. "I worked on the van earlier today while you were sleeping. I've rotated the tires and checked the oil. Providing you don't drive like an a-hole, it should get you where you're going."

"Thanks, Bill. You and Ruth have been too kind. I promise I'll take care of Buster." I climbed up into the van and started the engine. Whatever tweaks Bill had made to the van had done the trick. It was running much smoother and quieter than before. "It sounds good," I said through the open window.

"It's amazing the difference a little bit of maintenance can make," he said dryly.

I nodded in agreement and tried not to think about the van's young owner.

"Be real careful out there," he implored me.

"You bet."

He patted the driver's door and waved to the kids in the back seat. A lump formed in my throat as I watched him crouch down and ruffle Buster's fur as he said goodbye to the dog. Once Buster was safely loaded into the van, I drove out of the barn and headed down the driveway. The safety and comfort of the farm left behind.

Seventeen

It had been three days since we left the farm. We spent the daylight hours trying to sleep while crowded together in the van. At night we drove along the darkened roads at twenty miles an hour. On several occasions, we had to ease around wrecks blocking both lanes, crawling along the crumbling shoulder that dropped away steeply.

Fiona thought she'd seen a car following us once or twice, but I dismissed her concerns. Even with the threat of drones, other people were still going to use the road. At some point on our journey, Sasha had swapped places with Fiona. My sister now sat in the front seat beside me with a map spread across her lap as she tried to figure out our location. She held the torch above the crumpled sheet of paper (a necessary risk if we were going to figure out where the heck we were) while her finger traced a path along a squiggly line representing the road we were on.

"According to the map, there should be a town not too far ahead. If you take the next exit, the town should be two or three miles northeast. Maybe we should take a detour and check it out." I glanced at the fuel gauge. The needle was barely registering a quarter of a tank. Bill had given us a jerry can of gas, but it wouldn't be anywhere near enough to get us to the cabin.

"The kids could use a break from being stuck in the van," Fiona added. "They're getting restless. I'm not sure how much longer I can keep them occupied. I've exhausted my storytelling abilities, and we can't play I Spy in the dark."

"It might be worth taking a look," I conceded.

"Hey!" Fiona cried. "You just passed the exit."

Startled by her outburst, I put the van in reverse and watched the revision mirror as I backtracked. "What the fuck?" I said under my breath as I caught sight of the tiny glow of a lighter being held against a cigarette a short distance away. How could we have missed someone following so close behind us? The answer was obvious. We'd been so focused on the road ahead and the sky above us that we hadn't paid enough attention to what was happening in the background. Fuck. Fiona was right. I'd thought she was paranoid, but apparently not.

We were in the middle of who-the-heck knew where and someone was tailing us. "I think someone is following us," I announced quietly.

Sasha turned her head to look behind us. "Maybe it's nothing. As you said, we aren't the only ones using the roads."

I sniffed and shook my head. "No, I think Fiona is right. Some asshole is following us. Shine the torch on the sign so we can figure out where the hell we are."

Greensburg: Population 3, 573. It was probably considerably lower now, I thought darkly as I took the exit. I tried not to obsess about the possibility that someone was following us. It wasn't easy. Greensburg was over three miles away. I didn't like our chances of reaching the town and finding somewhere safe to bunker down before sunrise. The sky was already the faded purple of an old bruise. But I liked the prospect of spending another day cramped together in the van even less.

"We need to find somewhere to lay low for the day," I said as I pressed my foot down on the accelerator. Visibility was improving with every passing minute, and while it made my job easier, it also increased the risk of being discovered by a drone.

"Look. Over there! Do you think we could spend the day in that truck depot?" Fiona asked, pointing to the abandoned structure. A large shed loomed in the pre-dawn light, a covered loading dock was attached to it, which would provide adequate cover for the day. I pulled into the gravel lot and parked under the covered bay. Although the place had the unmistakable air of a building long since abandoned, I wanted to double-check before giving everyone the go-ahead to unload. "Give me a minute to look around and make sure we're alone out here," I told Fiona and my sister. I killed the engine and grabbed the shotgun. "Stay put until I say it's safe."

I climbed out of the van and pointed the shotgun out at the road. If someone really had been following us, they were going to get a nasty shock when I pointed the gun at their windscreen and pulled the trigger. My muscles were bunched and ready—the seconds ticked by. I was about to go check out the depot when the vehicle came into view. It slowly drove past the depot's driveway, and I aimed the gun. To my relief, it continued along the road. Although it was still too dark to get a good look at the driver, I got the impression that they were peering at the warehouse as they drove by.

"Do you think it was a coincidence?" Sasha asked from beside me. I was unaware she had climbed out of the van. "Maybe. Maybe not. I thought I saw someone behind us after we left the farm. And Fiona noticed a car behind us last night. It's hard to know if it's paranoia or something we need to be worried about."

"Come on," Sasha pulled me back toward the depot. "We are all exhausted. Let's find somewhere to sleep."

She was probably right. I climbed up the stairs beside the loading dock and was relieved to discover the padlock securing the double-wide sliding door had long since been busted open. Despite its weight, the door opened easily enough. It was still too dark to see clearly inside the warehouse. The pale dawn light was no match for the grimy windows positioned at wide intervals along the building walls. I switched on the flashlight and slowly swung it around the massive warehouse.

Sturdy metal shelving ran three-quarters of the length of the warehouse in evenly spaced rows. Judging by the dust and junk lining the abandoned shelves, it had been a long time since anyone used the building for its original purpose.

There was a doorway at the far end of the warehouse that opened onto a series of rooms. I stepped inside a carpeted space that had once been an office with a large window overlooking the warehouse. A stained and sagging mattress lay crammed into a corner, discarded condom wrappers littering the floor around it. Dozens of empty beer cans were stacked into a haphazard pyramid on the windowsill, melted candles placed on either side of the precarious tower.

I crossed the grubby room and poked my head into the doorway to my left. There was a dilapidated kitchenette. Graffiti covered the walls. I turned on the faucet and jumped back in surprise when a foul stream of brown water gushed into the sink. After a minute or so, it began to run clear. Shelter and ample running water, could the day get any better?

The final door revealed a cramped toilet cubicle plastered with busty centerfolds. I rolled my eyes at the tacky display as I stepped toward the swampy-smelling toilet. Although it probably hadn't been cleaned in years, it wasn't as filthy as I'd expected. I pressed the button and cheered when water filled the bowl. A huge grin split my face. No more shitting on the ground like an animal-at least, not for the next twelve hours. Life was looking up.

I hurried back to the van, eager to share the good news. "Come on inside. There's running water and a toilet that flushes."

"That's the best news I've heard in days," Fiona said happily. She shook the children awake and helped them out of the van. Buster bounded out after them, eager to stretch his legs and relieve himself against the side of the building. Sasha helped me collect the last of the food Ruth had packed for us. "Did that car come back?" I asked once Fiona was out of earshot.

"No. I watched the road the entire time you were gone, but I didn't see anything. We were probably getting worked up over nothing."

"Yeah, probably," I agreed. I took a quick inventory of the remaining food. We had been careful to eat only twice a day, and even then, we had consumed minimal portions. What food remained would only provide the five of us with a light breakfast. After a few hours of sleep, I'd have to go out and search for supplies.

I led everyone over to the abandoned office and ushered them inside. Fiona looked around the room in distaste. "It's filthy in here. I think we'd be better off out in the van."

"I know it's not ideal, but it won't be so bad if we drag the mattress out. Look on the bright side. We have running water and a toilet. We can wash, get some rest, and we'll be back on the road later tonight."

"Yeah, I guess. After staying at the farm and feeling like life was almost normal, it's hard going back to sleeping in places like this," Fiona admitted.

"We won't have to slum it in shit holes like this forever. Things will get better once we reach the cabin. I promise."

Sasha guided the children over to the desk. She kept them busy playing with a deck of cards Ruth had thoughtfully included in the care package while Fiona and I grappled with the putrid mattress. A giant cockroach ran out from beneath it, and Fiona screamed in horror as it scuttled toward her. She lunged forward and stomped on it, nearly losing her grip on the mattress in the process.

"Easy there, tiger. It was just a cockroach," I grunted as I struggled to maintain a hold on the musty-smelling mattress. We half dragged, half carried it across the room, panting with exhaustion by the time we eased it through the doorway and leaned it on the wall outside the office.

I followed Fiona over to the desk and watched as she rubbed her hands on her shorts before removing the remaining food from the carry bag. She arranged it on the desk like it was a king's ransom rather than the woefully inadequate pickings on offer. While Fiona lacked survival skills, she made up for it with her dedication to her children and her determination to shield them from the difficult situation we were in.

A single can of baked beans, half a packet of crackers, and a handful of raisins had to feed five people. Undeterred, Fiona peeled the lid off the baked beans and began scooping them onto the crackers. "Go on, eat up," she encouraged the children when they eyed the odd breakfast dubiously. Charlotte took a bite, and Harry giggled when a stray bean plopped into her lap. "Beans, beans, the magical fruit. The more you eat, the more you toot!" He cackled with delight at his little ditty, and we all joined in. Who didn't like fart jokes, right?

After we calmed down, everyone set about demolishing the beans on crackers. I even ate my share of raisins, which ordinarily I wouldn't touch. It took about thirty seconds to finish 'breakfast.' We were all so hungry; the food barely made a difference. If anything, it made it worse. "What are we going to do?" Fiona asked. "That won't keep Harry and Charlotte quiet for long."

She was right. As adults, we understood the pains associated with hunger. Although it felt uncomfortable, we knew it would pass. Sooner or later, we would have something else to eat, and the feeling would go away. But the children were too young to understand any of that. They were hungry, and their bellies hurt. Full stop.

"I know it's getting light outside, but I think I'll go scout around for some food in the nearby houses. We can't expect the children to go hungry all day."

"You don't have to do that," Fiona protested. "We've been driving all night; I know you must be exhausted."

"It's okay. I'd rather go now and get it over and done with. I'll try not to take too long."

"I'll come with you," Sasha offered.

"No way. I need you to stay here with Fiona."

"But I can help you carry stuff."

"You can help by staying here and helping Fiona look after Harry and Charlotte. Use the tap in the kitchenette to wash up while I'm gone." She knew better than to argue, and I was grateful. I was too fucking tired and hungry to fight with her.

"I'll be back as soon as I can," I told her.

"What if you don't come back?" she asked fearfully.

"If I'm not back by dark, I'm probably dead. We're close to the mountains now. It will be up to you to lead Fiona and the children to the cabin. Brent will take care of you."

"Don't even talk like that."

"I'm not trying to upset you," I said, wrapping her in a quick hug. "But we have to be realistic. I promise I'll try my best not to get myself killed, and hopefully, I'll find something to eat while I'm out there."

I grabbed my backpack and headed off, knowing Harry and Charlotte would soon distract my sister from her worrying. Buster was quick to follow me out of the office. He ignored my command to stay. Realizing he was probably feeling stir-crazy after being cooped up in the van for hours on end, I grudgingly allowed him to come with me.

In the time it had taken to get everyone settled inside the warehouse, the sun had risen, filling the sky with a delicious golden light that boosted my energy better than any fancy brewed coffee ever could. In our efforts to avoid the drones and roving gangs of homicidal lunatics, I'd overlooked the beneficial effects of regular exposure to good-old-fashioned sunshine. Buster and I relished the comforting warmth as we slowly trotted down the driveway toward the road.

By the time we reached the potholed blacktop, I'd slowed to a brisk walk. No matter how hard I tried, I just couldn't seem to convince my feet to maintain a faster pace. Buster bounded through the tall sun-bleached grass on the side of the road, his tail wagging as he sniffed for rabbits or rodents. In the distance, tendrils of smoke wound into the sky above Greensburg. We would probably have to pass through the town on our way to the cabin. But for now, I planned on avoiding the community at all costs.

Instead, I focused my attention on a run-down house set back from the road a quarter of a mile from the warehouse. It was impossible to discern if it was occupied before the drones or was sitting empty for years. Spurred on by the possibility of finding something more satisfying to eat than a few spoons of baked beans, I broke into a run.

The driveway was in poor condition, rutted and dotted with clumps of weeds determined to survive despite the adverse growing conditions. As I approached the property, I began to wonder if anyone even lived there. The paint was faded and peeling.   Nobody had washed the windows in years. It seemed unlikely that I'd find anything useful. When I made my way around to the rear of the house, I was relieved to discover that I'd been wrong.

There was a good-sized veggie patch out near the clothesline. While most of the vegetables had died from lack of care, a couple of tomato plants had survived. Without the benefit of regular watering, the leaves had wilted, and many of the tomatoes had begun to rot. However, there was still an abundance of edible fruit. I plucked a ripe tomato from the plant and held it up to my nose, inhaling the earthy scent before I sank my teeth into it. Juice and seeds squirted over my chin as I chewed.

I was startled by an explosion that couldn't have been more than a mile away. It reminded me of the peril of running around during the daylight hours. We hadn't seen a drone for a while, and I'd quickly become complacent, encouraged by the lack of sightings.

With over a dozen tomatoes stuffed inside the backpack, I continued my search. There was a doghouse near the back steps, a length of chain lying in the dirt. The dog was gone. A few sun-bleached turds and an overturned water bowl all that remained. I followed Buster over to the chicken coop abutting a rusted-out water tank. Rotting, feathery bodies littered the ground inside the coup.

I turned away, the tomato I'd eaten sitting uncomfortably in my stomach. Buster trotted along beside me as I turned my attention to the house. I climbed the steps to the back door and rattled the handle, but it was locked. "For fuck's sake. Did you have to lock the door?" I grumbled. I'd try the front door, but if it were locked too, I'd have to break a window to get in.

I was headed for the front of the house when I heard a car up on the road. Buster's ears pricked up, but he remained by my side as I crouched down behind an old wheelbarrow that had once been an ornamental flowerbed. I eased my head up over a clump of crispy brown marigolds and watched a cop car speed along the road. It was heading away from the town, and I saw with growing alarm that there was a drone closing in after it. My fingers locked around Buster's collar, holding him in place beside me as I watched on helplessly.

It only took the drone a few seconds to catch up with the black and white cruiser. There was a brilliant flash accompanied by the all too familiar screech of metal ripping apart. The burning vehicle rolled to a stop, and Buster whined at the pitiful cries of the injured driver before a second blast silenced them. The drone hovered above the mangled wreck, presumably waiting for the burnt and bleeding occupant to crawl out. It quickly lost interest, turning its focus to the farmhouse. There were twenty seconds, maybe less, before it reached me.

I darted around the old wheelbarrow and dived under the rotting timber rails that bordered the front porch, calling Buster up after me. I counted down the seconds as I got to my feet and ran across to the front door. Buster whined beside me, scratching at the door as I smashed my elbow through the pane of glass above the handle and reached inside to unlock it. The dog rushed inside, and I followed close behind, slamming the door shut behind me, but I was too slow. There was a deafening bang accompanied by a whoosh of superheated air that flung me off my feet. Then everything went black.

A groan escaped my lips as I slowly regained consciousness, my entire body stiff and sore from being slammed into the floor hard enough to loosen my teeth. A warm, moist tongue dragged across my cheek, and I grimaced. Encouraged by my reaction, Buster set to work licking every square inch of my face. "Yuck," I protested groggily. "Stop licking me." I pushed myself up onto my hands and knees, mentally cataloging the various aches and pains wracking my body. Blood trickled from a knick above my eyebrow, and I wiped it away as I stood up.

The front door was gone, obliterated by the drone. The area around the frame was black and charred in places. It was a miracle the whole house hadn't caught alight and burned to the ground while I was out cold on the floor. Buster nudged my hand, and I patted him. "Thanks for sticking around," I told the dog. He looked up at me and wagged his tail. "I guess we had better get moving. Who knows how long I was out for?" I said and made my way through to the kitchen at the back of the house. The kitchen was a mess. Piles of dirty dishes filled the sink, and the counters were thick with grease and old food spills.

Before moving on, the people living there had picked the cupboards clean. All I managed to find was half a box of oats and some powdered eggs that had reached their best before months ago. I considered leaving the eggs behind but decided to take them anyway. They were unopened, and it was best before, not a use-by date.

When I was satisfied that there was nothing else worth taking, I made my way along the hallway and out through the blasted hole where the door had been. I stood on the porch and watched, waiting to see if the drone reappeared. Judging by the position of the sun, I'd been unconscious for at least an hour. Probably longer. There was no sign of the drone, and I assumed it hadn't bothered to stick around.

Eighteen

$\mathbf{A}$fter my near-death experience, I decided to call it quits and make do with the few food items I'd found in the farmhouse. We headed back down the rutted driveway and out onto the road. When we reached the hurricane fence surrounding the warehouse, I noticed the gates had been pushed open. Frowning, I entered the property and latched the gates shut behind me. I was sure I'd taken the time to close them when I'd set out earlier in the morning. Maybe I was mistaken. It had been a long night, and I'd had other things on my mind, but still. I could have sworn I'd shut the damn things.

Buster ran ahead, frantically barking when he reached the loading dock. It was the first time I'd heard him bark since he had joined the group. He scratched at the steel door, barking and growling as he tried to force his way inside. The hairs on the back of my neck stood on end, and I sprinted towards him. I climbed the stairs two at a time and had the shotgun raised and ready.

I slid open the door and squeezed through the gap, waiting while my eyes adjusted to the gloomy interior. Buster shot off between the empty shelving units and made a beeline for the other end of the warehouse, his throaty barks echoing in the cavernous space. I discarded the backpack and followed him, unable to temper the panic rising inside me.

When I reached the rear of the building, I saw Sasha scuffling withing some random guy. She plunged her pocketknife in his back seconds before Buster reached them. The dog grabbed hold of the guy's leg and shook it violently. I pointed the barrel of the shotgun at them, but there was no way I could pull the trigger without risking my sister's safety. "Get out of the way!" I called to her. She looked back at me in surprise and stepped away from the man she had just stabbed.

My brain couldn't seem to make sense of what I was seeing. "What the hell is going on here?" I asked uncertainly. I kept looking past Sasha and the stranger at the female lying on the concrete behind them. There was something familiar about her blouse. I'd seen it before.

"Oh my God, Fiona," I cried and rushed toward the guy with the knife in his back. I cracked him in the head with the butt of the gun. He collapsed unconscious, and Buster released his leg. I ran over to Fiona and dropped to my knees beside her. If it hadn't been for the familiar flower pattern on her blouse and the small hibiscus tattoo on her ankle, I would not have recognized her.

I willed myself to remain calm. Fiona's face was a battered mess. One eye was already swelling shut, and her nose was broken. Blood bubbled from between the lips of her ruined mouth. A red stain was spreading across her chest at an alarming rate. I reached down and hurriedly unbuttoned her blouse, searching for the cause of the bleeding. Numerous stab wounds crisscrossed her breasts and ribs. "No. Oh, Fiona, what did he do to you?" I whispered between hitching breaths.

Her hand was limp when I reached down and enclosed it in mine. I couldn't understand how anyone could want to inflict such violence on Fiona. She was so gentle and easy-going. What could she have possibly done to enrage someone so much that they would beat and stab her until she was unrecognizable?

Sasha knelt opposite me and smoothed some stray hairs that were caught in the blood trickling down Fiona's face. "We have to help her."

I looked across at my sister and fought the urge to wrap her in my arms and comfort her. Tears ran down her cheeks, dripping off her chin, where they landed on the concrete with a plop. "We can't let her die," she implored me.

"Sasha, I don't think there is anything we can do. She's too badly hurt."

"You said there's a town nearby, so go and find a doctor. Bring someone back here who can save her."

"Even if I could find someone, there isn't time. Fiona has lost too much blood already."

My sister examined the puddle of blood spreading around Fiona and slowly nodded. "What are we going to do, Jess?" she sobbed. I felt my heart cracking into a thousand pieces for Sasha and the absolute devastation I saw in her eyes and for Fiona and the hideous attack she had endured. She didn't deserve to suffer like this. But worst of all, very soon, someone was going to have to go and tell Harry and Charlotte that they would never get to see their mom again. They would be utterly alone in the world.

Fiona's fingers lightly squeezed my hand, and I looked down in surprise. Her puffy eyelids opened a crack, and she groaned. I crawled around behind her and gently lifted her head, cradling it in my lap. "I should never have left you alone," I apologized. She blinked and shook her head slightly. Her lips moved as she tried to speak, accompanied by a spray of red droplets and a horrible whistling sound.

"Harry and Charlotte are fine," I assured her. She reached up and patted my arm, and I took her hand in mine once more.

"I promise we'll take care of them for you. The mountains are so close we can see them in the distance. It won't be much longer before we reach the cabin, and then they will be safe." I swallowed the lump forming in my throat.

Fiona sighed and blinked back the tears shimmering in her eyes. She looked at Sasha, who was still pressing down on her wounds and coughed up blood. Somehow, my baby sister managed to smile encouragingly, although I could tell she was falling apart inside. I was still looking at Sasha's strained expression when I felt Fiona's grip on my hand loosen. I squeezed her fingers, but she didn't respond.

"Fiona. Stay with me. Think of Harry and Charlotte; they need their mom," I implored her, but it was too late. She was gone. I lowered her hand to the floor and gently released it. I reached out and lightly ran my fingers across her puffy eyelids, closing them so I didn't have to look at her unseeing eyes. My heart felt like it was shattering into a million pieces, which surprised me. I hadn't realized that I cared so much. A dreadful howl erupted from deep within me, and I turned to my sister. My face twisted in agony and confusion; I asked, "What the fuck happened here?"

She jumped back, startled. I waited as she looked at Fiona then up to me before returning her gaze to Fiona. Just when I was about to prompt her, Sasha wiped away the tears streaming down her cheeks and began. "I must have fallen asleep for a while because I woke up feeling confused. It took me a moment to remember where I was. At first, I thought I must have been dreaming because I felt all fuzzy and disorientated, but then I heard a scream, and I jumped up. I was halfway out the door when I remembered the pocketknife you gave me. I grabbed it and ran out into the warehouse. By the time I reached Fiona, she'd already been beaten and stabbed. Some guy was kneeling over her, and I just ran at him. I was clutching the pocketknife you gave me, and I remember plunging it into the guy's back. I didn't know what else to do," she wailed.

"It's okay," I reached out and touched her arm. "You did what you had to do."

"He made this high-pitched squealing sound before he collapsed on the concrete. He loosened his grip on the knife he used on Fiona, and I kicked it out of reach. Then I saw you running toward us."

I crawled over to my sister and wrapped her in my arms. She collapsed against me, and we both sobbed uncontrollably. "You did good, Sasha. You did the right thing."

She pushed away from me. "No, I didn't. Fiona's dead."

"You stopped him. That's enough."

"It was my job to keep everyone safe while you were out looking for supplies. I failed, and now Harry and Charlotte don't have a mother."

"That was never your responsibility. You're just a child. I shouldn't have left you alone. It was reckless."

Behind us, Fiona's attacker began to stir. I gently pulled free of Sasha's desperate embrace and stood up. I watched as he slowly regained consciousness. He groaned and opened his eyes. An expression of pure hatred settled over his features when he saw me standing over him.

He struggled up into a sitting position, gritting his teeth as the knife embedded in his back restricted his movement. He was young. Probably younger than me, the stubble across his jaw was patchy and sparse. And aside from being dirty and thin, he looked like any other young guy I might have walked past in the street on a busy Saturday morning. If Sasha hadn't told me he was responsible for Fiona lying dead on the concrete floor behind me, I wouldn't have thought he was capable of such a dreadful act.

"Is she dead?" he asked, a bitter smile twisting his face into something cruel and ugly.

"What?" I heard myself ask.

"I asked if she's dead?" he repeated in a raspy voice.

"Yes," I nodded slowly. "She's dead. You killed her."

"Good," he replied. "How does it feel to watch someone you care about taken away from you?"

Rage pulsed through me, hot and seething like some ancient serpent woken from a dark slumber. I wanted to kick the guy in the face and watch his teeth skitter across the floor. "What the hell is wrong with you? She had two small children to look after. They have no one else."

He shrugged coldly. "I watched you stab my friend to death. He needed help, and instead, you chose to stick a knife between his ribs."

I puzzled over his accusation, at a loss. Then it hit me. It was the guy I'd seen running from the burning car back at the farm. He must have seen me silence the driver—his friend. "There was nothing I could do for him," I whispered, swallowing down a wave of nausea as it dawned on me what this was all about. "He was too severely injured. All that noise he was making- it would have gotten us all killed."

"Yeah, best just to silence him, right? You must be one hell of a cold-hearted killer," he said between clenched teeth.

"Did you attack Fiona because of what happened to your friend?"

He smirked and nodded. "I couldn't let you get away it. So, I followed you and waited for my chance. It took a while, but then I saw you hobble off this morning with that fucking dog, and I knew today was it. You would finally learn what it feels like to have someone taken from you for no good reason."

Fiona's death was on my hands. Maybe not directly, but I'd played my part, just as undoubtedly as the twisted fucker at my feet had played his. I screamed. Pain and hatred burst from me in a primal wailing as I swung my booted foot back and kicked him in the face. Blood spurted from his nose.

Sasha ran over and tried to pull me away, but I shook her off. I kicked him repeatedly, only stopping when I couldn't raise my leg anymore. Panting heavily, I wiped at the sweat dripping into my eyes before reaching down to pluck Sasha's pocketknife from his back. "Jess, no!" Sasha cried. Ignoring her pleas, I dropped to my knees and plunged the knife into his throat to finish him off—the merry-go-round of revenge and its brutal outcome playing over and over in my head.

Once I was sure he was dead, I got to my feet unsteadily and turned to my sister. She shrank away from me in terror. Her eyes darted between me and the bloodied body of Fiona's attacker. Buster trotted over to her, and she grabbed hold of his collar, placing him between us protectively. "What else did you expect me to do?" I asked flatly, keeping my eyes on the ground. "I couldn't let him walk away. Not after he killed Fiona."

"I'm glad he's dead," Sasha admitted reluctantly. "But the way you did it? You practically kicked him to death. There is a darkness inside you that frightens me, Jess. Sometimes, when I look at you, I don't see my big sister anymore. I'm always afraid. And it's not just because of the drones or people like him," she said, waving at the battered stranger lying nearby.

"What are you saying? You know I would never hurt you. Everything I do, I do to keep you safe," I muttered in dismay.

Sasha shook her head, doubtfully. "I'm not sure that's true anymore. I've watched you change since the drones appeared. Sometimes I wonder if you enjoy it."

"If you mean I enjoy killing people, you are wrong. Nothing could be further from the truth," but even as I said it, I wondered if she was right. Had I been kidding myself all this time? Was it possible that I'd just been waiting for the opportunity to vent my violent tendencies? And the arrival of the drones created the perfect environment to nurture my blood lust. The possibility that there was some truth to my sister's accusation left me reeling. I wanted to argue that it wasn't right, that I only did what was necessary to survive. But there wasn't time.

"We have to get rid of the bodies," I said. "Harry and Charlotte could wake up any minute now. They can't see their mother like this."

"You're right," she agreed. "We need to bury her."

"Sasha. I only meant we should move her someplace out of sight. We don't have a shovel, not to mention it hasn't rained in weeks, and the ground is as hard as a rock out in the lot. And I saw a drone blast a cop car off the road less than half a mile from here."

Sasha crossed her arms and glared at me. "I don't care what you saw. I don't care how hard the ground is. And I certainly don't give a shit if we don't have a shovel. I'll dig Fiona's grave with a stick if I have to."

"Okay. I understand that it's important to you. We'll figure something out. I just need time to think."

Her connection with Fiona was strong. I had watched the pair develop a close bond during the short, but intense time we had been together. The loss of another mother figure was undoubtedly dredging up painful memories of our mom's passing. "Can you go and sit with the children. If they wake up, try and distract them."

"What if they ask about Fiona? Should I tell them what happened?"

"No," I looked down at the young mother's ravaged remains. "I think it would be best to wait until after we bury her."

"Okay," she said, an anguished expression creasing her face as she looked down at Fiona before slowly turning away. I watched as she walked back to the room where the children were sleeping. She stopped outside the door; her shoulders slumped in defeat. I knew how she felt. More now than ever, she needed reassuring that everything would be okay, but with two bodies to dispose of, there wasn't time for cuddles and kind words. Plus, I was starting to feel like we were chasing an impossible outcome. There was no way of knowing if Brent was still waiting for us at the cabin. Or even worse if he was even alive. I hadn't been in contact with him for weeks, and I had no clue if we were clinging to a hopeless dream.

All I wanted to do was run away and forget what had happened or what I'd done. However, Sasha and the children were relying on me. I shook off the darkness that had settled over me like a heavy cloak and walked over to the dead guy and grabbed him by the ankles. Even though he was slim, I struggled to drag him across the concrete floor towards the door.

Acutely aware that I had limited time to remove the bodies before Harry and Charlotte became restless and started asking questions, I dragged Fiona's killer out onto the loading dock and rolled him over the edge. He flopped over the concrete lip and landed on the gravel below with a mushy thud. I flinched at the gruesome sound and hurried down the stairs after him. Without the energy or inclination to care about what happened to the body of Fiona's killer, I dragged him under the stairs and rolled him over so he was lying face down. Hopefully, Harry and Charlotte wouldn't notice him when we set off later in the evening.

While outside, I took the opportunity to scout a suitable location to bury Fiona. The compacted gravel lot was out of the question, so I made my way around the back of the warehouse. The ground behind the building was no better. But I did discover where the murdering bastard stalking us had stashed his vehicle. I searched his car for anything of value. However, it appeared that he had been doing it even tougher than us. Aside from a flashlight and a half-empty bottle of water, the vehicle was empty.

As I'd suspected, there wasn't anywhere to lay Fiona to rest. The ground was hard and impenetrable, thanks to the long dry summer. She deserved a decent burial, but I couldn't see any way of making that happen.

Something snapped inside me. Whether it was due to sleep deprivation- which was approaching a critical point, or I'd simply reached the end of my endurance with all the killing and constant state of fear; I couldn't say. It was probably a combination of the two. Either way, I felt emotionally and physically spent. All I wanted to do was curl up in a dark corner somewhere and sleep for days. Instead, I had to dispose of the body of someone I cared about and look after her two small children, despite not having a maternal bone in my bruised and battered body.

My legs would no longer support me, and I crumpled to the ground, my chest hitching as I began to weep uncontrollably. It was loud and ugly. Snot and tears streamed down my face as weeks of pent-up emotion were released.

When Sasha stepped around the side of the building and cautiously approached me, I quickly rubbed at my puffy eyes and climbed to my feet.

"You've been gone for a while, and I was starting to worry," Sasha said.

"Yeah, I needed some time," I sniffled.

"It might have been better if you had chosen somewhere less exposed to have a meltdown. I could hear you bawling the moment I stepped outside. It's a miracle the drone you saw earlier didn't show up," she gently admonished.

I nodded in agreement. Sasha was right. It was a fool move, and I was damn lucky. "I know. Shit just got on top of me. I'm sorry. I shouldn't have been so reckless. You would think I'd have learned my lesson by now."

Sasha stepped closer and wrapped her arms around my waist. "It's not your fault. I know you think you're to blame for what happened to Fiona, but that psycho was messed up in the head. He chose to kill someone who never did anything to him. That's on him-not you."

"I killed his friend. If I hadn't done that, Fiona would still be alive," I said. It felt cathartic to say it out loud.

Sasha squeezed me before breaking our embrace. "Maybe. But we all might have died back at the farmhouse if you hadn't silenced him. The rules have changed. Survival comes at a cost now. Sometimes people can't be saved. And when that happens, we have to choose between compassion and survival."

"Maybe compassion and survival are the same things?" I suggested.

My sister gave me a stern look that left me feeling mildly ashamed. "Maybe they are," she offered with a shrug. "Sometimes."

She walked to the edge of the building and glanced up at the sky. "The kids are still asleep, but we need to deal with Fiona's body soon."

"I know. But the ground is impenetrable," I complained, hating the whining tone of my voice.

"You're right. As much as I want us to do the right thing by Fiona, we have no way of digging a grave."

We stood in silence for a few minutes, wondering what to do with the body of our friend. My eyes kept drifting over to the abandoned car of her murderer, and I eventually said, "What if we place her in the car? It's not ideal, but it's the best option I can think of." Sasha looked at the car doubtfully before grudgingly agreeing. "Alright. I don't like it, but at least it will prevent animals from getting to her," she said.

"Come on. We need to move Fiona before Harry and Charlotte wake up."

***

After Sasha and I placed Fiona in the back seat of the killer's car, wiped the blood from her face, and smoothed her hair before covering her with a blanket taken from the van, I'd curled up and fallen asleep almost immediately. It was almost dark when I finally woke up. Buster was curled up on the floor beside me and raised his head eagerly, his tail thumping against my leg when he noticed I was awake. I ruffled his ears as I tried to shrug off the after-effects of the pain pills I'd taken before crashing.

We were alone in the room, and I wondered where Sasha and the children were. Every muscle in my body protested as I slowly dragged myself to my feet. The pills I'd taken earlier could only do so much. I'd liked it better when I was asleep. There's a lot to be said for the unconscious state. The sound of rain on the metal roof of the warehouse jolted me out of my funk. I couldn't remember the last time it had rained. It must have been sometime before the drones appeared.

Outside, Sasha and the children ran around under the covered loading dock playing a game of tag. I smiled sadly. It was a good strategy. Risky, but good. With the body of their mom's killer stashed under the stairs and the constant fear of drawing the attention of a drone, I was a little unnerved. Still, the children had been stuck in the van since leaving the farm, and an opportunity to run around and burn off some energy would do them a world of good. Watching the little ones running back and forth was a welcome distraction from the terrible news I'd have to share with them before we piled into the van and hit the road again.

Sasha caught my eye and smiled wanly. It must have been torture to run around with Harry and Charlotte, pretending everything was okay. She was so much stronger than me. And kinder. If I knew my sister, she would have wanted them to enjoy themselves one last time before their little lives changed forever.

I packed the camp cooker into the back of the van and motioned for Sasha to gather the children close. She nodded and knelt between them, hooking an arm around each child. I crouched down in front of the trio and took Harry and Charlotte's tiny plump hands in mine. My mouth opened and closed like a fish gasping for air as I struggled to find the right words. None were forthcoming. Eventually, Sasha intervened.

"We have to get back in the van now, guys," she said, giving each of them a loving squeeze.

"What about Mommy? Why didn't she have dinner with us?" Harry asked.

"Mommy won't be coming with us," Sasha told him and looked to me for assistance.

I swallowed the lump in my throat. "Mommy can't come with us, Harry. She's gone to sleep and can't wake up."

Tears were streaming down my sister's cheeks, and Harry looked up at her intently before returning his attention to me. His child-like innocence dissolved as realization transformed his features into something sad and impossibly grown-up at the same time. "Is she asleep like all those people the wasp machines hurt?" He asked, tears shimmering in his big blue eyes while Charlotte jammed a thumb in her mouth and stood quietly.

"Umm. Sort of," I said, a sharp stabbing pain in my chest trying to steal my breath. It was even more difficult than I'd imagined. He turned to Sasha and buried his face against her, his crying muffled against her shirt.

"I want my Mommy," Charlotte wailed.

I gently pried Harry away from my sister so that she could scoop up Charlotte and comfort her.

"Why did Mommy have to die?" Harry sobbed.

"Do you know what dying is?" I asked.

Harry nodded, his body violently shaking with the force of his grief. "Our goldfish died. His name was Fred-Fred the Fish. He was floating in the bowl one morning, and Mommy said he died. We buried him under a tree outside the apartments."

He was more switched on than I'd realized. Harry looked up at me mournfully. "I didn't want Mommy to die."

I crouched down in front of him, ignoring the pain radiating from my knee. "I didn't want her to die either," I admitted. "It makes me feel sad that she's gone." He wiped at my tears, and I swear I felt my heart splintering as his chubby fingers brushed my cheek.

"Are you going to look after us now?" he asked uncertainly.

I nodded. "Sasha and I will take care of you and your sister from now on. Is that alright with you?"

"Yep. That sounds good. But what will we do without Mommy? She knows all my favorite foods and which stories to read to me before bed."

I slowly stood up and lifted him onto my hip. "You can tell Sasha and me all the special things your mom did for you, and I promise we'll do our best to look after you like she did."

"Okay," he agreed. He rested his head against my shoulder and cried for a long time.

Eventually, when neither Sasha nor I could hold the children anymore, we gently loaded them into the van. They clung to each other as we secured their seat belts. Buster hopped up on the seat beside them and placed his head on Harry's lap. He looked up at them sadly, sharing their grief. I slid the van door closed and wondered how I could ever fill the void left by their mother. I had promised Fiona that I would keep her children safe, at least until this waking nightmare was over, and we could locate a more suitable carer. But the responsibility was immense. Suddenly, I was the mother of three children, having birthed not even one, burdened with the task of keeping them alive and well when everything and everyone seemed to want us dead.

Before climbing into the van, I stopped and took a moment to say a final goodbye to Fiona. Night had descended while the children grieved, and the warehouse was shrouded in darkness. Knowing its violent secrets gave it a sinister atmosphere, and I was glad to be leaving the place behind.

Nineteen

After watching the cop car blasted to shit and losing Fiona, I wasn't about to take any unnecessary risks. Although we had next to no supplies, I wasn't willing to risk a trip into the town. We would have to make do with the provisions we had. There were bound to be other small towns along the way that we could loot. Besides, the mountains were within spitting distance. Provided there were no more setbacks, we could reach the cabin sometime within the next few days.

The windscreen wipers squeaked against the glass as they swooshed back and forth across the windshield. If I'd thought driving out in the sticks without headlights had been difficult before, it was nothing compared to trying to drive in the rain. Although it was little more than a light mist, it still reduced visibility to practically nothing. Perhaps I'd been overly ambitious in my estimations. Under the current conditions, we would be lucky to reach Brent in a week. Possibly longer.

A while later, Harry and Charlotte cried themselves to sleep. It was a relief to no longer listen to their grief-stricken sobs. At some point, Buster decided to abandon the children and join us. He squeezed in beside my sister, breathing his hot doggy breath in her face. "Jesus, Buster. Your breath smells like garbage," she mumbled irritably. I tried not to laugh, but I found myself chuckling, nevertheless. She gave me a withering look, which just made me laugh harder.

"Keep it up, and you'll wake Harry and Charlotte," she warned.

She was right. The last thing we needed was for the children to start wailing again. I got myself under control and glanced over at her apologetically. "Sorry. It's been a rough day."

"No shit," she snapped.

"It's like that, is it?" I asked, provoking her.

"Yeah, it is. I'm so over this endless saga of death and destruction."

"Me too," I admitted. "I know you are hurting, but we have to keep it together. We're so close to reaching the cabin. Brent's there waiting for us. We just have to hold on for a bit longer."

Sasha studied me for longer than was comfortable before replying. "Do you believe that? After everything that's happened?"

I considered the question as I hunched over the steering wheel and squinted, struggling to make out the road ahead. "I have to believe it," I finally answered. "Otherwise, we are just running without purpose, and I'm all used up. I can't keep living like this. There must be some relief in sight. There just has to be."

It rained intermittently for the next two days, which slowed our progress as I had expected. The mountains were so damn close yet remained frustratingly out of reach. We had avoided the small town of Greensburg, too burnt out and damaged after Fiona's death to take any unnecessary risks. Even though it meant we couldn't stock up on food and water, I felt it was a worthwhile trade. We needed time to lick our wounds before we faced further challenges.

After bypassing the town via a convoluted series of detours, signs of human habitation rapidly diminished. Farmhouses became few and far between. When I eventually spotted a house set back from the road that I thought we could shelter in for the day, the owner had other ideas.

A suspicious face appeared at the door with a rifle pointed at my chest. It wasn't the first time someone greeted me in such a manner, but it didn't make it any easier. The man with the rifle pointed at me had no interest in my hard-luck story. He was unmoved by the three hungry children waiting in the van. Times were tough, and he was determined to protect his turf no matter what. I understood his position, although it did nothing to solve my problems.

I meekly retreated with my eyes lowered and my shoulders slumped, hoping his finger wouldn't squeeze the trigger. When I heard the door slam, I turned and hurried up the driveway to where I had parked the van. The mountain peaks were a dark smudge on the horizon, and I wondered if Brent was waiting for us. There was no way of knowing if he was still alive. It had been over three weeks since I'd last heard from him. Anything could have happened during that time. For all I knew, he'd given up hope of ever seeing us again and had relocated somewhere even more remote than the cabin.

It was with a heavy heart and hollow stomach that I climbed back into the van. Sasha looked across expectantly. "Any luck?" she asked. I quietly closed the door and shook my head.

"Folk out this way aren't too keen on having strangers knock on their door looking for handouts."

"What are we going to do?"

"What can we do? We don't have any choice but to keep going. Sooner or later, we'll find an abandoned house or maybe even a gas station."

"I don't know," Sasha said. "It feels pretty isolated. What if there's nothing else between here and the mountains?"

"There's a small town ten or so miles from the cabin. And there are still people that live out in the backcountry. They might be few and far between, but they exist. We've just got to be on the lookout and hope someone takes pity on us."

"I hope you're right. The kids need to eat something soon."

I nodded. Sasha seemed to forget that I'd had to listen while Charlotte repeatedly complained about how hungry she was. Harry managed to distract her with some ridiculous story about a farting dog that his preschool teacher read to the class. "I'll sort something out. I promise." I turned the key in the ignition, and the starter motor clicked, but the engine failed to turn over. That was strange. I'd never had trouble starting the van before. I tried again, and again it wouldn't start. "What the fuck?" I reached down and popped the hood before hopping out and walking around to the front of the vehicle. A few seconds later, I tapped on the passenger window, waiting impatiently for Sasha to unwind it. "Pass me the flashlight. I can't see dick."

"Is that safe?" my sister asked.

"Probably not, but I need to figure out why the hell the van won't start," I snapped as I took the flashlight from her. After a painstaking examination of the motor, I was no closer to discovering what was wrong with the van. Perplexed, I climbed back into the van and tried to start it again. It sputtered and shuddered but still wouldn't start. "Fuck," I cursed and thumped the steering wheel.

Sasha leaned over and pointed at the dashboard. "Look, I think it's out of gas."

She was right. The needle on the fuel gauge was dead on empty. We'd probably been driving on nothing but fumes for the last few miles. "I can't believe I missed that. How could I have forgotten to check the fucking fuel level?"

"Come on, Jess, it's not the end of the world."

I laughed bitterly. "I'm pretty fucking sure that's exactly what this is. And to top it off, we're now stranded in the middle of butt-fuck nowhere with two hungry kids." I could feel the pressure building inside me. It was like a wild animal trapped in a snare, the wire loop getting tighter and tighter the harder it fought to escape. I jumped out of the van before I flipped out, wincing as pain flared in my knee. My chest hitched as I strode down the middle of the empty blacktop. Tears dampened my cheeks, and I wiped at them angrily.

We had passed a total of three cars since leaving the warehouse, and that was on the first night. I hadn't seen another person foolish enough to travel the rutted back roads since then. So, it seemed unlikely that one of those murderous machines would suddenly appear as I was recklessly storming off. Still, I stopped before I got too far away from the van. Considering the run of bad luck we had been having, I wasn't about to tempt fate.

Standing in the middle of the road with my hands resting on my hips, I peered up at the sky. Stars twinkled between the clouds like tiny glimmering beacons of hope. Too bad, I was in no mood to appreciate their beauty. We were sitting in a rusty metal coffin, thanks to my ineptitude, and I couldn't think of a single thing that would help dig us out of our current situation. Time and time again, I'd fucked up, leading to one wrong decision after another. So much for having faith that we would make it to the cabin.

Footsteps thudded on the blacktop behind me, and I whirled around. Sasha froze mid-stride and looked up at me sheepishly. "Jess. You're scaring Harry and Charlotte," she said nervously.

"I didn't mean to scare anyone. I just needed to get away for a moment."

"I know," she said softly, stepping closer. She placed a comforting hand on my shoulder, and the physical contact released the knot of emotion building inside me. Great wracking sobs gripped my body, and I buckled over. Constant exhaustion, hunger, grief, and a state of permanent fear came to a head. The last thing I wanted was to frighten my sister with a disturbing outpouring of emotion, but I couldn't seem to stop. My life had become an endless loop of killing and crying. I wanted to give up, throw in the towel, and let someone else take responsibility. Too bad, Sasha had other ideas.

"It's okay to let it out. Nobody expects you to be tough all the time," Sasha said behind me. Tears continued to pour down my cheeks, the sobs refusing to abate. I gulped for air, willing myself to pull it together.

"I have to be," I managed to stutter between hitching breaths.

"Not true. I can't even begin to imagine how you must be feeling."

"What are you talking about?"

"Jess. I know you have had to do things that must be tearing you apart inside. Dodging the drones is just a tiny part of what you've had to do to protect us. Whatever you have done, I understand."

My sister was a smart girl. It was damn near impossible to fool her. Her acknowledgment and acceptance of the heinous acts that weighed so heavily on my conscience dissolved the last vestiges of my tough girl facade. My limbs turned to jelly, and I sank to my hands and knees, my head hanging low like a beaten dog.

"I didn't protect Fiona. Or Phil. If they hadn't met me, they would probably both be still alive. Thank God Bec and Dylan bailed before I could kill them too."

Sasha knelt beside me and gently stroked my back in a soothing motion. I wanted to shoo her away. Tell her it was too risky exposing herself like this, but I couldn't bring myself to send her away.

"It's a miracle that we're still alive at all. Without you, I would have died in the park beside the church. And there is no way Harry and Charlotte would still be here if Fiona hadn't begged

you to help her. She knew that you were the best chance her children had of surviving. You didn't kill Fiona. Just like you didn't kill Phil. I know you want to blame yourself for their deaths, but you aren't responsible. However, you are responsible for those two little kids sitting in the van. They don't have anyone else. Fiona trusted you. She believed you when you told her you could keep her little ones safe. I believed you. And that hasn't changed."

"Fiona is dead. Her children are starving, and we've run out of gas. It's time to face facts. I fucking failed."

There was a drawn-out silence before my sister responded. "How far is it to the cabin, do you think?"

I sniffled and considered her question. "It's probably thirty or forty miles to the little town at the base of the mountains. Then another nine or ten miles to the cabin."

"Okay. That's too far to walk, so we'll just need to find another vehicle."

I scoffed. Sasha made it all sound so simple. "You make it sound so easy," I replied. "I don't know if you have noticed, but there isn't exactly an abundance of available cars just waiting for us to climb inside and continue our journey," I said as I raised myself into a kneeling position.

"We'll walk if we can't find a car," Sasha snapped. "Are you done with the pity party? Because, let me tell you, feeling sorry for yourself doesn't put food in Harry and Charlotte's tummies. Nor does it get us any closer to Brent and the cabin. We're all scared and hungry, Jess. The difference is, you're the only one that can keep us safe."

I wiped the tears from my face and smoothed the hair back from my forehead while I took a moment to process what she had said.

"If you quit now, everything you've done since that first drone appeared in the sky beside the church will have been for nothing. The ones we've lost and the people you have killed, all that has happened will have been for absolutely nothing."

"Okay," I sighed. "Point taken."

"No, I don't think you get it. We're in this together. Instead of running off and having some mammoth meltdown, talk to me. Let me know what's bothering you."

"Sometimes I wish you didn't sound so damn grown-up. It makes me seem like a complete asshole," I admitted.

Sasha grinned impishly and hooked her arm through mine. "You *are* an asshole, Jess. But I wouldn't have it any other way. Come on, let's head back to the van and figure out our next move."

When we reached the van, I slid open the back door, and Buster leaped out, running off to relieve himself. "Hey guys, I'm sorry if I frightened you."

"Why did you leave us?" Harry asked uncertainly. Charlotte snuggled up against her brother and watched me from beneath her wispy blond fringe. "Did we do something wrong?"

"No, of course not," I assured them, shocked that they would believe they were somehow responsible for my actions. "I got a bit upset because the van ran out of gas, and I know everyone's hungry, but we have nothing left to eat."

Harry reached out and took my hand, gently stroking it in a soothing motion with the tips of his fingers. I started to choke up again. This roller coaster of emotions was seriously messing me up. "That sucks," he said with an earnest expression on his face. I held back a snort of laughter. "Yeah, it does suck, doesn't it?"

"How are we going to get to the cabin now?"

I looked back at my sister and shrugged. "I guess we'll have to walk the rest of the way. It might take a bit longer, but the sooner we leave, the sooner we'll get there."

"But, I only have little legs," he said.

"You've got little legs," I agreed, "and I've got a bung knee. So, I think that makes us just about even. What do you say?"

He shrugged, seemingly satisfied with my answer.

"I'm cold," Charlotte complained.

"Come here, and I'll find you something warmer to wear."

She climbed across her brother, oblivious to his groans of discomfort as she unwittingly jabbed him with elbows and knees. I shrugged out of Bill's old work shirt I'd been wearing at night when it cooled off and got Charlotte to thread her arms into the sleeves. It swamped her tiny frame. "It's so big," she giggled.

"I know," I agreed. "Let's roll up the sleeves and see if that makes a difference." I folded the sleeves over and over until her small starfish-shaped hands poked out. She fumbled with the buttons, determined to secure them herself, but hard as she tried, she couldn't manage the job. "Buttons can be super tricky," I said, helping guide the button through the hole. "Mommy has been teaching me, but I still can't do it yet." A shadow crossed her face, and I knew she was missing her mom.

"With a bit more practice, you'll be a button expert in no time," I said, hoping to distract her.

"Do you think so?"

"Absolutely. I bet if you ask nicely, Harry can help you while I quickly collect our things."

It didn't take long to stuff the few worthwhile belongings we had into the backpack Phil had given us. I topped up everyone's water bottles and handed them out, silently hoping we would find somewhere to refill them along the way. Although there were still over three gallons left in the back of the van, it wouldn't be possible to take it with us.

"We'll be leaving in a minute, so grab anything that you want to take with you," I told the children over my shoulder. I hooked my arms through the shoulder straps on the backpack before grabbing the shotgun. Sasha led the children over while I quietly called out to Buster, who was snuffling the scrubby growth along the roadside.

I crouched down to talk to Harry and Charlotte. "Since we won't have the van to hide in anymore, it's super important that you are very quiet. If we see a drone, try to find somewhere to hide. Otherwise, drop down, and stay still. Don't move until either Sasha or myself tell you it is safe. Do you understand?"

"We can't make any noise, and if one of those stupid drones shows up, we have to hide or pretend we're dead."

I ruffled his hair affectionately. "Good boy, that's exactly right. Come on, let's go. We have a long walk ahead of us." Sasha took them by the hand and started down the road with me following behind.

Nearly three hours passed before the children started to show signs of fatigue. They were far more resilient than I'd expected. By one in the morning, they had had enough, and I knew we would have to rest for a while. There was an unpleasant chill to the air, and the rain was threatening to start up again. A few errant drops had plopped on my face, reminding me how exposed to the elements we were. If the weather turned bad, we would have no choice but to stop and find some sort of shelter. The last thing I needed was for Harry or Charlotte to come down with a cold.

"Jess. Can we sit down for a bit? Everyone's feet hurt, and I can't carry Charlotte for much longer." I couldn't even remember when she'd picked the little girl up. "How long have you been carrying her for?" I asked, disturbed that I hadn't noticed my sister stopped to pick Charlotte up.

"It's only been for the last mile or so. But I can't carry her for much longer. My arms feel like jelly." Charlotte's head was resting on Sasha's shoulder. The poor kid had fallen asleep while we marched along in the dark toward an uncertain future. Harry wasn't doing much better. He leaned against my sister, too exhausted to support himself anymore. Sasha was right. We needed to take a break. "We'll stop soon. We just need to go a bit further until we find somewhere to rest."

Desperation made me wonder if I'd risk hailing down a car if one happened along the road at some point. I tried to convince myself that not every stranger was out to kill us. Sure, we had had a few bad experiences, but we'd also been met with kindness and generosity by people that owed us nothing. People had exposed themselves to considerable personal risk to help us at a time when everyone was too busy thinking only of themselves.

I had to remind myself that Fiona's murder was on me. My actions were responsible for leading a disturbed young man hell-bent on revenge to the warehouse that fateful morning. It had been avoidable, and one day, if we survived the drones and the lawless abyss that had become the norm, I'd have to admit my guilt to Harry and Charlotte.

"Hey Jess, did you see that light up ahead?" Sasha asked.

"What? I didn't see anything," I replied while searching the darkness around us.

"I think there's a house somewhere nearby. I'm sure I saw slashes of light through that clump of trees over there. You should go and see if they have an old stroller of something."

"Okay. One, I can't see any house. Two, I think the chances of a house out in the middle of nowhere having a spare stroller just sitting around is non-existent, and three, banging on some stranger's door in the middle of the night is liable to get me my head blown off."

"Well, we won't know if we don't give it a try. If you don't want to do it, I will." She quickened the pace, dragging Harry and Charlotte along behind her. There was nothing to do but jog after them. "Hey, Sasha. Wait up. You're right." If we didn't figure out how to speed things along, I couldn't see us getting much further. It wasn't realistic to expect the children to walk over forty miles with empty bellies and nothing to protect them from the elements. And if I was honest with myself, my knee was throbbing like a motherfucker. "I'll go and check it out. But I won't be around to tell you I told you so if some toothless redneck fills me with bullets."

Sasha shook her head and cracked a smile while she waited for me to catch up. "If somebody shoots you dead, I'll be sure to stick them with my pocketknife."

"Very funny. Just sit down with the kids until I get back." A light rain began falling, spurring me on and hardening my resolve. "Keep your eyes open," I said before leaving my sister to lead Harry and Charlotte over to an old tree stump, where they sank to the ground to rest. I turned to go then reconsidered. "Here," I carefully eased my way down the grassy embankment and handed the shotgun to Sasha. "Be careful. It's loaded." She nodded solemnly and placed it across her lap; the barrel pointed away from the children. "Good luck," she said, and I smiled grimly and left her sitting there, hoping nothing terrible would befall them while I was gone. It would likely be me that ran into trouble, but that did little to ease my concerns.

Sure enough, a quarter mile or so down the road, I spotted the sliver of light my sister had mentioned. I kept walking until I reached the entrance to the property. A heavy padlock and chain secured the gate. If I'd been driving a car, it might have posed a problem, but since I was on foot, I climbed over the gate and continued down the driveway, hoping like hell there weren't any killer guard dogs roaming the property.

Twenty

The closer I got to the house, the more nervous I became. Without the shotgun, I felt naked. I was entirely at the mercy of whoever was hiding within the walls of the sprawling ranch-style house with its expansive lawn. Even in the dark, I could feel the springy grass beneath my boots. There was no way of knowing if the occupants would be sympathetic or coldly indifferent to our cause. When I reached the porch, I took a steadying breath to calm my nerves before approaching the door and knocking.

After a brief pause, I heard approaching footsteps, followed by the distinctive click of a deadbolt unlocking. The door opened a crack, and a woman's face peered out at me suspiciously.

"I'm sorry to disturb you at this late hour," I offered as a way of an icebreaker.

"If you were sorry, you wouldn't have trespassed in the first place," she retorted.

"That's true, I suppose," I conceded. "I'm here because I need your help. We ran out of gas a few miles back, and three kids are waiting by the road who haven't eaten for days." The woman gave me an icy once over, and I was confident that she would slam the door in my face. Then she loosened her grip on the door, and her expression softened. "How do I know you aren't lying?" she challenged.

"I guess you don't. But I promise you, there are three young kids out there, and they haven't eaten for days. They're hungry and completely exposed to the elements. Maybe you have a spare can of beans or an old stroller you no longer need."

The woman scoffed. "Are you right in the head? I'm childless and in my fifties. We don't have anything like that around here."

"I understand. I'll go now. Again, I'm sorry that I disturbed you." I took a step back, resigned to another day of hunger, and delayed progress.

"Wait. You said you ran out of gas. Maybe you passed my brother on the road. He was driving a red pick-up with a black bumper. He went to look for feed for the livestock, but he hasn't returned. It's been almost a week. Surely he would have found his way back here by now if he were alright."

"I'm sorry to hear about your brother. But we only saw a few vehicles since passing Greensburg. And none of them match the description."

The woman sagged against the door frame, defeated by the prospect of never seeing her brother again. "I shouldn't have let him leave. The paddocks are bare, and he didn't want the animals to starve. I only agreed to let him go because I haven't seen a single *drone*," she emphasized the word the way people do when using a term outside their regular vocabulary. "I thought they were only in the cities. We'd heard there had been some attacks in Thompson's Creek, buildings destroyed, and lives lost, but it's such a small town. I thought people were exaggerating. It just seemed so unlikely for drones to bother with our community."

"The drones are everywhere. There aren't as many in rural areas, but there are still enough to cause trouble. Perhaps your brother is trapped in town. If there are drones in Thompson's Creek, he may be laying low."

"I hope you are right," the woman agreed.

"I'll keep my eye out for a red pick-up,"

"With a black bumper," she added hastily. "It's the only one around here that looks like that."

"If I see it, I'll tell him his sister is worried, and he should get home as soon as he can."

My willingness to try and help find her kin shook something loose inside her, and she choked back a sob. "Wait there. I might have a spare can of beans or something that you can feed to your children."

"They aren't my kids. One is my little sister, and the other two just lost their mother, who was traveling with us," I was quick to correct her.

The floorboards creaked on the other side of the door, betraying the presence of another person. Furious at myself for failing to notice that someone had been lurking nearby, I took a quick step back and reached behind me for the blade tucked into the waistband of my jeans. I was getting sloppy, and it was liable to get me killed.

The door swung open, and I braced myself, preparing for fight or flight. My damn heart was pounding like a drum. Then a massive beast of a man stepped forward, filling the doorway. A prodigious beard covered his face and trailed halfway down his chest, where it ended in a tidy plait tipped with a metal bead of some sort. I swallowed, madly calculating my odds if I had to go up against him. I quickly surmised he could snap me like a twig. Better if I just tried making a run for it, gimpy leg, and all.

Sensing my panic, he raised his large hands in a consolatory gesture. "There's no need to get all fired up. I'm just here protecting my woman. Someone comes knocking at this hour; it usually means trouble." There was a rifle propped against the wall where he could easily reach it. I was still tensed to run, but I knew that he had the upper hand. And, if he genuinely wanted to hurt me, I'd probably be nursing a bullet wound by now.

"I don't reckon you'll have much luck finding a stroller out this way. There aren't any young families around these parts. But I might have something that will do the job if you don't want those kids walking to Thompson's Creek. Stick around-I'll be back in a couple of minutes."

He swiftly shut the door, and I was left standing alone in the dark, wondering about my decision to leave Sasha and the kids alone by the roadside. I'd almost convinced myself to leave empty-handed and return to my sister when the front door opened, and the woman stepped down into the yard with a reusable grocery bag held out in front of her. "Here. As I said, it's not much. There are a few cans of creamed corn and some beans. And I popped a loaf of bread in there as well."

She handed me the bag, and I peeked at the contents in disbelief. "Where did you get the bread?" I asked in awe. She smiled at my reaction and explained, "I bake bread as we need it. That's yesterday's loaf. It might be a bit stale by now."

"I don't care. Thank you so much. The kids are going to flip when they see it." We heard the crunch of gravel underfoot as the bearded man rounded the corner of the house, pulling a garden cart along behind him. "I know it's probably not what you were hoping for," he said when he reached us, "but it's sturdy, and the rubber tires should hold up, at least until you reach Thompson's Creek." He was right. I hadn't imagined myself hauling Harry and Charlotte along in a cart designed for use around the yard.

"We use it to haul firewood up to the house, so you shouldn't have any trouble pulling a couple of kids in it. It won't be too comfortable, and there's more rain coming, so I threw an old horse blanket in there. The canvas is still waterproof, and it has a nice thick wool lining. It should keep them warm and dry."

I stepped closer and picked up the blanket. It was heavy and smelt strongly of a horse, but the bearded man was correct. It would keep the rain off the little ones. "I can't thank you both enough. We might make it to Thompson's Creek now."

"Don't forget to keep an eye out for my brother. He drives a red pick-up with a black bumper," the woman reminded me.

"I haven't forgotten. If I see your brother, I'll let him know that you are worried sick, and he should try to return as soon as possible."

"I'll escort you down to the road and unlock the gate," the man said. He pulled the cart along behind him as we walked down the driveway.

"Be careful out there," my bearded benefactor warned. "There'll be fuckin drones in Thompson's Creek for sure."

"Yeah, I've come from the city, and it was crawling with them, so I know what to expect."

When we reached the gate, he removed a key chain and slipped a key into the padlock securing the property. I waited for him to swing the gate open before I grabbed the cart's plastic-covered handle and pulled it through the opening. He was already securing the gate behind me when I turned to say goodbye. He waved and hurried back up the driveway, eager to return to the house and the woman within.

After hastily gobbling down the first meal any of us had eaten in days, Sasha lifted Charlotte into the garden cart while Harry insisted on climbing in unaided. They sat one in front of the other, and I gently draped the horse blanket over them so that only their faces were showing. "Yuck!" Harry complained. "It smells weird."

"Yeah," Charlotte agreed. "It's stinky."

There was undoubtedly a strong odor of horse, but it wasn't a bad smell. At least I didn't think so. After enduring the pervasive stink of barbecued human flesh, an old horse blanket was nothing.

"Well, you can either be warm and dry and put up with the 'stinky' part, or you can be cold and wet. Your choice."

Sasha chuckled and said, "That's a bit harsh, don't you think?"

I shrugged. "It seems fair to me. I'd happily swap places with them if I could."

"Yeah, me too," she grudgingly agreed. "My feet are killing me."

I returned my attention to the cart and its sullen occupants. "Is that a yes to the horse blanket?"

They nodded in unison. "Good, now that's settled; let's get moving while we still have a few hours of darkness left."

The cart was an absolute lifesaver. Even with my knee throbbing like the devil, we still managed to cover over ten miles before I reluctantly called it quits for the night. Dawn was rapidly approaching, and it was tempting to push on and squeeze out an extra mile or two, but Sasha convinced me to find somewhere to shelter for the day instead. "Thompson's Creek can't be far off," she mused while squinting down the road. "But I don't think it's worth the risk."

"You're right. We can't afford to get caught out in the open once the sun comes up. Now that we're getting close to town, there is no telling when a drone will show up. It probably isn't likely since we've got another five or six miles till we reach the outskirts of Thompson's Creek, but still."

"Let's find somewhere safe to hide so we can get some rest, and by this time tomorrow, we'll be sleeping somewhere warm and dry. Preferably somewhere with a bath," she smiled wanly.

"Now, you're pushing your luck," I replied.

"A girl can dream," she quipped and took the cart from me. It was time to pack it in for the night, so I allowed her to take over while I scouted for shelter.

***

It was late afternoon when the patter of rain on the roof woke me. I stretched and took a minute to massage the stiffness from my neck. Water dripped from the iron sheeting above, creating small muddy puddles in a few places, but overall, the crude three-sided animal shelter remained dry. Harry and Charlotte were wrapped in the horse blanket, still sleeping despite the late hour. Sasha was sitting with her back against the shelter's rough timber frame, looking out at the rain while Buster lay curled up beside her.

"How long have you been awake?" I asked.

Sasha turned her attention to me and shrugged. "Awhile. I heard a car drive by. It was headed toward Thompson's Creek. I couldn't get back to sleep after that."

"I didn't hear a thing. I must have slept pretty soundly, despite having hard-packed dirt for a mattress."

"You were snoring like a chainsaw at one point," Sasha informed me with a smirk.

"How cute. I'm sure Brent's gonna appreciate that newly acquired habit."

"It's just another thing for him to love about you."

"What are you talking about?"

"I don't know, just that Brent is super devoted to you. And I know you feel the same. Even if you won't admit it."

"Far out. I just woke up. I can't handle some deep and meaningful conversation about my relationship with my kid sister no less." Truthfully, there wasn't enough coffee (or booze) in the world to adequately prepare me for that.

"Fine. But you're not fooling anyone. You get this dreamy, faraway look whenever you're thinking about the big hairy lumberjack."

I glared at her, my mouth agog. Hairy lumberjack? She made him sound like some uncouth beast rather than a dude with a beard. A meticulously trimmed and oiled beard that received more grooming than her unruly mop, I pointed out.

"Sure, sure," she chuckled. "But seriously, you should be nicer to Brent- even if he is hairy."

She was determined to rile me up. "What are you banging on about now?" I asked against my better judgment.

Sasha considered for a moment before explaining. "Just that I like Brent. He's always been nice to me, and he is super patient with you. It wouldn't hurt to ease up on him. Let him know that you feel the same way. You two make a good couple. And I'll be pissed off if you mess it up."

"If I mess it up? Gee, thanks for the vote of confidence. It's good to know who you will side with if things don't work out," I said dryly.

"I'm just saying it doesn't hurt to tell someone that you care about them."

"Aside from questioning the relationship advice dished out by a twelve-year-old that, to the best of my knowledge, hasn't ever had a boyfriend, don't you think I already know that?"

She sighed loudly and rolled her eyes, like a long-suffering parent talking to a wayward child.

"It's true," I insisted. "Why do you think we're on this insane mission to the mountains?"

"Because you think hiding out in a cabin in the middle of nowhere will be the safest place for us."

"Yes, but I also want to be with Brent. I'm scared shitless every damn second of the day, and I feel like I might stop being so afraid if Brent's there beside me."

Sasha looked at me thoughtfully before changing the subject. "Do you think we should wake the children? It'll be dark enough to leave in half an hour. Plus, I'm hungry, and I can't stop thinking about the bread."

"Sure, wake them up. They've slept for long enough anyway."

Twenty-one

We passed a sign pock-marked with bullet holes welcoming us to Thompson's Creek. "Hmm. That fills me with confidence," Sasha drawled sarcastically. We would have reached the town hours ago, except something had upset Sasha's stomach, and we'd had to camp out under a tree while she alternated between vomiting and evacuating her bowels with an alarming frequency. Eventually, the cramps subsided, and she was able to continue, but we lost precious time.

I studied the faded sign. "Relax, I have a feeling those were there long before the drones started blowing everything to shit. It's probably just the drunken antics of bored teenagers with too much time on their hands."

A steady drizzle had continued all through the night, soaking Sasha and me to the core. Harry and Charlotte had fared better, thanks to the canvas horse blanket, but even they were damp and miserable. "Are we there yet?" Harry asked in a whiny tone.

"Almost," I assured him. We should be there by the time the sun comes up."

"When will that be?" he persisted.

"Soon, buddy. I know you've had enough. We all have."

Ten minutes later, the first buildings loomed ahead of us. As we approached the burned-out shells of commercial premises, my unease grew. We knew there were drones in Thompson's Creek, but I hadn't expected this degree of destruction. The warped and bubbled sign for a joinery business with twenty years of experience was all that remained of the single-level building. Beside it, there was an auto repair garage gutted in the ferocious blaze that had ripped through another four or five buildings lining the road.

"Jess, I thought the whole idea was to get as far from the drones as possible. If we aren't far from the cabin, how are we going to be safe from attack?"

"The cabin is at least a twenty-minute drive from here," I answered uncertainly. Seeing the blackened ruins around us filled me with doubt. We had traveled so far and lost so much to reach this mythical haven, only to discover the nearest town was crawling with drones.

"We knew there would be drones here. The couple that gave us the garden cart for Harry and Charlotte told me as much. I guess I'd hoped it wouldn't be this bad."

"The sun is coming up. Do you think it's safe to continue?" Sasha asked, looking around nervously.

"No, but until we find somewhere to hide for the day, we have to keep going."

"I don't like it here," she said, "it feels like a ghost town."

We reached an intersection and turned left, the commercial buildings thinning out before being replaced by large residential lots. "There are people about," I assured her. I was sure I'd just seen a curtain shift as we passed a narrow two-story house with a wind chime hanging out front. "They are probably laying low to avoid drawing attention to themselves."

"That's what we should be doing," Sasha said, clearly rattled. If I'd been alone, I probably would have taken the risk and continued through town. However, it wasn't an option when I was stuck pulling two kids along behind me in an old cart. All we could do was bunker down for the day and wait for the cover of nightfall before heading out once more. As if on cue, there was an explosion nearby that shattered the early morning stillness. It was somewhere north of us, a block or two away at least, but it still raised the hairs on the back of my neck. "Quick, we need to get off the street," I said, picking up the pace. Sasha pointed to a buttercup yellow house. The front door was hanging open. There was no way of knowing if the occupants had fled in search of safer lodgings or were lying dead someplace inside. Not that it mattered. Nothing could be worse than when we'd had to hide among the bloated and seeping bodies on the overturned bus.

I dragged the cart up onto the sidewalk and hurried over to the house, hustling Harry and Charlotte onto the narrow tiled entry. "Come on, Buster," I called over my shoulder. Detecting the urgency in my voice, the dog bounded up the walk and joined us. "Good boy." I ruffled his ears before raising the shotgun out in front of me. "I'll go first. Stay close behind me."

Before I'd stepped over the threshold, someone started screaming out in the street. Followed a moment later by a blast that cut the cries short. "Quick," I ran inside, the floorboards creaking underfoot as I made my way down the hall. The rooms we passed were empty, furniture overturned, anything of value stolen. Petty crime was thriving in small-town America.

Buster raced ahead, sniffing around the floor as I led everyone into the living room. "Sit on the couch while I go back and secure the door." Sasha nodded and helped Charlotte up onto the couch beside her brother. Everyone was enormously relieved to be out of the elements. After days spent trudging along back roads in the rain, a roof and four walls with an overstuffed couch felt like the Ritz-Carlton.

Once the drone moved on and the immediate danger passed, Sasha helped me put together a makeshift meal from what we managed to scrounge from the pantry. It mainly consisted of rice and canned vegetables, but nobody complained. It was hot and filling, and every one of us licked our bowls clean. With their bellies full, it didn't take Harry and Charlotte long to crash. I found a musty-smelling blanket in the linen closet and draped it over the sleeping siblings before retreating to the bathroom.

The door clicked shut behind me, and I sighed with pleasure. It was a rare treat to have a moment to myself, even if it was in the bathroom of some stranger who was likely dead. When I peered in the mirror, the person that looked back at me was almost unrecognizable. I had aged at least ten years. I'd never been vain, but seeing a much older version of myself, ravaged by time and circumstance, gave me pause. Truthfully, I barely recognized my reflection. It made me wonder if Brent would still want me.

There was a knock on the door. "Jess, are you alright? You've been in there a while."

"Yeah, I'm fine."

"Can I come in?" she asked.

My shoulders slumped. So much for some privacy. "Sure."

Sasha let herself in, reaching out to stroke my patchy hair. "I know you probably don't want to hear this, but I think it's time to cut your hair."

"What do you mean?" I asked.

"You look like shit," she replied bluntly.

"I know. Brent won't recognize me."

"I think Brent loves you for more than what you look like."

I burst into tears, overcome with emotions that I'd been refusing to acknowledge ever since that fateful day back at the church. Sasha wrapped her arms around me and locked me in one of her non-negotiable hugs. "We're almost there, Jess. And it's all thanks to you. I know it's cost you more than anyone will ever know, but I'm glad as heck to have you as my sister. Even if you do look like hell," she finished with an apologetic smile.

Her words were like a soothing balm on the blistered and scabbed over burns dotting my scalp. "It means a lot to hear that. Now, do you think you can let me go and do something with my hair?" She released me and took stock of my singed and patchy head. "Yeah, I don't think we can save it." She admitted. I sighed and lowered myself onto the closed lid of the toilet. I pressed the palms of my hands against my eyes, savoring the momentary escape. "Jess, it's just hair. It will grow back."

I raised my face to meet Sasha's concerned gaze. "I know. I'm just so damn tired all the time. Tired and hungry. I'm over stinking like a dog, and I'd kill for a long hot bath with a glass of bourbon. Followed by a stretch of uninterrupted sleep in a real bed with clean sheets and no worries to keep me awake."

Sasha leaned back against the tiled wall and slid her hands into the pockets of her jeans. "Do you know what I miss?"

"No, tell me?" I asked, curious to hear what she wanted.

She smiled wistfully. "Eating choc chip cookie dough ice cream in bed while reading something on my book list."

"That does sound good," I agreed. "Ice cream, bourbon, and books."

"When was the last time you picked up a book?" Sasha asked playfully.

"Steady on. I like to read. It's just difficult to find the time. Before the drones, I'd started listening to books on my phone when I was working."

"Does that count as reading, though?" my sister asked.

"Possibly not," I conceded. "But it's better than nothing, right?"

"Yeah, it's a start."

"Anyway, that's enough wishful thinking. Let's find some scissors, so you can give me a makeover," I said with a grimace.

Sasha chuckled darkly and waggled her eyebrows. She rifled through the medicine cabinet taking inventory of all the lotions and spot treatments left on the shelf by the previous occupants. "Bingo." Sasha turned to me, making snipping motions in the air with a tiny pair of nail scissors.

"Wow. Is that the best you can come up with?" I asked doubtfully. It was hard to imagine nail scissors chopping through an entire head of hair- even one as patchy as mine.

My sister shrugged, seemingly unfazed by the prospect of butchering my hair. "Are we going to do this or what?"

"Fine. But you don't have to look so damn pleased with yourself," I grumbled half-heartedly.

"Think of it as payback for all those times you made me wear a skirt or, worse still-something sparkly."

"I thought you liked sparkles," I said defensively.

"Yeah. When I was in the third grade." She took my plait in her hand and started hacking away close to the base of my skull. When it finally came free, I shook my head. The shorter length felt lighter, and I wondered why I hadn't given it the chop sooner. "Maybe I can keep it like this," I suggested while examining the choppy chin-length bob.

"You can leave it if you want, but it doesn't look so good from the back," she reminded me.

"Fine. Keep cutting then," I told her and sat back down with a sigh.

By the time Sasha finished, I was dozing off.

"All done," she announced, startling me. "You won't win any beauty contests."

"Lucky for me, that was never something I've had to worry about."

I braced myself before checking out my new 'do in the mirror over the vanity. "It isn't as short as I was expecting."

"I couldn't exactly give you a buzz cut with nail scissors. And I didn't think you would want me raking a razor blade over the burns."

"Fair point." I turned from one side to the other, feeling the contours of my head. It was probably up there as one of the worst haircuts of all time, but it still looked a shit load better trimmed close to my scalp than before.

"It makes me look like a badass."

"Jess, you *are* badass."

"Hey. Watch your language," I chastised.

Sasha rolled her eyes, and I shooed her out the door. "Keep an eye on the kids while I wash up."

"Do you want me to see if I can find you something clean to wear?"

"That would be amazing."

She returned a few minutes later, and I opened the bathroom door wrapped in a towel, my skin still damp from the shower. "Any luck?"

Sasha passed me a fresh change of clothes. I held up the long-sleeved plaid shirt and faded jeans and wrinkled my nose in distaste. "They look like they came straight off the rack in Walmart."

"They probably did. I got the jeans from the boy's room. The woman that lived here was too generously proportioned."

I raised my eyebrows, a faint smirk tugging at the corners of my mouth. "How very politically correct of you."

My sister shrugged and held out a piece of paper. "I also found this on the dresser in the master bedroom. I thought you might want to take a look at it."

Curious, I took the flyer from her and read it.

Community Refuge at William Street High School basketball stadium. ALL WELCOME. Please bring food staples and bedding. Nightly blackout strictly enforced. Law and order maintained by local police. Entry via the south parking lot. All weapons to be surrendered before entry. STAY SAFE.

"Do you think we should check it out?" Sasha asked.

"It doesn't change anything for us. We are still going to the mountains to find the cabin. Besides, the idea of a large group of people all gathered together in one place worries me."

"Wouldn't it be better for everyone to stick together?"

"In theory, yes. But it's a lot harder to control everyone's actions in a situation like that. Plus, they would make one hell of a target locked away in that stadium."

"I see your point. It would be difficult to control a group that large."

"Impossible more like it. And the more people there are, the greater the likelihood of something going wrong."

"Do you think the people at the school are alright?" she asked in concern.

"I hope so, but there is no way of knowing without going to the school and checking it out."

She opened her mouth to say something, but I silenced her. "And before you ask, we are not going anywhere near that school. We are so close to the mountains. Brent is less than ten miles away. I'm not willing to take any more unnecessary risks. Now, if you don't have any objections, I'm going to dress up like a teenage boy and then try and get a few hours of sleep."

The day was almost over when I awoke. Charlotte was standing over me with a troubled expression scrunching up her button nose. "Where is your hair?"

I stifled a yawn. "I asked Sasha to cut it off while you were asleep."

"I liked it better when you had long hair," she stated with a small child's honesty.

"I liked my long hair too, but it got burnt, so we needed to cut it off. It will grow back eventually," I said as I climbed to my feet. "How about I rustle up something to eat before we take off?"

Harry followed me to the kitchen and watched as I put a pot of water on the stovetop. "I hope you like tuna and pasta because that's all that's left in this place."

Harry made a face as if he'd just caught a whiff of excrement stuck to his shoe. "That sounds disgusting."

I chuckled and nodded in agreement. "It sure does, but it's better than nothing, right? And it won't be long before we reach the cabin where there will be more than just stinky old tuna to eat. Brent is waiting there for us."

"Is Brent your boyfriend?" he asked shyly. Charlotte and Sasha joined us in the kitchen right as Harry asked the question. I caught my sister smirking, and she quickly covered it with an unconvincing cough, averting her eyes to avoid the dirty look I gave her.

I grudgingly returned my attention to Harry, reluctant to get involved in a conversation about my relationship with a five-year-old. "Yes, Harry, Brent is my boyfriend."

Harry studied his shoes intently before looking up at me. "Do you think he will like Charlotte and me?"

"Of course, he will like you," I assured him and drew the boy close to me. "Why did you ask me that?"

Harry pushed away from me and shrugged. "Sometimes Mom worried her boyfriends wouldn't like us. It made her sad."

I glanced across Sasha, shocked by the boy's admission, and she shook her head sadly. I placed my hands on his shoulders, looking him dead in the eyes. "Harry, that isn't something you ever have to worry about while you're with Sasha and me. Brent will be so happy to meet you and your sister. Especially when I tell him how you have helped look after Buster."

"Okay. That's all I wanted to know. You can cook the stinky tuna pasta now," Harry said.

I ruffled his hair before turning my attention to the water bubbling in the pot on the stove. *Yum, yum. Tuna pasta here we come*, I thought with a distinct lack of enthusiasm. I was pouring some pasta shells into the pot when I heard a commotion at the front of the house. "Watch the stove," I told my sister as I hurried out of the kitchen and into the lounge room.

Buster was jumping up and down in front of the curtain covering the picture window; the dogs hackles up as he growled menacingly. His lips pulled back to expose his teeth. He didn't even acknowledge me when I cautiously stepped up beside him. "Hey, Buster, what's going on?" I whispered as I drew back the curtain to peer out into the late afternoon shadows.

A stray dog stood out on the lawn, sniffing the air, probably attracted to the cooking smells, or perhaps the scent of a strange dog invading its territory. Its dull and matted coat did little to conceal its jutting hips and protruding ribs. Buster lunged forward, his jaws snapping against the glass as he locked eyes with the dog outside. I had to grab hold of his collar with both hands to drag him away from the window.

Fuck. It wasn't enough that we had to worry about pyromaniac drones and homicidal humans. Now we could add starving, desperate dogs to the list of things that wanted to harm us. I dragged Buster across the room and locked him in the bathroom, hoping it would give him a chance to calm the fuck down while I finished cooking. As we sat down to an unappetizing meal of pasta with canned tuna stirred through, topped with a generous seasoning of Parmesan and cracked pepper, I tried not to worry about the mangy dog lurking outside the house.

"Is everything alright?" Sasha asked around a mouthful of pasta. I glanced over at Harry and Charlotte, reluctant to say anything that might upset them. However, we were probably way beyond that now. They had seen too much and lost even more. It was impossible to shield them from the danger we faced. "I'm just worried about that damn dog. A hungry dog can be desperate and unpredictable."

"It will be okay," Sasha tried to assure me. "We have the shotgun, and Buster won't let anything happen to the kids."

"Yeah, maybe. If it's still hanging around when we're ready to leave, we might have to stick around for another day." I shoveled food into my mouth, chewing mechanically while privately doubting my sister's blind optimism.

Twenty-two

The days were shorter now that summer was behind us, so we could leave soon after finishing our makeshift meal. After carefully checking for drones and the mangy stray dog, I helped the kids into the cart before threading Buster's leash through the loop on my jeans. It was the first time we had had to restrain him since leaving the farm, but I didn't want him running off and getting into a fight.

We headed straight for downtown, my eagerness to reach Brent trumping any reservations I had about exposing ourselves to unnecessary risk. Besides, I figured the busy main street would have been one of the first places hit in such a small town. It was unlikely there was much of anything left to attract the killer drones. By now, they would be terrorizing the residential areas, stalking, and killing anything that moved.

Walking along the middle of the wide tree-lined street, the sound of Buster's claws clicking on the road, a feeling of absolute desolation settled over me. Time and the rain had doused the fires that had blackened many of the storefronts. I couldn't help but wonder if the town would rebuild after the threat from the drones passed. Such a small community would probably never recover from the destruction heaped upon it.

"It looks so empty," Sasha whispered, "but I feel like we're being watched."

I glanced around us at the shuttered windows of the few buildings unaffected by fire and looting. "I know what you mean." Weeks of living in full-blown survival mode had honed our instincts, and although we couldn't see anyone, I felt eyes on us. Probably from the apartments over some of the stores. With no way of knowing if they were hostile, my finger remained on the shotgun's trigger. We were utterly exposed as we passed ruined businesses, and I had to force myself to maintain a steady pace and refrain from bolting down the road in a blind panic.

It wasn't until we had crossed the only intersection with a traffic light and the buildings began to thin out that I lowered the shotgun. Sasha pulled the wagon, and I kept pace with her, afraid to get too far ahead since Buster was acting up. He kept pulling at the lead and turning back the way we had come, a low growl rumbling deep in his chest.

Unsure of the route, I motioned for Sasha to pause while I removed the map from the backpack and checked where we were supposed to be going. "When we reach Dean Street, we need to turn right and continue until we pass the meatpacking plant on the outskirts of town. The turn-off to the logging road should be a mile or so after that."

"So, we're almost there," Sasha said happily.

"Almost," I agreed. "Brent said the cabin is around nine miles up the logging road."

"Damn. It still sounds so far away," she said, clearly disappointed by my reply.

"Well, we won't get there by standing around complaining about it."

She mumbled something incoherent and set off once more, pulling the wagon along behind her sullenly. I slipped my arms into the backpack and hurried after her. The rain had started again as we passed through downtown, and now it was falling in earnest. Sasha and I were soaked. Harry and Charlotte were mostly dry thanks to the horse blanket draped over them.

We walked in silence for a while, turning onto Dean Street and continuing until the dark outline of the abattoir loomed ahead. It had an eerie and somewhat dangerous vibe that I couldn't quite shake.

"Do you think there are animals trapped in the holding yards?" Sasha asked.

I turned to check if the children were listening, but the rain had sent them burrowing under the horse blanket.

"I don't think so. If there were, they would have died of starvation by now. And even the rain couldn't dampen the stench of so much decay."

"That's good. I can't bear the thought of a bunch of animals slowly dying of hunger and thirst."

My heart hurt a little bit at my sister's kind and gentle soul. Even when she was cold and shivering, brushing water from her eyes, she was thinking of the suffering of others.

"I still don't like it. The place gives me the creeps," Sasha admitted.

"Yeah, I know how you feel. It isn't a nice place," I agreed.

Buster must have picked up on our anxiety because he started to growl, a deep and persistent rumbling that made the hairs on the back of my neck stand on end. He lunged forward, nearly pulling me off my feet as he let out a series of ferocious barks. I held the shotgun one-handed while I took hold of the lead in the other, wrestling with the agitated dog as he slowly dragged me along the road toward the abattoirs.

"What's going on?" Sasha cried out in alarm.

"I don't know! Something over near the meatpacking plant has him all riled up," I explained as I tried to bring the dog under control. He danced back and forth, jerking me around like a marionette doll. "I can't fucking control him," I said, panicking as I almost lost my balance.

A cacophony of barking from somewhere within the abattoirs alerted us to the cause of Buster's agitation. "Oh shit," Sasha exclaimed.

Buster lunged forward, and I lost my balance. I fell to my knees, and he dragged me along the blacktop as I tried unsuccessfully to rein him in. Sasha rushed over to help me up, and together we managed to stop him from breaking free. He wouldn't stand a chance against a starving pack of dogs left to go feral and fend for themselves, no matter how bravely he fought to defend us. None of us would. I was almost out of ammunition, and my skills with a shotgun didn't extend to taking out a fasting moving dog-or three.

"We need to shut the gates," I cried as a pale streak appeared from behind the nearest building and charged toward us, followed closely by three other dogs.

"I've got it," Sasha said and sprinted for the entrance in a life and death race against the vicious pack of animals. All I could do was watch on helplessly as time seemed to grind to a halt. Buster strained against me, choking on the collar as he tried to take off after my sister. I blinked rain from my eyes and raised the shotgun, anchoring my feet against Buster's frantic attempts to break free as I prepared to shoot.

Sasha reached the first gate and swung it across the driveway, dropping the bolt into the metal keeper in the concrete before dashing over to grab the second gate and pull it closed behind her. The snarling pack was almost on top of her. The large gray dog at the front leaped into the air. Its jaws were snapping in anticipation as it sailed toward my sister.

I dropped Buster's lead and raised the shotgun to my shoulder, fighting the urge to squeeze my eyes shut against what was to come. Then Sasha slammed the gate closed as the first dog threw itself against the gates in a frenzy. They rattled and bowed outward under the weight of the furious animals, but Sasha didn't flinch. She held firm despite the snapping jaws and frenzied barking on the other side of the chain-link. It wasn't until she squatted down and secured the second bolt in the ground that I dared to breathe again.

She jogged over to me, breathing heavily, and I hugged her quickly before reaching down to snatch up Buster's lead as he danced around us in excitement. "I didn't think you were going to make it," I admitted over the din.

"Neither did I. It was close. That gray dog almost got me. I felt its breath against my cheek, but I didn't have a choice," she replied shakily. "You never would have made it with your knee and Buster attached to your waist."

There was no point arguing about it. Sasha was right. I would never have reached the gates in time. "I know. You did well. But we need to get out of here. It's a slaughterhouse, not a maximum-security prison. They'll eventually find a way out. There might be another exit, or they'll dig a hole under the fence. Either way, we need to be long gone when it happens."

"Do you think they will try to follow us?" Sasha asked as we joined Harry and Charlotte. I shrugged uncertainly. "They're desperate enough, but I'm hoping the rain will mask our scent. Can you pull the wagon while I try to control Buster?"

"Sure. Are you going to manage?" She asked, her voice heavy with doubt as she looked down at my knees. The jeans were ripped open, and I could feel the warm trickle of blood oozing from the scrapes. The dark helped conceal the extent of the injuries. "It's all good. Those Walmart jeans took the brunt of it. The skin's barely even broken," I said, downplaying it.

She crouched down to reassure the children and adjust the horse blanket before picking up the handle. "Let's jog for a bit," I suggested as I tugged on Buster's lead, "It's not just the dogs that we have to worry about. A drone is bound to show up any time now."

The emaciated dogs bounded along the fence line, continuing to bark and bite at each other in frustration as we drew away from them. We kept up the faster pace even after turning onto the logging road, gravel crunching loosely underfoot as we distanced ourselves from the abattoir and the pack of dogs trapped within. Harry and Charlotte started complaining the moment we hit the unpaved road. The cart wasn't designed for transporting small humans along a heavily potholed road frequented by heavy vehicles. They bounced around uncomfortably, holding on for dear life as Sasha dragged them along after her.

It wasn't until we started climbing a hill that felt like it went on forever that I finally slowed to a walk. "I've got to stop," I panted breathlessly. Confident Buster was no longer intent on running off to battle, I stopped to unclip his lead. My legs were shaky with fatigue, and my lungs burned with every inhalation. It was mildly satisfying to notice Sasha wasn't faring much better. But then, unlike me, she had been pulling a cart along behind her, loaded with two small kids.

When we could finally breathe again without feeling like we were going to puke, Sasha asked me how much further I thought we had to go. I stared ahead into the darkness, calculating the distance. "If we can maintain a steady pace, we should reach the cabin in a few hours. We must have covered nearly a mile since turning onto the logging road. It would be quicker if we weren't stuck walking uphill most of the way. Plus, my knee's starting to play up."

Sasha nodded in understanding, hair sticking to her face in wet clumps. "That's okay. I'm amazed you didn't collapse in a heap back at the turn-off to the logging road. I thought I'd have to kick Harry and Charlotte out of the cart and drag you along in it instead."

"I don't mind walking," Harry piped up. "My butt's getting sore anyway."

Sasha laughed. "I guess it is a bumpy ride in the cart."

Harry nodded enthusiastically. "It sure is. Super-duper bumpy."

"I bet it's uncomfortable," I sympathized. "But do you think you can stay there with your sister for a little while longer? Just until the rain stops. I'd hate for you to get wet and cold."

Harry scowled at me, and I sensed an atomic tantrum brewing. Fortunately, Sasha intervened, diffusing the situation before the boy had a chance to erupt. "I tell you what, if you stay in the cart with Charlotte until it stops raining, you can use your big muscles to help me pull it up the steep hills."

He huddled under the horse blanket with Charlotte snuggled against him for warmth while he considered the offer. There was a moment when I was sure he would have a meltdown, but then he shrugged and agreed. "You can pull the cart," he said. "I'll walk with Buster."

"Deal." Sasha grinned at him and held out her hand so that they could shake on it. I gave her an approving nod. She was quite the negotiator-a handy skill to possess when our family had recently expanded to include two small children under five. She was far more patient than I would ever be.

"Thanks for stepping in back there," I said once we started walking again. "I don't think I could have handled a full-blown tantrum right now."

She shrugged nonchalantly. "What can I say? Saving your ass is my new thing," she teased and continued pulling the cart up the hill.

I scoffed, taken aback by her newfound attitude.

Twenty-three

As usual, I had been overly ambitious in estimating the time it would take to reach the cabin. Inclement weather and the steep winding road had taken a toll. We were deep in the foothills, navigating around ankle-high puddles and sloshing through runoff, hours spent taking turns pulling the cart in the rain, leaving Sasha and me in a foul mood. Brent had warned me the driveway was hard to spot. The entrance was overgrown and easily missed. I could only hope we hadn't walked past the cabin without realizing it.

Something caught Buster's attention, and his ears pricked. He stopped and turned to look down the road behind us. "Hey, Buster, what's up? You find a rabbit or something?" I said, thinking he must have found some small prey feeding in the pre-dawn hour. "Come on, Buster." The dog continued to ignore me, too intent on whatever it was down the hill that held his interest. Irritated, I clipped the lead to his collar and tugged on it, but he didn't budge. "For fuck's sake, dog," I complained, my patience all but spent. Then he began to growl, and I felt my bowels loosen.

I glanced back at Sasha. She continued up the road. Her shoulders slumped in fatigue as she hauled the cart along behind her, unaware that I had stopped. Buster surged forward, barking as he struggled to get free. "Oh fuck," I whispered when I caught sight of the pack of dogs that I'd thought we'd left behind at the meat processing plant.

"Get the kids and run!" I screamed. She stopped and looked back in my direction, confused. I jerked on Buster's leash, dragging him up the hill as I ran to meet my sister.

"The dogs are coming. We need to run. Now!"

Sasha flung the horse blanket off the cart and scooped Harry and Charlotte out. "Quick, we have to go. The dogs are back," she exclaimed. Taking hold of their hands, she urged them up the road, their legs not moving nearly fast enough. Buster kept barking and spinning to face the approaching pack. They were faster than us. Rapidly gaining ground now that they had us in their sights.

Fear kept me moving, helping me push through the burst of pain when I stumbled into a pothole and rolled my ankle. We had come too damn far to be picked off by a bunch of feral dogs, especially when we were so close to the very refuge that had been the driving force for our entire fucked up journey. I caught up to my sister, and she stared up at me fearfully. "What are we going to do?" she panted. It was too late for reassurance. And I didn't want my last words to my little sister to be a lie.

"Keep running, and don't stop for anything. No matter what happens, you have to keep going. The cabin can't be far," I told her with a sense of calm that surprised me.

"I'm not leaving you behind," Sasha argued.

"You don't have a choice. If you stop, those dogs will rip Harry and Charlotte apart," I said unkindly as the pack, sensing a victory, howled one after the other.

I smiled at her sadly. "No, Jess. Don't do it," she cried as I dropped back and turned to face the approaching pack. Buster was going mental, and I couldn't hold him and aim the shotgun. Knowing it would almost certainly get him killed, I dropped the lead with a heavy heart. Without him tugging at me, I'd have a better chance of shooting one of the dogs.

Going against every instinct for survival, I stopped, tamping down the urge to turn and run after my sister. My hands trembled, and my heart was hammering like a jackrabbit. As I aimed the gun at the dog at the head of the pack, Buster shot off down the hill to meet them, despite being hopelessly outnumbered. They were twenty yards away. It was now or never, and my finger tightened on the trigger.

From somewhere behind me, the unmistakable crack of a hunting rifle echoed through the hills. The bony gray dog yelped, continued to run at me for two or three strides, then dropped dead on the road. The others quickly overtook it, and I trained the shotgun on a shaggy coated dog to my right. I squeezed the trigger, but the shot went wide.

Buster collided with the nearest dog, the pair locking onto each other in a violent brawl. They reared up on their hind legs in a life or death battle, jaws snapping as they ripped and bit and growled. I aimed again and pulled the trigger a second time. The bullet grazed the flank of a short, muscular dog at the rear of the pack, and it emitted a startled cry. The injury slowed the animal, but it wasn't enough to stop it altogether.

Out of ammunition and with no time to reload, I dropped the shotgun and whipped out my knife as a last resort, determined to go down fighting. There was another rifle shot, and a second dog collapsed within spitting distance of me, its body twitching as it died. I had no idea who was picking the mongrels off, but I was desperately grateful. A minute ago, we were facing certain death; now Sasha and the children might have a future.

The dog I'd shot launched itself into the air and sailed toward me with grace at odds with its stocky build. I raised my arm in front of my face protectively as it plowed into me, and we went crashing to the ground. It pinned me beneath its substantial weight, and all I could do was thrust the knife up into its muscular chest. The dog's head whipped from side to side, its teeth gnashing together inches from my face. It was too powerful. I couldn't hold it back for much longer. The knife wound only seemed to aggravate it. Spittle flew from its jaws, and I stabbed it again, hoping to hit an artery. The knife plunged into the thrashing dog, over and over. Blood spewed from the wounds, splashing my chest and face.

Then I heard heavy footsteps approaching, and a rifle butt smashed into the dog's head with a sickening crunch. It collapsed on top of me, its body going limp, and I felt its life slip away. Weakened and in shock, I couldn't shift the dead dog off me.

Nearby, Buster and the remaining dog from the feral pack continued to fight in a terrifying dance. Blood flowed freely from each dog as they circled and lunged at each other. The other dog was gaining the upper hand. Its jaws locked around Buster's throat as it shook him around. Another shot rang out, and the fight was over. The rogue mutt slumped down dead. Buster whimpered and slowly crawled toward me.

Then someone lifted the dog off my chest, and I could breathe again. I wiped blood and rain from my eyes. A figure stood over me; a rifle slung over his shoulder. "Brent? Is that you?" I stammered.

He reached down and took hold of my hand, pulling me to my feet. "Jesus Christ, Jess. I didn't recognize you."

I burst into tears and collapsed against him. "I thought that fucking dog was going to rip my throat out. A few more seconds, and I'd be dead."

"I didn't know it was you. What the hell happened on your way here?" he eventually asked once I'd pulled myself together. I reached up and ran a hand over my close-cropped head self-consciously. "What? You don't like the new haircut?"

"It's as sexy as hell," he replied, and we both laughed. "Seriously, what happened? I'd almost given up."

I let out a deep sigh. "It's been a rough journey."

"I'd say that's the understatement of the century," he replied, holding me at arm's length, presumably cataloging my almost endless collection of injuries.

"How did you know it was us coming up the hill?" I asked.

Brent shook his head. "I didn't. I was out hunting game and not having much success, I might add, when I spotted the dogs stalking you all. Next thing, they started barking, and all hell broke loose. The little kids threw me off. And your chrome dome," he added cheekily. "I wasn't expecting that."

"Get used to it, buddy. I kind of like the patchy, feminazi look," I teased.

"Careful," he warned, "the PC police will come after you."

I scoffed. "They're probably all dead."

"All jokes aside," Brent continued, "I couldn't let them maul people to death. No matter how hungry and desperate they were."

"Well, you saved us. The dogs must have tracked us from the meatpacking plant. I thought we'd gotten away, but I was wrong."

Buster gave a pained whine, and I limped over to him and knelt beside the injured dog. He raised his head and licked me when I reached out to pat his head gently. It looked like he was bleeding from everywhere. "You poor brave boy," I said, swallowing down the lump forming in my throat. Brent crouched beside me and carefully checked the dog over. "I think it looks worse than it is. A lot of that blood is from the dog I shot. I'll be able to take a better look when I get him up to the cabin."

"How far away is it? Because I'm not sure that I can go much further," I admitted.

"It's literally around the next bend." He touched my cheek with the back of his hand and kissed my wet, bloody forehead ever so gently. "The kids should already be safely inside. If you don't think that you can make it, you can wait here, and I will come back for you."

"No fucking way. I'm not letting you out of my sight. It would be just my luck that a plane would drop on me while you were lugging that damn dog up the hill."

He chuckled. "I haven't seen many planes since the drones appeared."

"Come to think of it, neither have I. But I'm still not risking it. The sun is almost up, and I don't want to sit around, waiting for a drone to appear."

Brent scooped Buster up into his arms, being careful not to aggravate the animal's injuries, and we started up the hill. I managed a few unsteady steps before Brent demanded that I hold onto him for support. A few minutes later, we reached the cabin. It was set back from the road on the high side of the hill. Thanks to the dense foliage of the trees surrounding the property, it was almost invisible from the road.

I opened the cabin door and stepped over the threshold. Sasha and the children rushed over when they saw Brent carrying Buster. He gently lowered the dog onto the table, and I knew the damn mutt would be alright. He raised his head for pats when Harry and Charlotte began fawning over him, his tail madly thumping as they were reunited.

Sasha stepped over to me and looped her arm around my waist while we watched Brent and the little ones take care of Buster.

"You did it," Sasha said in awe. "You got us all here safely."

"Not all of us," I corrected her, thinking of Phil and Fiona. "But you kids are here, and I think this is where we're meant to be. For now, at least."

I felt the tension drain from my body. We made it. After all the horror and bloodshed, it was finally over. Sasha and the children would be safe. Or as safe as was possible with killer drones prowling the skies. For the first time since I saw that drone appear on the church grounds, I felt genuine hope. Perhaps we really could survive the end of the world.

ABOUT THE AUTHOR

Naomi H Brown is an Australian writer who lives in a crumbling cottage with a sprawling back garden. She is run ragged by three demanding cats and a fluffy black pom-pom that may or may not be a dog.

She enjoys curling up by the fire with a cup of Earl Grey tea, or if she is feeling naughty, a vodka lime and soda (easy on the lime and soda), Netflix binges, bumblebees, and Josh Homme from QOTSA.

When she isn't working on her latest book, she can often be found rescuing unwanted furniture from the side of the road and giving it a makeover with a little bit of imagination and lashings of paint.

Discover more at naomihbrown.com

ALSO BY

Taylor's End

Ella. A mysterious outsider with holes in her memory and a malignant darkness lurking inside her.

A sleepy rural community rocked by the discovery of a mutilated body at a rest stop on the outskirts of town.

As the violence and body count rises, Nick Bremner, the local Chief of Police, is desperate to find the killer before anyone else gets hurt. But he doesn't realize what he's up against. Only a teenage boy with no job and even less hope knows the truth.

Something inhuman is preying on the innocent. And it has an insatiable appetite.

Welcome to Taylor's End.